A Week at the Woods

A novel by Rebecca Taylor

Printed in Canada
Paperback ISBN: 978-1-7773070-2-8
E-Book ISBN: 978-1-7773070-1-1

rebeccataylorwrites.com

To my very own large, loud, and crazy family.

I wouldn't be me without you.

1

She pulled up in her blue Mini Cooper. The tires rolled over the gravel and she looked out to survey the land, the sun peaked down between the lush fir trees that surrounded the driveway and lined the hill down toward the lake behind the cottage. A turn of the century log cabin in the woods, in the height of a hot New England summer, it was an idyllic landscape, the type most used as an escape.

Rachel's hand trembled as she reached into her glove compartment. *Thank God.* Clasping the small orange bottle of valium, she leaned into her seat and popped two little yellow pills into her mouth, followed by a swig of now cold coffee. She pinched her big blue eyes shut, took a deep breath, and stepped out of the car.

Into this nightmare.

A family reunion.

How can one person's paradise be another's hell, she wondered? But enough of that now. Knowing her family, cocktail hour would already be going strong at 11 a.m. She threw her duffel bag over her shoulder and headed for the front door.

2

"Everyone come here! Rachel's home!" Her mom, Judy, shouted into the living room. Seven years ago, Rachel was twenty-three, and back home in rural Vermont, on a break from grad school in New York for the week to catch up on sleep, binge on her mother's famous sugar cookies and prepare for her next semester. The scene was set just as magically as every other year before. Her mom must have been Mrs. Claus in another life—every December, their home would be transformed into a red and green holiday wonderland. Little reindeer and snowmen would replace the usual figurines above the fireplace, green garland snaked its way across every ledge and windowsill. Autumnal farm paintings were stored away, to make room for winter landscapes, while little twinkling lights adorned every doorway.

The house was a hive of activity. Rachel's older brother Max, twenty-eight, tall with a shaggy brunette mop of hair that fell down into his soft blue eyes, was home from his job as a philosophy professor upstate, and busy helping their dad, John, string the lights outside. Maggie, twenty-six, tall blonde and lean with legs her sisters would kill for, was making cookies in between pouring Sancerre for everyone. Ever since she took a year off to live in France, she likened herself to French aristocracy, turning up her nose up at most of the things her 'silly American' family partook in. The same could be said for the wine Rachel put down on the counter.

"Oh, how quaint, I didn't know you could still buy this wine. Remember how we loved it as teens since it was so cheap and fruity?"

Rachel took a deep breath, smiled tightly and poured herself an oversized glass of their mom's famous hard eggnog, determined not to let it sour the mood just yet.

"Hey little one, how's senior year going?" she asked her little sister Erica as she walked down the two steps into the den.

Erica, seventeen, blonde like her sisters, and wearing the latest fashions of Forever 21 barely looked up from her cell phone. "Yeah fine, whatever." Such a charming age.

"Girls come on, help us with the rest of these cookies. Dad's had a terrible week trying to finish up his latest construction project before the holidays, I want to make him a little treat."

Mom had a little twinkle in her eye as she floated to the kitchen. Would Rachel ever find a love like that?

"So, how's school, honey? I love the new hair by the way, I always said a nice bob would look great on you." She popped a loose strand behind Rachel's ear as she Erica rolled up their sleeves to help.

"Thanks Mom. School is…busy this semester. I got that internship with the school paper." She tried but failed to hold back the excited chirp in her voice.

"Well done, sweetie! No time for boys then?" Mom poked her with her elbow.

"God Mom, you know that isn't the be all to end all! I beat out hundreds of applicants for that job! Besides, who knows if I'll ever get married—the guys at NYU are all so pretentious." She rolled her eyes and licked some stray icing off her finger.

"Ugh, I know exactly what you mean," Maggie chimed in, "that's why I'm so happy with Pierre! You really should get yourself a European man, sis, they really are *so* much more cultured than the boys 'round here."

Ah, the famous Pierre. They had yet to meet the guy whom Maggie spent hours texting. Nothing like racking up the monthly bill for "cultured" Eurotrash.

"Don't these cookies look amazing? You'd never know they're low fat and salt free for your dad's diet." Mom smiled triumphantly as she started to drop cookies by the spoonful onto her baking tray.

Erica took a whiff of the batter and tried to choke down a piece. "Sure Mom, just like Nannie used to make!"

Rachel excused herself from the kitchen with the eggnog to check on the boys outside. Rachel always felt most at ease with the men in the family. So much less drama. Go figure.

She grabbed her NYU beanie off the stairs and pulled it down tight over her now short, strawberry blonde hair. She zipped her puffy jacket up tight to protect herself from the infamous New England winters, pulled her boots over her jeans, and took her eggnog outside to see how the boys were getting on.

"Hey Pop, how's it going?"

"Oh, you know babe, just trying to keep your mom happy with all this junk!" He waved his gloved hand over the big box of lights and plastic reindeer in front of him.

Ever the joker, Rachel knew she could count on him for the comedy factor. Much as he'd hate to admit it, he loved being a part of all the noise. Yet what choice did he have? The man was outnumbered in a house full of women.

"Well, good to hear you haven't lost that Christmas spirit!" She poked him in the ribs.

"Surprised the graduate had time to come home at all." Max sniffed as he tested the bulbs. Poor guy has had that same job since he was about six years old.

"You're one to talk, Professor." She put a hand on her hip.

"So spill Rach, what's the deal with this paper? Are you gonna be running the show now? Fulfilling the prophecy of globe-trotting journalist?"

"It's a pretty great opportunity, you know, just happy to be involved." A diplomatic response.

"And how's the job going, bro? Reckon you'll get tenure over there some day?"

"Hoping so! I've spent eight years in university so I figure I might as well make a career out of it." Only he could make the prospect of teaching philosophy to a bunch of despondent undergrad students looking for a fluff course, sound like the golden ticket.

"How about the chicks in the philosophy department huh, Maxy?" Dad said, wrestling with a tangled ball of lights.

"Come on Dad, you know I'm just struggling to keep them at bay!" Max said. For the romantic game he lacked, it was a wonder their friends always found Max the mysterious, hot older brother. But then, as a philosopher, if the girls aren't there, did the interest even exist?

Rachel shivered, glanced sadly at her empty glass and headed back inside. Ready for a refill, she braced herself for a classically loud family dinner. She loved the chaos that surrounded her family. Without a screaming match, complete and total-destruction of the house, and someone (or several) ending up in tears—how could you even call it a get together? Or have cozy reconciling?

<h1>3</h1>

Back at the lake, Rachel took one last deep breath before she turned the antique knob on the cottage door. "Oh Rachel, you made it!" Mom shouted as she entered.

"Hi Mom!" She dropped her bags and leaned down to wrap her mom in a hug. Standing tall at a mere five foot five, the kids all got their great height from their father. Rachel's head rested atop her mother's cropped silver hair.

A whiff of Estée Lauder perfume transported Rachel onto a carousel of childhood memories—*mom.*

"It's so good to see you, honey." Her mom's eyes began to well. "Your hair is so long, I love it," she whispered.

"Jeez Mom, not so tight! And if you start crying already, you're going to get me going. And it's too early, and we're all far too sober for that just yet."

"I know sweetie." Mom laughed as she pulled away. "I just feel it's been so long since you've been around. With your sudden move to London and then the divorce..."

She was right. She knew she was. For a long time now, Rachel had carried this burden of guilt. How could she let it go so long? They had all been so close and then suddenly one year turned to two, and then two to three. It all just sort of got easier that way: out of sight, out of mind.

"I know, I hate it's taken me this long." She picked at a piece of lint on her arm. "So, where's Maggie and Erica? Max called me from the airport to say he's missed his flight and to get the beers chilled."

"Maggie has the girls in their room downstairs. Pierre hasn't arrived yet and who knows if he will. Erica is in her room with a box of wine-on-the-go." She lowered her voice, "you know how tense things are between them."

Yes, she did. Everyone knew why there was so much tension. The drama that finally came to a head three years ago. She shook off the thought, grabbed a glass, and headed into Erica's room.

"Yo, little sis, give me a dose of the good stuff," she said and handed her glass to Erica.

"Sure, and a welcome home to you too!" Erica jumped up and gave her big sister a long embrace.

Rachel was struggling to maintain her stoic exterior as they pulled away. "Rach, what's up?"

Rachel shrugged, kept her eyes to the floor. "I just can't believe it's been so long."

Erica handed her back a very full glass. "Hey, forget it, we've got wine, we've got Wi-Fi….it can't be so bad!"

"Touché!" Rachel took a deep breath and glugged back some wine. "Can't believe you still buy this basic shit."

"Hey, I was going for quantity over quality for all this family time."

Can't argue with that.

4

The sound of loose gravel under tires woke Erica and Rachel from their reunion. Rachel jumped up to look out the big window in Erica's room. "It's Max!" She left Erica to her wine and ran out to see her big brother. Even though it had been awhile, she could always rely on her brother, the rock, to give her a sense of comfort.

"Hey sis! What's it been, five years or something? God you've aged." He laughed as he pulled her in for a big hug.

Somehow even Max's jokes helped during these times. She breathed in her brother's shampoo and felt the strength of his arms around her, bringing her back into the embrace of her family.

"Whatever old man, did these elbow patches come with the corn cob pipe, or do you buy those separately from the Professor store? Plus you're looking a lot more salt than pepper up top these days!"

"Aunt Rachel!" Chloe said running across the gravel.

"There's my gorgeous girl!" Rachel picked up her niece and twirled her around. Until now, she had only seen her newest niece on video chat or through photos, a thought that sparked tears.

"Where's Uncle Peter?" Chloe asked the question everyone had been avoiding. "Is he gone 'cause you got a divorce?"

"Yes honey, we got a divorce, but don't worry, Peter is fine and still asks about all of you," she lied.

"Come Chloe, let's go find your cousins." Max saved her from any more questions. She mouthed thank you and followed them inside to grab a beer with her brother. "Where's the other wicked sisters?" He shouted as the door banged open.

"Dear, keep it down please, your father is still asleep," Mom whispered from the kitchen.

"He seems to be doing that an awful lot now, Mom. What's up with the old man?" he asked.

Mom's cheeks flushed as she jumped up, eager to change the topic. "Okay! Chloe come, let's find the girls!"

"Hey big brother! How's school treating ya these days?" Erica asked as she crossed the living room to join them. Having struggled to finish fashion school, Erica couldn't believe her brother chose to stay in higher education of his own free will.

"Pretty awesome. For those that can hack it anyway," he said and stuck his tongue out at her.

She punched him in the arm and grabbed one of his beers. "Not everyone is blessed with these looks."

"The modeling thing turning out okay then?" he asked.

A leggy five foot eleven, with thick blonde hair and a thin physique, Erica had initially found it somewhat easy starting a modeling career. But the few decent jobs posing for average magazines aside, she was still struggling to crack into the world of high fashion.

"I have a few promising gigs lined up, lots of fires on and all that," she said. She watched the sweat from her beer bottle leave little circles on the marble counter top.

"I think you'll find it's lots of irons in the fires there, Ms. Universe," he teased. "Shouldn't you be watching the carbs there anyway?"

"Don't be jealous all your students Google me while they should be listening to your boring lectures!" she said triumphantly and jumped away before he could give her a punch back.

The laughter began to die down as Maggie came up the stairs from the basement, her girls, Anna and Abby, at her heels. "Don't stop on my account please," Maggie said pushing past Erica.

"Max, hey, good to see you." She gave him a warm hug, then the same for Rachel. Rachel scooped up Abby, another new niece to join the family since she had been living in London.

"Hey Mags, no hug for me?" Erica asked, feeling brave from an afternoon of drinking.

Maggie turned, narrowing her gaze on Erica. "Hey Erica, don't worry, I'm not sure Pierre is coming, mostly thanks to you."

Rachel shifted uncomfortably in her flip flops. She let Abby slide back down to play with her sister in the adjoining living room, avoiding all eye contact. Erica slammed her beer down on the island and ran out of the room.

"God Mags, couldn't you be chill for like five minutes?" Max hissed.

"I can't help it if she nearly broke up my marriage!" Maggie shouted.

"Hey girls, why don't we go see what Chloe found out back?" he slid a hand into each of theirs and made a beeline for the screen door.

"I think she just wants to clear the air Mags. If you remember, it was a pretty shit time for everyone," Rachel said, reaching to lay a hand on Maggie's shoulder before she pulled away.

"Oh yeah, your wedding day was a really terrible time for you, wasn't it?" she asked, forgetting for a moment all the events that led to three years of anger, hatred, and awkward phone calls.

5

Rachel took an ungraceful swig of champagne out of her 'Bride' flute. "Oh god, I'm so nervous." She hadn't yet finished her hair and makeup before she polished off her second glass.

"Maybe let's take it easy," Maggie suggested, offering her a strong coffee.

"Is it normal to suddenly doubt this whole thing?" Rachel panicked. "I mean, I know we're meant to be together, right? Oh god, what if we aren't?" She waved away the makeup artist to give her a minute to compose herself.

Maggie took out her cell phone to try and find Erica. She needed back-up this morning. This was not a time to flake. "I'm going to find Erica. Take five, beautiful bride, and don't worry. Just focus on how stunning you're going to look in your wedding dress!"

Mags felt the suite door click closed behind her and leaned her head against it. How could she tell her beautiful baby sister that everyone thought Peter was the wrong choice? That she was sacrificing her own goals and aspirations, for his?

If only her sister could find what she had with Pierre! She dialed his number again wondering why she didn't see him for the final tux fittings this morning either. "Hi darling, where are you?"

"Just in our room, getting organized mon amour," he cooed in that sexy French accent Maggie still couldn't resist after seven years together. "I can't talk though, I need to call the office, kisses, bisous." He hung up quickly before she could respond. She checked the time and realized she had to get Anna ready for her flower girl duties. At only one year old, Maggie was going to have to stroll her down the aisle, and being a heavy seven months pregnant, was dreading the thought.

"Erica, thank god!" Rachel shouted when she finally walked into the bridal suite, "I'm so goddamn nervous; am I making the right choice?" She studied her little sister's face, knowing she would tell her the truth.

"Rach, it's just nerves, come on, everyone gets them," she soothed, topping their champagne glasses.

"Then why do I feel sick? Tell me something to take my mind off things."

Erica paused and looked around to make sure no one else was around. "Okay, here's something. I had to bring the boys their boutonnieres and I think Pierre has already been into the whiskey," she raised an eyebrow. Ever since Mags finally brought him home, everyone struggled to warm to him. It wasn't just a cultural clash, it was the sensual comments, the lingering looks, the slimy kisses at family gatherings. Is that what Mags truly wanted? She deserved a man that respected their marriage (and healthy boundaries).

"That's good, this is helping!" Rachel nodded, "What else? What did he do?"

Erica sighed and pinched the bridge of her nose. "Well, he asked for my help tying his bowtie, but as I was doing that he leaned in, and well, he kissed me." Erica shivered at the memory.

Rachel shook her head. "We've all been there." Even poor Max caught the receiving end of one after a particularly boozy New Year's Eve.

"No, he *really* kissed me—pulled me in close and everything. It was like he'd been planning it for months." Erica twirled her now empty champagne glass between her fingers. "Did you see his slutty assistant drop off some files for him this morning? I don't trust that relationship."

"So, are you going to tell Mags?"

"Tell Maggie what? Oh my gosh, darling you look absolutely stunning!" Mom gushed upon entering. The conversation would have to wait.

"Thanks Mom, you don't think the veil is too much?"

"Or the white?" Max joked as he gave his kid sister a kiss on the cheek. "You look great, Ray."

Maggie wasn't far behind as she ran into the room with Dad in tow, holding Anna in his arms, adorable in her little white dress.

Dad smiled and grabbed a glass of champagne from the table and raised his glass, "To Rachel…may your future be as bright as you are, babe."

The family clinked glasses. She'd never felt happier to have the people she loved most beside her.

Standing outside of the church, the butterflies were still rattling around Rachel's stomach. She cursed herself for not eating something. She couldn't help but stop her father once more for a final piece of reassurance. "Hey Pop, you're sure this is the right guy for me? The father of your grandkids, the one I'll grow old with, all that stuff?" she searched his eyes for answers.

"Look kiddo, it's just nerves. When your mother and I got married, she was a wreck the day of the wedding—and she was marrying me, a total catch!" he winked.

"I know but, I mean, you and Peter never exactly got on the best."

"Yeah, but honey, he's just not the same kind of guy that's all; he's more white collar and I'm blue. It's just hard to relate. I wouldn't ever tell you not to marry someone based on what I think," he said, trying to be as honest as possible without crushing his daughter.

"Hm, not sure that was the pillar of strength I was after there, Pop!" She adjusted the pearl bracelet on her wrist.

"Look babe, you love him, right? You've been through quite a bit together: college, jobs, moving cities. And he's been supportive, right? You just have to continue to work on things that's all. It isn't some fairy tale like in the movies. It's just like building a house: if you've got a good foundation, like it seems you do, things will be just fine." He kissed her on the cheek and looped her arm into his, then searched her face for the okay. She took a deep breath and nodded for the doors to open.

"May we present for the first time as Mr. and Mrs. Mitchell, your bride and groom!" the emcee announced as Rachel and Peter ran into their reception amid great applause. It was a slightly more extravagant affair than Rachel ever imagined—a country club in Maine with spectacular views over the ocean. Peter's family had insisted on covering majority of the costs to see their only child married in style. Rachel scanned the room and took a contented breath. So happy and swept away by the celebrations, it was strange to think hours ago she'd been so uncertain. She found Peter in the crowd, drinking whiskey at the bar with his groomsmen—looking confident, happy.

She headed for the large French doors that opened up on to the patio, the starry night sky coating everything in a golden glow. She grabbed a flute of champagne from the outside bar, ducked under the twinkling lights on the pergola and headed to look for her family—she wanted to enjoy this moment with them.

"Erica!" she shouted as she saw her sister rushing around the side gardens.

"Oh, there's the gorgeous little bride!" Erica slurred, looking a bit distraught.

"Not gonna lie, little Ernie, you've definitely looked fresher," Rachel dabbed her sister's eye, clearing her smudged mascara. "Have you been crying?"

"That pompous Pierre. Did you know his assistant, Leslie, is still hanging around the lobby? I saw them together and tried to confront him. Anyway, it doesn't matter, where is Max?" Erica tried changing the subject.

"I haven't seen him since he was downing whiskeys during the main course with Kailey and Mike." She raised her eyebrows, referring to their neighbors, the Conroy's, from back home. Not to mention, Kailey spent most of their childhood chasing after Max, who couldn't have been more oblivious to her intentions.

"Here comes the love doctor now!" Rachel laughed as Max walked towards them. He was looking quite disheveled but a cheeky grin was plastered across his face.

"And what have you been up to?" she slapped her brother on the back as Kailey walked out behind him, smiling from ear to ear.

"A man never kisses and tells," he hiccupped. "God, I hate weddings. No offense, sis." He clumsily threw his arms around her, nearly collapsing onto her. "Don't tell anyone I slept with Kailey tonight, okay?"

Rachel laughed, welcoming the distraction. "She finally wore you down! This is awesome; for sure going in the next Christmas card."

"What's that you're saying, Max?" Dad asked as he and Mom walked over, ready to head in for the night with a sleeping Anna in his arms.

"Yeah, we saw you with Kailey. You really dodged a bullet with that one, son." Dad jabbed him in the ribs as Max struggled to remain upright.

"Erica, are you ok hon?" Mom said, putting her arms around Erica.

Before she could respond, Maggie was stomping across the manicured country club grass, her heels digging into the soil with every thump.

"Mags, what's the problem?" Rachel asked.

"Why don't you ask our lying little sister??" Maggie practically shouted, her balled up fists turning white.

"Whoa whoa, ladies," Max tried to get between the girls but tripped in his drunken stupor, nearly taking Rachel down with him.

Erica stared at her sister, afraid of how to respond.

"Nothing to say huh? How about telling us why you and Pierre were missing at the exact time and Leslie tells me you were practically his shadow all night? I confront him and he tells me you threw yourself at him this morning!"

"It isn't like that!" Erica jerked her head up and shouted. "Look, I didn't want to say anything before but," she stammered, then shook her head. "Why is Leslie is even here?! Just ask your husband what we were doing. You should it hear it from him anyway," she stumbled back, losing her nerve and footing all at once.

The sounds of Twist and Shout blared across the lawn, crickets could be heard adding their own song to the chorus. Maggie took a step back, "so, it's true huh? I knew you were pathetic, I just didn't think you'd stoop this low."

"Maggie hon, let's call it a night and just chat in the morning," Mom said, looking from one girl to the other.

"No, screw this whole charade. We shouldn't even be here celebrating." Maggie's voice had gone from shaky to enraged.

"We've all had quite a bit to drink, let's get some sleep and talk about it with clear heads in the morning," Dad urged. Anna was getting heavy in his arms as he shifted her to the other shoulder.

"You're the worst of it, Dad!" Maggie shouted, "you're the one who told us all to just lie and pretend everything is okay when you fucking hate that guy Rachel just married! Don't lie and tell her you didn't!"

"Dad, is this true?" Rachel could no longer hear the music, just her heart beating in her chest, the champagne banging against her temples. "But you said...I just asked you again today and you said..."

"Honey, it's not that—look your father is right, everyone has had a lot to drink and we're all going to say something we regret in the morning," Mom pleaded, grabbing Rachel's arm reassuringly.

"No, I want to hear it now! Is this true? Do you all hate Peter? Peter, as in my new husband?!" Rachel noted the hysteria in her tone as she wiggled out of her mom's grasp. The champagne and lack of food all day was finally catching up to her. The trees seemed to blur around her, melting into one another. She angrily swiped the fresh hot tears from her eyes before they could spill over, allowing the dam to break and a river to flow.

"It's just we worry about you sometimes," Dad said soothingly, "I don't want you giving up your own dreams or sacrificing all of your hard work. We only want the best for you, but I meant what I said before, if you love him and choose him, then so do we."

"Somehow that just sounds a bit fucking hollow right now, Dad" Rachel finally let the levee break and the tears were coming in fast and hot. She quickly turned to go. Where, she didn't know, but it had to be away from here.

"Honey don't go like that," Mom called, but Rachel was already halfway across the grounds and headed for the bridal suite.

"I'd appreciate it if you stayed away from me and my family," Maggie looked coldly at Erica as she turned to grab her sleeping daughter from Dad and leave.

"Wait, what happened?" Max picked himself back up to see only Erica and his parents remaining, the tension palpable. "I think I'm gonna be sick," he groaned. Mom and Dad propped him up and practically carried he and a distraught Erica back to the hotel.

6

There was a thud behind them as Dad opened his bedroom door and started across the large living room and past the original wood fireplace of the cabin.

Before the girls could reminisce too much, Rachel ran excitedly to give her dad a hug. In the three years since she'd seen her family in person, her parents had developed deeper lines and a worn disposition she didn't remember noting. Did she really miss that much?

"You look great Dad." She nuzzled in closer to his chest, his towering six foot three frame enveloping her.

"Bullshit Cricket, I look awful. I'm still trying to get rid of this old beer belly and I can count the hairs left up on top of this bald head." He laughed and gave her a kiss on the head. "We're just thankful you finally moved home and stopped playing around in Europe, even if you did come back with that funny accent."

"You mean came back to my senses?" she said smiling up at him.

After Rachel and Peter married, they decided to spend some time living and working abroad. Getting her wish to bust out of the small town, they were off to London where Rachel worked her way up from lowly intern to in-demand reporter at The Times. She figured if she and Peter could create a bubble for themselves, and keep the negativity of her friends and family away from them, she could grow to be happy in her marriage.

It didn't take long for that dream to backfire.

7

"Hey, you're Rachel right?" She looked up from her arm full of books to see a tall, sandy haired, guy, his backpack slung over one shoulder, exposing his NYU Violets football jersey. She had just finished her shift at the paper and already risked running late for her next class.

"Yes, and you're...Phil?"

"Close! Peter." He put his hand forward to introduce himself.

"Nice to meet you," she said. "But I'm, uh just rushing off to my next class." She nodded to the books and laptop she pressed into her chest.

"Here, let me help," he offered.

She handed over her books. "Thanks, I'm prepping for my thesis next year and they don't warn you about the upper body strength needed to complete."

Walking with Peter to her class, Rachel remembered seeing him once or twice over their years on campus, even had a mutual friend here and there. He was cute, athletic, and planned to follow in his dad's footsteps into the world of finance after finishing his MBA next year. Having had little time (or desire) to date much during university, she found herself agreeing to a drink the next week before finals got underway.

During their first date, Rachel couldn't believe they hadn't crossed paths before. Sure, she had dabbled with guys during her undergrad but once she started her Master's in Journalism, the pool got smaller and smaller. Not exactly a winning lottery, was it? It wasn't long after their first date that the two become inseparable. Peter was never shy about showing his love for Rachel: bringing her flowers, constantly texting, picking up her favorite wine and making special reservations for them. She was blown away by his attentiveness and found herself quite enjoying being in a relationship after all.

By summer, Rachel hated the idea of Peter staying in New York without her, so instead of spending another four months bumming around her hometown, getting hours at the local paper, she and Peter decided to move in together and spend the summer working in New York. She secured a small but paid internship at New York News, and he managed to get a decent entry level job through his dad's contacts at Goldman Sachs.

Rachel's dream of long walks in Central Park and brunches spent on the patio together quickly became nothing but that, a dream. With her friends back home for the summer and Peter working such long hours, she found the time incredibly lonely. By the time the Fourth of July long weekend rolled around, she packed her bags and headed home for some much needed family time.

Rachel told the taxi driver to pull over in front of 2561 Apple Orchard Lane, the familial turkey mailbox bringing a smile to her face. She got out and looked up at the only home she'd ever known: bright blue shutters set amidst the windows of the two story home complete with white vinyl siding, still bearing a crack under the living room window from when Max thankfully missed launching his soccer ball straight through the window. She paid her fare and headed for the front door.

"I'm home!" she shouted. Erica got to the door first and gave her a tight squeeze.

"Geez cool it little sis," she said, stepping out of the embrace. "It's not like I've returned from war."

"I've just missed you," Erica said quietly. Rachel pulled Erica back in for a proper hug, and allowed herself to be comforted. So much had happened since she last saw everyone, maybe she needed family time more than she'd like to admit.

"Come on, let the poor girl in!" Dad called, jogging through from the kitchen. "Hey Cricket!" he hugged Rachel, then helped her out of her coat and tossed it onto the hook on the wall.

"Now tell us about this guy stealing you away from us!" Mom called from the kitchen. "I've put a fresh pot of coffee on and there's fresh cookies here." Mom never did disappoint.

"Give me a minute, Mom," she said, despite grabbing a warm chocolate chip cookie. "There's nothing to tell! We've got a teeny tiny apartment in Brooklyn, the paper is good. I mean, I wish I could get more features but New York News is good experience, covering lots of local events so at least I'm able to explore the city—even if on my own."

"Who is this Peter guy then?" Dad asked, "you do know I need to approve of any and all suitors, right?" He went to grab a second cookie but Mom smacked his hand and gave him a knowing look.

He must be on another diet, Rachel thought.

"What decade is this, Pop?" she laughed. "He really wanted to come this weekend but work is so hectic at the minute and he's trying to make a good impression for after graduation." She wondered if they could tell she was lying.

Peter hadn't once feigned interest in coming back with her. Yes, work was a bit crazy but in his words, "it wasn't for him". Growing up an only child in a relatively cold family, she sensed the noise and chaos orbiting hers was more than most could handle. Alas, she'd come on her own.

"As long as you're happy dear," Mom offered Rachel another cookie. "I just can't wait to meet him! Labor Day right?"

"Definitely! I've told him he cannot miss our big end-of-summer BBQ," she kissed her mom on the cheek, slipped off her shoes, and headed out to the pool to relax. It was good to be home.

Rachel slowly found her parents contact in her cell phone and hit dial. She nervously waited for her mom to pick up. Mom was likely putting the final touches on her famous American flag sheet cake. It was the annual Woods Labor Day party and it just wouldn't be complete without it.

"Hello?" her mom said upon answering.

"Mom! Hey, it's Rach!" she said cheerily down the line.

"Oh hi darling, are you guys on your way? Cake is all done and your dad should be firing up the grill soon. He's out on a bike ride after the doctor told him light exercise was no longer optional!"

Rachel cleared her throat. "Uh, not quite Mom…it doesn't look like we'll be able to make it after all," she stammered.

"Oh Ray Ray, come on, we haven't seen you in almost two months! Plus no Woods has ever missed it…"

"Mom, we're just busy! I've told you guys a thousand times," Rachel said exasperated, widening her eyes at Peter.

"Just hang up the phone," he whispered.

"I mean, we've never even spoken to him…"

"It's not like he doesn't exist," she held the phone out to Peter. "Here, he'll say hello to you now."

Peter threw his hands up in front of his face, aggressively shaking his head before running out of the room.

"Sorry Mom, he's just gotten a call," she lied, padding down the hallway after Peter. "Look, we'll see you guys at Thanksgiving and you'll see why he's so great, okay?" she hung up and stared blankly at her phone for a minute. She hated fighting with her parents; she hated not going home most weekends like she used to. She hated lying.

Peter was sitting slouched on their bed, mindlessly flipping through a magazine. "Why didn't you want to talk to my mom just now?"

He slammed the magazine shut. "God Rach, I've never even met the woman and you just want me to hop on a phone call with her?"

"Well, it's not my fault you haven't met them yet," she mumbled.

"You wanna go so badly to some lame party in the suburbs, then just go for it."

"It's not that and you know it's not about the party. I want you to *want* to come and meet my family! I'm so close with them and yet, these days I barely see them anymore. Ever consider my feelings?" she shouted as she angrily threw her hair into a bun.

"Yeah, well excuuuuse me if we didn't all grow up in some rosy colored house where every day was an after school special." He walked to the dresser and mindlessly tinkered with the few things on it. Clearly, he was in no mood to continue the conversation.

Rachel left the room and grabbed a beer in the kitchen, letting the first few cold sips hit her stomach. She knew Peter had a hard childhood with an absentee dad who worked long hours and a mom addicted to prescription pills. Poor guy didn't even have any siblings to keep him company. She had a feeling her home life intimidated him and as a result, he chose to stay away rather than get too close.

Peter stormed out mumbling something about needing to work on an account and Rachel was left alone, yet again, with her thoughts. She grabbed another beer, took a deep breath and called Erica.

"Hi, who's this?" her sister asked jokingly.

"This isn't 1992, we all have caller ID now," Rachel said, as she flopped down on the leather sofa.

"What's up, sis? Aren't you and Peter off somewhere fantastic, too busy for all us wee folk?" Although she was joking, the words stung.

"No, he's just gone into the office. You know he's getting more and more hours as he wraps up college, they're even trusting him with his own accounts." She chided herself for faking enthusiasm.

"Oh yes, he's very important, I know. Guess Daddy is really helping him to get his foot on the ladder huh?" Erica started, when Rachel let out a little sigh. "Okay I'll stop, last one! What's up?"

"I don't know, I just asked him why he never wants to meet or talk to anyone and he totally blew up at me."

"Really? I thought you guys never fought?" Erica said.

Because that was just it. Rachel never shared the true nitty gritty of their relationship with anyone. She stayed stoic and tried to paint a pretty picture. She hated the idea of people seeing past the shiny veneer she shared with the world and noticing the imperfections. The cracks that seemed to be appearing on the surface, threatening to swallow Rachel whole.

"No, I mean it's rare," she lied. "He's just so stressed with work, and I'm spending more and more time alone so just having time to think I guess."

"Think about what?" Erica pried.

"I don't know, never mind, forget I ever said anything." Rachel said, getting up and tossing her beer bottle into the recycling bin. She headed back into the living room and took a seat along the window sill to watch the busy street below. Maybe a change of scenery would help her mood?

"Hey sis, come on. We never talk like we used to. Remember all the times we'd get into trouble as kids together, pissing off Max and Maggie? Or those hours spent in our room because we *clearly* were up to no good. Or how every time I've struggled with this modeling thing, and all the loser guys, you've always been there for me," she said quietly. "Let me do the same for you."

"I know, Ernie, you're right. I just don't know what happened. When we first got together, he was a total charmer. Spoiling me, leaving me little notes all the time, helping around the apartment. And now I just barely see him. And when I do, it usually ends with a fight. I think it will all be better once grad school is done and we can just focus on work. Plus, he finally gets to meet you all at Thanksgiving!"

"Exactly! Chin up sis, pour a glass of wine, switch on a chick flick and just enjoy the peace and quiet!" Rachel smiled. She knew Erica was trying really hard to be there for her and supportive of her relationship with Peter, even if she got the impression Peter hadn't quite won everyone over just yet.

She longed to share everything with her sister, and her entire family for that matter. She wanted to spill every bean, vent all her frustrations about Peter and just have that shoulder to lean on. He could be so terrible with his temper at times. But he would always make it up to her, and she wanted to be there for him, to show him that not everyone would abandon him.

Rachel's phone started vibrating as she rolled out of Grand Central Station and away from the busy city, with its dusting of winter's first snow. "Happy Thanksgiving, Mom!" Rachel cheered to her mom down the line.

"You too, honey! Are you guys on your way? Daddy's wondering when to get you at the train station. He even cleaned out the truck to make a good impression for Peter." She laughed.

Rachel took a deep breath and rubbed her forehead. "Actually, it's just going to be me, Mom."

"What? Is everything okay? Why isn't Peter coming?"

"He wanted to prep for finals and has a meeting with one of his dad's contacts next week at JPMorgan Chase so he's staying home to prepare." The lies just rolled off her tongue now.

"Okay, dear...it's just, we missed you on Labor Day and now he's leaving you alone again on a holiday is all."

"I'm not alone, he knows I've got you guys! Anyway, my train gets in at 5:30, I'll see Dad there. Can't wait for the pumpkin pie!" Rachel tried to end on a good note before hanging up.

She put her phone away and leaned back in her seat. She and Peter had a huge blowout right before she left. He couldn't believe she would just leave him on a holiday, especially when he had such an important meeting coming up. Why couldn't he see how important her family were to her? Because he hadn't grown up that way himself, something for which Rachel held a soft spot. There were no camping holidays in the middle of nowhere, fighting, laughing and making s'mores around the campfire for him. No long drives to visit relatives the next state over. While she looked forward to making new memories around the major holidays, he became reclusive and distant.

She stopped the snack cart attendant for a coffee as he passed by. After paying she was still wondering: how did they work with so little in common? When they first met, it seemed they were two peas in a pod but soon the differences became more and more apparent. She had decided to broach the conversation with Peter last week over the red and white checkered table at their corner Italian restaurant, Antonio's. A long overdue date night, not exactly the time to stoke an argument. Half a bottle of chianti down however, and she felt emboldened to ask.

"Don't you think it's great how we are a great example of how opposites attract?" she asked followed by a big gulp of wine.

Peter stopped chewing and wiped his mouth with the black cloth napkin. "What does that mean?"

"Oh, just you know, some couples have endless things in common but I like that we're one of those couples that complement the other's strengths and weaknesses," she said laying a hand on his.

"Yeah, you drive me crazy and yet I'm a dream to live with." He smirked, running his thumb along the top of her hand.

"Not exactly, but something like that." She smiled as she leaned over for a kiss. He kissed her back and gave her a peck on the nose before she pulled away. Something he'd always done which made Rachel smile.

As he signaled for the check, she knew the conversation was over. She was sure it was just the usual thoughts of the grass is always greener that everyone had, right?

As Peter turned his BMW 3 Series into her parents snowy drive, Rachel could hardly contain her excitement that everyone was finally going to meet her great love. She bounded through the door ecstatic for everyone to finally meet Peter.

"Merry Christmas everyone! This is Peter!"

Peter followed Rachel inside, tapping away on his Blackberry.

"Peter...put it away," she whispered.

"So sorry, everyone! Really nice to finally meet you all." He smiled naturally, reaching out to shake her Dad's hand.

"That's quite the ride there Peter." Dad motioned out the window at Peter's shiny silver new wheels.

"Thank you sir. That's a little perk from JPMorgan for accepting their offer. Start the first of May after school."

"Wow, now that's impressive! Best I ever got from an employer was a beat up FORD F150 for site." He chuckled.

"Yes well, I guess they want me to make a good impression for clients." He shifted uncomfortably.

Mom hustled in from the kitchen, wiping her hands on the dish towel thrown across her shoulder. "That's enough car talk for me! Peter, great to finally meet you!" she said, going straight in for the hug.

Peter hugged her quickly and awkwardly before his phone started vibrating in his pocket.

"Uh, so sorry Mrs. Woods, but I need to take this." He slipped his coat back on to take the call on the front doorstep.

"Wow, I feel like I know him already," Max mumbled, coming down the stairs.

"Shut up!" Rachel gave him a smack on the shoulder. "It's intimidating coming into a big house meeting this lot."

"He seems very nice, dear," Mom said putting her arm in Rachel's. "Come, help me finish icing these cookies while he's on his call." She threw a dirty look over her shoulder before following Rachel out.

While Peter was out on his call, Rachel tried to lighten the mood. "So how long did it take to get the lights up this year, Pops?"

"Easy peasy, just like that," he said snapping his fingers.

Erica snorted from behind. "Sorry, cookie went down the wrong way," she said stifling a laugh. "Not that Dad kept me up last night cursing at those damn lights ending up in a ball again!" she said mimicking Dad.

He tousled her hair and gave her a wink. "Christmas traditions and all that, kiddo."

"So, tell us about this guy," Dad asked. "Is it serious?"

"I think so, Dad. Look, everyone just give him a bit of a break, okay? He's really stressed about this new job. It's an incredible opportunity for him." She hated how desperate she sounded. Was she always so shrill?

"Yes, dear, it's fine!" Mom reassured. "Why don't you go check on him for dinner, honey?"

Rachel managed to get Peter to finally hang up the call and join everyone for some eggnog, but he still spent the majority of the night on the phone.

After yet another day spent with an absent Peter, Rachel cornered him up in her old room. "You haven't even tried to get to know them."

"God, Rach, get off my back! You know I'm under it right now and don't really need added shit from you."

"Fine, fine. Sorry I said anything." Rachel paced the bedroom. "It's just, we came all this way and they've been dying to meet you. I want them to see why I love you so much." She tried to give him a kiss but he moved away.

"Look, I'm sorry, babe. You know how much I've wanted to meet everyone. Just leave me to sort this out, okay? It's gonna take me hours to look over this file on this Wi-Fi connection." He gave her a quick peck on the cheek before shuffling her out the door. She knew he'd make it up to her another time: a beautiful bouquet of flowers, tickets to a Broadway show.

Rachel left the room to find Maggie standing in the hall. "Come on, we've just opened some fantastic wine from Pierre!" She put her arm around Rachel and they headed down to the kitchen. Rachel leaned her head on Maggie's shoulder and walked toward the laughter downstairs.

29

8

Back at the cottage, Rachel was in desperate need for air. Crossing the lush green grass, she made her way down to the long wooden dock to see Max sitting on the side with his feet dangling in the cool water.

"Pretty nice place, isn't it?" she said walking up behind him.

"Yeah, it's awesome, thank god Mom is so organized and managed to find a place that fits this entire brood!" He handed her a beer from the mini cooler beside him. Did this place come stocked or did Mom waste no time casting her spell? Rachel knew it was the latter.

She sat down beside him and let her toes make little circles in the water.

"So, what took ya so long, Crick?" He asked quietly bumping shoulders with her. A single loon called as it glided across the calm surface of the lake.

She turned to the side to really scan her brother's face. He was showing no shortage of grey hairs poking out from under his baseball cap, and she noted his laugh lines seemed to be a little deeper. And yet, the mischievous smile of his youth remained untouched.

"I know...I just didn't know, I mean, I wanted to," she stumbled, her voice catching in her throat.

"Hey sis, it's no biggie," he pulled her in for a long hug, "hasn't been a piece of cake around here either to tell you the truth."

"I bet…I think I've dodged a bit of a shitstorm over here," she mumbled before taking a long refreshing sip of her beer.

"Yeah, things have definitely changed," he stated sadly.

"Is everything else okay? With Mom? And Dad?" she asked, worried about what he might say.

"I don't think the stress has been good for either of them. They don't look so good, huh?"

She started to cry openly. "I can't take it if something is wrong, Max. If

I've missed out on these years only to find out something isn't right."

"Hey, hey, no shh. Look, it's all getting a bit heavy right out the gate!" He joked. "Come check out this boat they have here!"

He helped her up and they walked to the end of the dock, but before she had a chance to catch herself, Max threw her in.

"Max!" she shouted after she resurfaced. "Still the same annoying big brother then!" She splashed up at him.

He laughed as he cannon balled in after her. The kids ran down to the dock after hearing the splashing, and it didn't take long before they were excitedly jumping into the cool water too.

Floating on her back, the hot sun on her face and the laughter of her family nearby, Rachel closed her eyes and took it all in.

9

Two weeks after the disastrous wedding confessions, Rachel had just returned home to Philadelphia from honeymoon. They had moved there after grad school for Peter's job at JPMorgan Chase and now, barely home an hour, he had already gone into the office for a few hours to catch up on work. Trying to avoid unpacking and tackling the mass amount of laundry that would ensue, she took out her phone and with a deep breath, dialed her parents.

"Rachel sweetie, hi!" her mom shouted.

"Hey Mom! Can you hear me, where are you?"

"Just finishing at the supermarket, what's up, honey? How was the honeymoon?" she asked as she paid and turned to leave the store.

Rachel hadn't spoken to any one in her family since the night of the wedding. She took advantage of an early flight to Tahiti and limited cell signal to spend time with her new husband and try to put the events from the wedding out of her mind.

"It was fine, beautiful actually. Only mildly tainted by the fact that my family hates my new husband." Rachel noted the hostility in her voice. She hated taking it out on her mom but she was jet-lagged and the pent-up anger had nowhere else to go.

"Sweetie, we feel terrible about it all really. Why don't you come out this weekend and have dinner? Just the four of us?"

"Um, I don't know," Rachel didn't even want to suggest it to Peter. Knowing it was unlike her to not at least try and get in touch with her family while away so long, he asked her one night over dinner on yet another white sand beach, why she seemed so distracted and whether she wanted to use his work phone to call them. She just lied and said she wanted to truly embrace being incommunicado for a bit. Peter was more than happy to leave it at that.

"Please dear, your father hasn't slept a wink since the wedding night. We really want to see you. Just think about it, honey, and call me, okay?" she pleaded before hanging up.

Rachel hung up and stared down at her phone. She suddenly threw it against the bedroom wall and flopped down on the bed. She let the tears finally flow as she let go of the anger she was holding onto. She'd normally reach out to her sisters but even now she didn't know where everyone stood. Who could she trust? Who could she depend on? When did everything get so complicated?

Her phone started to ring from under the bed. She wiped the tears off her cheeks and cursed as she crawled under the bed to grab her phone.

"There's that Woods temper," she mumbled as she looked at the Caller ID.

Erica. "Hey Rach, how was the honeymoon?" she asked cheerily.

"Hope we gave you a good send-off!"

"What a fucking train wreck that whole thing was," Rachel's voice trembled.

"Hey, come on now, it's all part of it. Big families, big events—there's gonna be big drama!"

"Yeah, I just wish it wasn't something I was already worried about. Making the right choice..." she trailed off and started picking at the luggage tag on her suitcase.

"You don't still have those doubts do you, Rach?" Erica asked quietly.

The door to their apartment slammed shut, and Rachel jerked her head up.

"Hey babe, come on, we're going for dinner to celebrate!" Peter yelled as he kicked off his shoes and walked down the hallway.

"Look, just forget it, okay? We've gotta go. Chat later?" she asked without waiting for Erica's response before hanging up.

A few minutes later, Rachel and Peter were back at Antonio's as a waiter brought over a silver ice bucket with a bottle of Veuve Clicquot. The waiter popped the cork and topped up their flutes with the chilled amber bubbles.

"Ahem, a toast please," Peter raised his glass of champagne up to meet Rachel's.

"And to what are we toasting exactly?" she asked him.

"Not only have I been promoted but get this! They want to send me over to the London office!" Peter nearly shouted. "Can you believe it, Rach? It's all happening for us."

"Wow! Well done, Peter! Of course, you're the perfect man for the job!" Rachel smiled, trying to push her family out of her mind for now.

"You can get some fabulous job writing for The Times or The Telegraph, sipping lattes in the same place as Dickens." His grin would give the Cheshire cat a run for his money.

"If only!" she said catching his excitement. "So, when do they need you? Guess we have some time to work out the logistics. I'll need to give notice at The Inquirer, and of course plan something with the..." she looked away, "family." What would they think of all this?

"They want me to fly out this weekend to meet everyone and then get started ASAP! I can't believe it. This is it!" He gulped down the rest of his champagne and started to pour another.

"Wait, so when do we have to move? What about our apartment?"

"They're going to sort it all—we don't have to do a thing! As soon as we're done here, we can go home, start packing and start all over again in Europe." He smiled and laid his hand over hers. "Look babe, I know things haven't been quite right since the wedding, I don't know what happened with your family, and frankly, the less Woods drama I know about, the better. But this is a real chance for us to start our own lives. Together. Me and you—a family."

He kissed her hand. He looked so hopeful, excited even, for this next chapter. "I wouldn't be here if it wasn't for your support, baby. To us," he said raising his glass again.

"Cheers to you, Peter, I'm so proud of you," she raised her flute. *What the hell*, she thought, *if not now, when?* "To us," she smiled as they clinked glasses.

The next day Rachel awoke with a pounding head. Too much champagne for a Sunday night. She shook her head awake as the realization of their big move came crashing down on her. Unsure of where to start and the overwhelm washing over her, she wandered down into the kitchen. She must not have heard Peter leave this morning as his briefcase was gone from the kitchen table and just a whiff of his Dior cologne hung in the air. She clicked the coffee pot on. If she was going to completely pack up her life, she was going to need copious amounts of caffeine to help.

The next few days passed by in a blur of packing, phone calls, and life admin. After avoiding too many calls from her family, Rachel headed into her parents for dinner to share the news.

"Thanks for having me for dinner tonight, Mom and Dad...I know it was short notice." She was fidgeting with the napkin on her lap nervously.

"Oh, honey, you never need to say thanks for that. This is still your home dear," Mom said passing Rachel a glass of red wine across the table. Rachel took it greedily, she needed extra courage.

"Okay well, I don't know how to tell you this, but Peter was offered a promotion with amazing chance for advancement but it's not here. I guess his dad has a good connection from his days at Barclays who says Peter would be an excellent asset at the London office of JPMorgan." She took a very large sip of her wine after rushing out the news.

"Oh wow," Dad said, "Cricket that's amazing news! When do you leave?"

"Well that's just it, we leave tomorrow." Rachel couldn't bring herself to look them in the eyes.

Time stopped. The sound of her mother's fork clinking against the plate, the neighbor's dog barking in the distance, the dryer running in the basement. Rachel started to pick her fingernails, her head firmly down, willing them to say something.

"What do you mean tomorrow?! How long have you known?" Mom nearly choked on her wine.

"We only found out on the weekend, so we've been packing things up, trying to get visas expedited; luckily his company is sorting most of the details so we just need to show up at the airport tomorrow. First class if you can imagine." Rachel tried to lighten the mood.

Mom started to cry, "I just can't believe it's so soon! When are you going to tell your brother and sisters? Are you going to go and see everyone?"

"I don't know. Look, I had a hard enough time coming here after everything at the wedding. As far as I know, Erica and Maggie haven't seen or spoken to each other in weeks and Max has dropped off the face of the earth—what's happened to him anyway?" Rachel diverted the conversation and looked at her plate of untouched food—Mom's classic lasagna. She took a bite and it hit her: there would be no Mom's lasagna in London.

"Let's not get off topic here. Rachel, hon, I wish you'd forgive me over all of that," Dad said. "It's just what any parent would say, a dad has a right to look out for his daughter," he said his voice cracking.

Rachel let a lone tear roll down her cheek before aggressively wiping it away. "Do you have any idea how hard it was to hear you guys say that?" She asked slamming her wine glass down, the red liquid splattering across the wooden table. Her voice croaked as the tears threatened to come faster and stronger. "It's just. This is where we are, okay?" She wiped another stray tear away. "I'm married to Peter, we're going to start our lives together in London and that's that. Please try and get onboard." She got up and put her glass in the kitchen sink. "I should really go and finish packing. Thanks for dinner." The tears were pouring too quickly to wipe them away now.

"You're not even going to finish supper?" Mom cried.

"I'm so sorry, but I should really get going." Rachel hung her head guiltily, unable to look at her mom so upset. A pain that she had caused. She headed for the door and slipped on her Converse. Her parents followed close behind and switched on the outdoor light. The cool autumn air breezed in through the screen door.

"We love you so much, honey," Dad admitted defeat and wrapped her in a bear hug. Rachel didn't want to let go but knew she must.

"You better visit! And call, and Skype!" Mom said as she hugged her tightly. Rachel breathed in her mom's perfume and gave her an extra squeeze.

"Love you guys, too. I'll probably see you in a few months anyway! Tell the sibs I'll call them from London, okay?" Rachel walked back to Peter's car. She couldn't look back for fear she'd crumble right there on the walkway. She took a deep breath, put the car in drive and gave a wave to her crying parents on the front step.

Max was sitting in the doctor's office, nervously flipping through a magazine. He kept his head down, avoiding the eyes of the other patients. Happy couples eager to start a new phase of their lives, a mom with a toddler playing at her feet, her baby bump just visible beneath her magazine. Those were the types of people who should be in this room. Not him!

Max had never had a one night stand in his life and chose Rachel's wedding to give it a try. And with Kailey no less. She had called him yesterday to say she booked an appointment—her period was five days late. Apparently, an oddity for her. Even with three sisters he had always avoided discussions about periods, cramps, and lady issues: he simply plugged his ears and left the room. But he knew what it meant to be late, and this was not the time to plug his ears and walk away.

His phone rang loudly from his briefcase. *Didn't he turn the sound off when he came in?* He fumbled through his bag, the ringtone getting louder, which attracted several annoyed glances in his direction across the room. "So sorry," he mumbled as he finally picked up.

"Mom? What's up?" she sounded like she'd been crying.

"Oh, honey," she tried to get the words out but struggled. Dad took the phone. "Hi son, your mother and I wanted to let you know that Rachel just left."

"Is she okay? Why are you both being so dramatic?" His heart began to race, fearing the worst, he got up and walked into the hallway.

"Peter got offered a very lucrative job in London. He's taking it and they're moving. Tomorrow morning." Dad said, the last bit in a breathy rush.

"What? Was she even going to try and see us? Why hasn't she called?" Max tried to keep his voice down as others passed by in the hallway.

"She said it's something she needs to do. I'm sure she'll call everyone." Mom was back on the phone, "we just wanted to let you know, can you call Maggie and we'll get Erica?"

"Of course, Mom." Frustrated as he was, Max knew how much this must be killing her.

Max stood in the bright white hallway staring down at his phone. Before he could turn to go back inside, Kailey walked out of the doctor's office. Her normally round face hung long with her wide brown eyes cast to the floor. "It's positive," she said.

"Hey Mom! Sorry I can't really talk, I'm rushing out for an audition, can I call you back?" Erica said putting the finishing touches on her makeup.

"Hon, we just wanted to fill you in on some news…it's Rach and Peter. They're moving to London," she rushed out matter-of-factly.

"Whoa," Erica set her mascara down. "Well, that's a good thing, right?

Weren't they planning to eventually?" She ignored the sinking in her stomach. How could she withstand not living near her best friend? Or how their last get together went. God, the guilt.

"Yes, a great opportunity for Peter...I just feel responsible somehow," Mom said, her voice catching in her throat.

"Mom, don't do that! We sort of knew they were looking at some options. I know we didn't think it would be so quick though. I hate how that whole wedding went," Erica said sadly. "Feels like a bad omen."

"Don't say that—" Mom cleared her throat—"any word from Maggie?"

"Sadly not. I text her daily and get nothing in return. Not every call goes unanswered though, she did pick it up only to hang up on me once," Erica tried to make her voice sound light. "It was just so stupid. I just wish she'd hear me out, I'm not even sure I'm the bad guy here."

"I know Ernie, it'll all come out in the wash. Max is going to call Maggie and let her know. Do you know why he's been so tense lately?"

"Hmm, no...maybe just his term schedule? I know he's teaching quite a few classes this year. Anyway Mom, I really should go—I'll miss this audition."

"Okay...love you, sweetie."

"Love you too, Mom. It'll be fine, don't worry," Erica clicked the phone off and tried to put everything out of her mind for now. She willed herself to keep it together just until tonight. She needed to nail this casting call at the agency if she had any hopes of making rent this month.

Mags, call me ASAP. Stop ignoring the family calls!

Maggie saw Max's text but put her phone back down. The whole happy family thing was getting old. How can everyone just ignore what happened? She'd never felt so betrayed. And by her family no less! It was bad enough she kept getting calls from Erica but then her family seemed to tag team when to check up on her. It was bigger than the wedding—she had been denying Pierre's wandering eye for years. How could she face her family and look them in the eye, knowing she lacked the confidence to leave someone who was unfaithful? She was so humiliated.

Mags! I'm serious—it's about Rachel. CALL ME

Worried something happened on the honeymoon, she picked up the phone and called him back.

"Max, what is it?" she said shortly. "I'm just not ready to deal with all of that shit from the wedding, so don't even bother asking. Just let me know what's going on with Rach."

"Peter got a job in London…they're moving in the morning."

Maggie stopped folding laundry and sat back onto the sofa.

"Maggie?"

"Yeah, I'm still here…I'm just shocked. I didn't know that was a serious option for them. And now they're going? Tomorrow? What the hell?"

"I know, it shocked us all quite a bit. Mom and Dad aren't taking it so well," he said.

"She couldn't even call us or come see us to say bye properly?" Bile started to rise in her stomach as she pictured that final confrontation at the wedding. "When did everything get so fucked up Max?"

10

As Max rushed the girls off to get changed out of their wet clothes, Rachel sat on the dock letting the water beads drip off her hair onto the warm dock. She grabbed a fluffy towel from the chair her mom had left when unpacking. She lifted the towel up to her nose and inhaled—the same Tide detergent her mom had used for years.

She started to dab her hair dry and head back up to the cabin. The smell of charcoal and searing steaks suddenly made her stomach growl. As she made her way past the bonfire pit, she saw Dad tending the barbecue, cold beer in hand.

He looked up from the grill. "There's my girl! How's the lake? Have to say, saw that one coming, kiddo." He chuckled, his little beer belly bouncing up and down.

"Yeah guess I kind of walked right into that one," she said grabbing one of his light beers. Rachel took a big gulp, letting the bubbles fill her. She let out a satisfied sigh.

"Now you know your mother and I are over the moon you are home. We all are kid, but are we going talk about the elephant in the room at some point this week, or should we just keep knocking back the cold ones?"

In lieu of responding, Rachel polished off the beer then grabbed another.

"Well, guess we could do both," she said popping the cap off.

He laid the tongs down and took a step toward Rachel. "Do you forgive me yet, babe?"

She noticed the faintest sign of tears in his eyes. Seeing her father's emotion signaled her own tears to flow. "You know I never punished you, Dad. In fact, in hindsight, you were right...and I kind of hate that."

"Dad's really do know best," he said with a self-satisfied smile. "So, you wanna tell me how you ended up back home now? I mean, we didn't even hear you were unhappy or thinking about divorce, and next thing we know, you call Mom to tell her you've moved out. What happened in between 'I do' and being here today? Not that we aren't thrilled to have our girl back," he threw his big arm over her shoulder and kissed her wet head.

"It wasn't one thing that just happened. It was a lot of little things."

"Okay, let's start at the beginning. All good stories do."

Rachel played with the label of her beer until it curled off, then set it down. "You know what, Dad? It's feeling just a little intense for the first day."

"Hey guys! How are the steaks coming?" Mom asked coming out on the patio.

"I'm gonna go lie down…think I drank those too fast," Rachel said making her exit.

"Rach, come back" she called.

~

Judy turned to fix her gaze on John. "What did you do?!" She whispered as Rachel slid the patio door closed.

"Nothing! She said she wanted to talk about the divorce so I just asked her what happened." He shrugged.

"I lost her for three years—I won't have her leaving us again!" Tears welled in her eyes.

"Look, don't worry, honey, she's here now…we just need to go easier on her I guess." John gave her a hug. "How's things with Maggie and Erica? World War III call a truce yet?"

"No further fires so far but the week has only just started!" She laughed.

"Do you think we should fill the kids in on the other reason for this trip?" Judy stood on her tip toes to whisper into John's ear.

John took a deep breath in and ran his hands through his wife's short hair, something he must have done thousands of times by now.

He quickly reflected on the past year: the shortness of breath, the inexplicable exhaustion, months of specialist tests, the EKG's showing partial blockages. The list went on. "No. Not yet, I just want to enjoy this week with my family…like we used to." He pulled Judy in closer, her contented sigh signaling her agreement to avoid reality for just a little bit longer.

～

Rachel found Erica inside watching reality TV, her glass of wine perpetually refilled. "I can't believe this show is still on," Rachel said, snuggling into to her little sister. "How many real housewives do they need to have shows about?"

"Apparently one in every city. I won't complain since it's a nice escape from our own real life drama," Erica said, reaching out and tickling Rachel's arm. They sat there in silence for a few minutes, letting the show drown out the real world.

"I never thought I'd miss having your stinky feet in my face," Rachel joked giving her sister's toes a nudge.

"Too many nights crammed into a shared bed hasn't put you off me completely then?" Erica said rubbing them right in her face.

"Ah gross!" Rachel laughed as she shoved them away. "Spoken to Maggie much more today?"

"Nope," Erica said sadly. "I can't even tell you how many times I've tried to call her over the past three years. I've sent letters, texted, called, gone to the door—she just acts as if I've dropped off the face of the planet. Meanwhile, how am I even the one in the wrong here? I was just trying to look out for her."

"What actually happened at the wedding? Maybe if you let us in, we could help patch things up," Rachel tried to finally make sense of things.

"I don't really wanna talk about it Rach, maybe another time," she took a greedy gulp of her wine. Rachel could tell she was hurting so decided to switch gears.

"Well what about holidays? There's no way Mom and Dad would let you guys avoid each other for those."

"Oh, there have been plenty of awkward run-ins and enough polite chit chat. You know we haven't even seen Pierre in over a year?"

"Really?" Rachel had no idea. "Are they still together?"

"We're not sure, you know she's a vault. She won't let anyone in."

"Why didn't anyone tell me this stuff?" Rachel muttered.

"Come on sis, you weren't exactly an open book yourself this past while," Erica said bluntly. "You know Mom and Dad would never intentionally hurt you, or any of us for that matter. They just love you so much. They didn't want to overstep again. And every time you've called or we've seen you on video chat, you've been...I don't know, distant. In both senses of the word I guess."

"Yeah, that's probably fair," Rachel frowned.

"So, what happened? You're my best friend, you gotta tell me something!" Erica gave her a gentle prod.

"I know, I think I've adjusted myself over the years with Peter. I see it, and I feel it too. You guys aren't crazy, it's like I totally forgot who I was. I know it's cliché, but it wasn't one thing, it was a lot of things over time. I wanted so badly for Peter to have the home life we had growing up, and he was constantly promising me this fairy tale. According to my therapist, I'm a sucker for punishment, and that, coupled with his complete narcissism meant there was a lot of chipping away at myself over the years, until I just lost the plot somewhere."

"Lost the plot - that how you Brits say you got lost? Okay, well how does it go from that to 'sign on the dotted line, you're now divorced'?"

Anna ran in, interrupting the girls, swinging her baby doll around. "Nannie says it's time for dinner!!"

Saved by the bell, Rachel thought. Walking toward the kitchen she considered Erica's question.

11

"You're working late again?" Rachel was sitting at the kitchen table in their flat, nursing a glass of red wine. She had gotten dressed up in a brand new black cocktail dress and kitten heels she had decided to splurge on just for the occasion. She was ready and waiting to go for dinner with Peter. It had been weeks since they had eaten a meal together.

She waited on the line for his excuse.

"Look babe, you know how important this account is to me! To us! It's going to get me an awesome bonus we can put toward that big Thailand trip we've been talking about."

"I know, I just miss you is all. Every night you come home after I've gone to bed and you're gone before I even wake up...it's like I live with a ghost," she mumbled.

"Look I don't want to get into this now, Rach, you know how stressed I am at the moment," his voice rising down the line.

"Okay, so tell me when we can discuss it?" she shouted back as the tears started. "All I want is to spend time with my husband, you can't get mad at me for that!"

"Of course not, babe. It's only for a little while. Please try not to be ungrateful, it's like you think I'm doing this for the glory or something and not because I want to look after us."

"Ungrateful! How could you ever think I'm being ungrateful? Who has fiercely defended you over the years to my family? Who has been there every late night, every missed weekend and at every corner, supporting you and your work? Who has missed out on multiple promotions at work because you can't stand me being away when I need to travel?" It was too late to turn back now, years of pent up frustrations were ready to for release. "I mean for fuck's sakes, Peter, I practically deserted my family to be with you over here and I've seen you less and less since we arrived!"

She could her him typing over the line.

"Peter? Are you there? Can you stop typing for one fucking minute?" She sucked in a breath of air.

"I didn't realize this was such a fucking inconvenience for you, living in this incredible city, in the beautiful flat my firm pays for. If you really want to visit all those small towns in Europe that were on that dinky press tour, I'll take you there myself."

His words struck her like a blow to the stomach. She felt winded. Rachel took a heel off and chucked it across the room. She watched as it left a nice little dent next to the hideous mosaic painting Peter had picked out, before falling to the floor. "I guess my dreams just aren't as important as yours then?" she asked.

"Dreams? Come on, Rach…you wanted to travel and leave the small town behind. Isn't that what we're doing? I'm giving you everything you've ever wanted! Look, I can't talk about this right now or I won't make it to dinner. I'll text you later." He clicked off the phone.

She stared at her cell phone. A photo of Rachel and Peter sitting in sunny Central Park after they had just moved in together in New York. Such big smiles with the promise of many adventures together. Rachel shook her head, and dialed her friend Ellie from The Times. They had gotten quite close working together recently and she knew she'd be able to help her calm down. When there was no answer, she grabbed her purse and heel off the floor before heading for the door. Just because he was bailing didn't mean she had to pass up on reservations they had been waiting months for.

She took a seat at the bar and ordered a martini. "Better make it a double," she said to the bartender. He was quite cute. Her drink came and she spent some time looking down at her ring, rolling it between her fingers, a fidget she'd recently acquired.

Rachel finished her drink and ordered another. How had it been almost two years they'd been here already? The feelings of homesickness were getting more constant by the day.

"Hey, y'alright miss? Here all by yourself tonight?" the Aussie bartender asked, bringing over her fresh drink. He had thick black hair that cascaded down his neck and across broad shoulders with the hint of tattoos peeking from under his short sleeves.

"Uh, yeah, looks that way! Cheers!" she looked up before taking another sip. She always was a sucker for that Australian drawl. "God these are good! Is it some secret recipe you've got or something?"

"Nah, the secret is all in the shaker," he smirked, giving his very large bicep a flex.

She smiled. It had been ages since she felt attention from someone.

Now, sitting at the bar solo, surrounded by happy young couples and girlfriends out for drinks, she'd never felt more alone. Is this what marriage was supposed to feel like?

"You really are in another world, aren't you?" She looked up to lock eyes with the bartender. His eyes were such a dark brown, they seemed almost black as they looked her squarely in the eyes.

"Oh sorry! Did you say something?" She blushed.

"Just wondering if it was a stupid Yank or Pommy that stood you up tonight?" he asked, leaning across the bar.

Being surrounded by so many Australian and New Zealand expats in London, she didn't skip a beat with his asking if her husband was American or British. "How do you know I'm not just an independent gal out on the town?" Gal? Did she just say gal? God, she really was rusty at this.

"My apologies if that's the case. I see a beautiful Sheila staring down at her ring and looking pretty sad—I make an assumption."

"No...you're right. Bartender intuition I guess?" she said letting herself relax. "Life just doesn't seem to be turning out how I thought it would."

"Things rarely do. Here, let me get you another…on me," he said mixing her up another martini.

Three martinis deep, Rachel stood to excuse herself and hit the loo when the drinks hit her. Thinking it better to go home than wait for her table, she grabbed her jacket from the back of her chair and snuck out the front door. She slipped her jacket on, the damp London air sinking straight into her bones. She pulled out her phone. No messages and no texts from Peter. Just typical.

While their flat was only a fifteen minute walk away, she decided to hail a black cab to get home. Her feet were killing her from the stupid new heels as she silently berated herself for making such a ridiculous purchase.

After the cabbie dropped her off, Rachel spent the next hour pacing back and forth across their carpeted living room. She took stock of their years in London, promises of weekend getaways to Paris and sampling all the local pubs were long gone. She figured she and Peter had shared maybe two formal dinners together in the last year. She worked hard to make friends with her colleagues at The Times, and had a great ally in Ellie who's boyfriend worked nights as a bouncer. They often got after work drinks together or watched rom-coms over a pint of ice cream and wine while the boys were at work. But Peter was never around to meet anyone. She felt torn between two worlds.

Growing up as an only child with only nannies around for friends, Peter always made Rachel feel guilty if she had things going on in her life other than him. "Oh, you want to go out with the girls? You sound just like my mom when she'd be on a break from her meds. Don't worry, I'll just fend for myself," he would say sarcastically. Or the fact that he was too blind to see he was recreating a world exactly like his father's. All this work for them to have this fantasy future together when nothing would ever be good enough, would it? All the long hours that led to one promotion would only be a building block for the next. Trying to be the husband and future father his dad never was, when really history was simply repeating itself.

She started to sort through some old papers on her desk. She wanted to find that list of places they wanted to go. During their honeymoon, they daydreamed of their next adventure and she felt like escaping now. In the midst of the junk, a folder with her portfolio clippings fell over. A mix of everything really: some amateur pieces she wrote at university, some of her features from her gigs at New York News and the Philadelphia Inquirer. And then randomly, her own 'life list' fell out. The one she made when applying to universities.

- *Editor at a major daily newspaper*
- *Make a difference*
- *Live in a big city*
- *Find someone who fits into my big crazy family*
- *Regular family reunions*
- *Be happy*

She scanned the list. Part of her laughed at the naivety. Another part was sad. Some of the items she could tick off, but then why did she feel like a fraud? This wasn't it. This wasn't what she wanted when she said live in a big city; or be happy. In the last couple of years, if she was honest with herself, had she even been happy?

A pang of nausea swept across her stomach. The martini aftermath started to give her a headache. It was like finding out Santa wasn't real and knowing you couldn't keep living a lie. She knew this wasn't the life for her. She struggled to pull in a deep breath and ran to open their large window overlooking Hyde Park. She leaned her head right out as she gasped for air. She would have to talk to Peter. And it would have to be tonight.

It was 2 a.m. when Rachel finally heard the door open and shut. Peter. She threw the blanket off her and sat up on the sofa. She must have passed out but wanted to wake when he came in. She leaned over and switched the lamp on beside her.

"Babe, what are you doin' up so late?" he slurred. She could smell the whiskey on his breath as he clumsily leaned onto the sofa and in for a kiss. Rachel barely moved.

"Sorry, one of the partners was working late too, so we cracked a bottle of excellent 30 year-old scotch. Felt we deserved it...we closed that deal, babe! It's gonna be a huge bonus for us this Christmas!" he smiled and loosened his tie.

She continued to stare at him. "I don't want to talk about another goddamn bonus Peter! I want to finish our conversation from earlier." She tried to remain calm and keep her courage. Hours of waiting caused her emotions to deepen and build like a tsunami headed for shore.

"What? The dinner cancellation? Come on, Rach, it's no big deal," he waved his hand away at the mere thought.

"Maybe not this time, but what about every other time you've cancelled? What about every fucking night I've had to sit alone in this flat because you're too busy? What about the fact that I'm completely isolated here?" she was standing now as she screamed the last sentence.

"Whoa! Rachel, what the hell? Calm down, okay? Look I'm gonna take a shower and we can talk about it tomorrow when I'm home from work." He turned to head toward the bathroom as he unbuttoned his shirt.

Rachel quickly followed behind, " Nope. Sorry, I can't and won't live this life anymore, Peter."

"And if not, then what? Huh? You're telling me you don't love this big flat? Or the clothes you have? You're telling me you can afford all that on your salary? Babe, I'm not doing this for me, it's all for you!" he was now shouting back in his underwear.

"I never said I wanted all this stuff!" she shouted.

"Pah, not like you were turning it down either." He looked down at her expensive new shoes by the sofa.

"I want a marriage! I want a partnership! I want...I don't know...what my parents have!" she cried.

"Oh please! They fight all the time, always over money, the house is falling apart and even your siblings aren't talking to each other, Rach. It's time to get over this fantasy you have in your head about them. And while we're at it, what the fuck did you mean earlier when you said you're always defending me to them? Who's got a problem with me?" The argument transformed his drunken nonchalance into sober anger.

"It's not a fantasy!" she shouted through a sob. "It's not my problem you had such a shit childhood, okay? But don't try and take mine away too! They've always had my back. I should have just listened to them years ago."

"What the hell does that mean?" Peter said, his eyes narrowing, hands bawling into fists at his sides.

Worried she stepped over the line, Rachel stopped. "They were just worried, you know, about us settling down so quickly, then this sudden move over here, it was a lot for them to handle."

"Liar. You know I hate you talking to them about me!" He quickly unfurled a fist and lifted it in the air. Before he had time to stop himself, he had cut her clean across the face with a slap.

Rachel's head flew to the side. Her eyes were burning as she lifted her head back to look at Peter. She lifted a hand to her cheek and could feel it throbbing—tears coming on fast and strong.

"Fuck, Rach, I'm so sorry. Listen baby, I've just been so stressed and, oh god, I didn't mean to do that baby, please let's just forget about this and talk in the morning, okay?"

She stood still, dumbstruck.

"Rach, come on! Say something, baby." He took a step forward to try and make amends. She shifted back, scared of him touching her in any way.

"How fucking dare you." She said calmly, cajoling all of her nerves to finish what she'd started. "My family just wanted to make sure I was making the right choice..."

"Well big fucking surprise there. Loveable John put ideas in your head about me!" His remorse clearly evaporating.

"All I'm saying is this is not what I signed up for when we got married! I thought we'd be building a life together, instead I'm sitting here alone watching yours take off."

"Well fine! You know what, Rach? You don't like it? There's the fucking door. Now I'm going to go and shower and go to bed, I've had a long day and don't appreciate a spectacle every time you want a bit of attention." And with that, he left the room.

Her cheek was still stinging. She couldn't believe he actually hit her. She looked in the mirror hanging over their dresser. With the red finger prints splayed across her face she kept replaying it in her head.

She looked around their apartment. Not one piece of home hung on the walls or any evidence of her existence in 'their' apartment. She heard the shower turn on and before she knew what she was doing, Rachel threw whatever she could fit into a small bag. She grabbed her purse, all the cash she could find, and headed for the door.

12

With the steaks cooked a perfect medium rare and the table set with a big fresh salad and corn they'd picked up on the side of the road, Dad tapped his wine glass with his knife, gathering everyone's attention. "I'd like to raise a toast," he said, as he stood with his glass of red. "To my family," his voice was shaky, "when your mom and I got married and decided to start a family, we never would have thought we'd be so blessed." He quickly wiped a stray tear away.

Mom jumped to his rescue. "We're just so happy you could all put your differences aside and join us for this week…just like the old days, right guys? Cheers to the good ol' days." She giggled and raised her glass. She gave her husband's hand a squeeze as they sat down.

"Yeah cheers, guys!" Max said. Forever trying to be the peacemaker, he tried a light subject everyone could agree on. "Anyone remember that kid Neil, down the road from us? He had the big bottle cap glasses and gap between his front teeth?"

They all looked at him eagerly, waiting for the punchline. A lot was weighing on this opening conversation.

"Yeah! Whatever happened to that guy?" Erica asked, trying to help him out.

"Well, I saw a photo the other day, he got his teeth fixed. Looks like a whole new guy. Cute too for the ladies."

Erica gave him a shove. "Wow bro, hope you keep your students this entertained in class!" She cut a steak in half, before scooping a tiny bit of salad and skipping the corn as it passed by.

"I'm just saying, I know a few single ladies who might be interested!" He laughed before taking a gulp of his wine.

"We're not all single, ya know," Maggie mumbled across the table, looking down at the salad she kept pushing around her plate. No mention of Pierre but Maggie wasn't ready to share that story just yet.

"Shit of course not, Mags! I meant...majority. Say Pop, pass the steak would ya?" he said, his eyes pleading across to Rachel's to move the conversation along.

The kids were eating their hot dogs on the deck, oblivious to the tensions running high at the kitchen table.

"This place is beautiful, Mom. How did you ever find it?" Rachel asked.

"Oh, one of the women in my book club recommended it, said it was perfect for a big family! Can't wait to get out on the water tomorrow properly," she smiled.

"That's if we survive the night," Max whispered across to Rachel. She threw him a dirty look to zip it before starting something else.

"Well, I've got some good news!" Erica said excitedly. "You know that modeling agency I did a few runway shows for last year? They've asked to sign me...three-year contract!"

"Oh, hon that's excellent news!" Mom beamed. "When did you find out?"

"They just confirmed today! Truth is I was getting kind of worried there!" she said only half joking.

"Well we all were, kiddo," Dad joked. "Hey, does this mean you won't be doing laundry and eating our food all the time now?"

"John!" Mom gave him a tap. "I'll miss having one of my kids around so much," she said sadly.

"Mom, it's a good thing, right?! Your twenty-four-year-old daughter can finally stand on her own two feet! They're even helping pay towards my apartment in New York so I can finally ditch the random roommates."

"No, it's amazing news, hon! Well done," Mom said as everyone offered their congrats.

Erica looked hopefully at Maggie. "What do you think, Mags? Couldn't have done it without you teaching me and Rach all those catwalk moves in the basement growing up."

Maggie kept her head down and didn't look up from her plate. "Look, I've got a bit of headache; I think I'll take this chance to put the kids to bed."

"Mags! Hey, it's our first night!" Rachel called as she left the room.

"It's fine. It's been this way for years now, Rach. She's never going to get over it," Erica said moving her untouched plate away before topping up her wine glass.

After finally getting the girls to sleep following four books, two songs and a couple of pats on the back, Maggie flopped down on her bed. She was tired. Tired of being angry. Tired of punishing her sister. Tired of always being the grouchy one at the table. She was just plain tired. Pierre had barely been home in a year. Nearly an entire year without seeing his kids.

She hadn't even worked up the guts to tell everyone yet, although she was pretty sure they already knew. She just kept making excuses. And the hardest part was, regardless of what happened at the wedding, she couldn't blame anyone else but *him*. It was Pierre and his wandering eye, his business trips that were always more than that. She knew about the slip-ups, but always attributed them to how busy he was working to provide a good life for himself and his girls. They tried therapy, group counseling, self-help books, and even paid the top marriage counselor in the country to take them on a couple's retreat. Whatever void Pierre was trying to fill, it was obvious he wasn't going to find it at home.

But Maggie was still tired. Tired of hiding it all. She'd try better tomorrow she told herself as she switched the light off and willed herself to fall asleep.

Upstairs, Rachel finished washing the dishes as Erica dried, while Mom and Dad set up Scrabble. "Is that the same game board from when we were kids?" Rachel asked in amazement. "I thought we lost all the pieces and Max broke the board during that infamous fight of '99." She laughed.

"Hey! Muzjiks is a word! It's a Russian peasant. Wouldn't a soon-to-be professor have known such words?" Max claimed, defending his win.

"You know it wouldn't be right to kick off a family vacation without it!" Dad said. "Should we wait and play with Mags tomorrow?"

"I don't think we should hold our breath for much of that," Max said. "Does anyone know where Pierre is anyway?" he whispered.

"No! I was wondering that. I haven't even heard his name mentioned since...Christmas? And they couldn't come because of work or something?" Erica said. "Doesn't he own the company? I think he could take the time off if he wanted."

"Well, she'll come around when she's ready" Mom said. "Now come on, I've got a fresh bottle of wine ready to go and seven letters burning a hole over here!"

"Gee Mom, you can be a forceful badass when you wanna be," Rachel said, giving her mom a hug. "I've missed this."

"I know dear...so happy to have you back."

13

The stage was all set: CLASS of 2011 was sprawled across the large cloth hanging from the ceiling. Rachel was finally graduating from her Master's degree and she was ecstatic to finally enter the 'real world' and start making a name for herself as a journalist at New York News. Her parents were proudly snapping pictures of her in her cap and gown, chatting about her future.

"Are you guys going to stay in the Big Apple?" Erica asked.

"Yes, yes, little one. Don't worry, the couch still has your name on it!" Rachel said giving her a little pat on the head.

"I can't believe you're a graduate…again!" Maggie gave her a big hug. Pierre came over with a big bouquet of flowers from them both.

"*Félicitations,* Raquel" Pierre said giving her a lingering kiss on both cheeks. Uncomfortable, Rachel pulled away quickly.

"Thank you, guys! You didn't have to spend so much on this gorgeous bouquet! Just having you guys here is enough!" she said beaming at her family.

"So, where's Peter?" Dad asked, "I wanted to ask him about that position at JPMorgan was it? Is he taking it?"

"I'm not sure, Pop, he should be along soon. He couldn't make the ceremony because of that meeting at the office. I know his dad pulled a lot of strings so I'm sure he's got it! Hopefully we'll know more at lunch."

"Speaking of which, we better get over there for our reservation; it's not every day your dad and I splurge on lunch at The Ritz to celebrate!" Mom exclaimed, hustling the kids out.

"Mom, you really didn't have to do that! It must be costing a fortune," Rachel pleaded as they walked out.

"Hey! If I wanna treat my little girl, I can do just that," Dad said, as he mimed for her to zip it.

"Still no word from Peter?" Max asked as their starters were taken away.

"He should be here soon. Top up the fizz, would you?" Rachel asked. Her excitement was starting to fade and she just wanted another drink to keep the buzz going.

"Hi everyone! I'm sorry I'm late," Peter said as he rushed in to take his seat.

"No problem, son, here grab a drink and we'll have a toast to you both now," Dad said filling Peter's glass.

"To our little Cricket and Peter graduating! Well done you two," Mom exclaimed as they all clinked glasses.

Peter took a small sip and cleared his throat. "I, um have an update on the meeting I had this morning."

"Yes, tell me all about it, baby!" Rachel said with a smile.

"They want me to join a brand new department, meaning I'll have amazing opportunities for advancement! I'll get an expense account, corner office, the whole deal!" he said smiling as he grabbed a piece of bread.

"Wow! That's incredible!" Maggie said, "starving students no more!"

"What do your parents think? They must be so proud!" Judy smiled.

"Oh yeah, Dad's off on business but sent an email with his regards, mother is off on another retreat somewhere so I'm sure she'll pick the message up and get back to me," Peter mumbled, rolling his bread in the oil and vinegar.

"So, babe, when do you start?" Rachel sensed his needs and piped up.

"Well that's just it, Rach, I wanted to speak to you later about it but they want me to start immediately. And it's in Philly."

"Philadelphia!" the Woods women chimed in unison.

"Yeah...they have the space there and need a rejig to the team so they thought it would be a good fit. It wouldn't be for long though, babe, and we could even do long distance for a bit if you don't want to give up that internship." He squeezed her hand under the table.

"Philly," Rachel whispered looking down at her main dish. The chicken was getting cold, yet she had no appetite. "What about all of our plans for New York?"

"Let's talk about it later, k? This is your day," Peter said, refilling his champagne flute.

Mom gave her a little tap under the table and a reassuring wink. She'd leave it alone for now

14

The morning sun streaked through the windows, waking Rachel. She glanced at her phone: 6:30 a.m. Why couldn't she sleep in? She reached over to grab the water on her nightstand. The three additional bottles of Malbec during Scrabble had caused one hell of a red wine hangover.

She laid there, taking in a moment of calm before the first full day of the so-called perfect family reunion began. Mom took the liberty of issuing schedules to everyone so they could prepare for what she'd deemed, non-stop Woods family fun time! She always did love trying to keep the kids entertained during summer vacations camping. Somehow this big cottage felt more oppressive than the tiniest of tents they had growing up.

"I don't want Cheerios!! I *hate* Cheerios!" Rachel heard Anna yelling from the kitchen. Guess that wrapped up the peace and quiet portion of the schedule.

She grabbed her robe and opened the door, Erica nearly knocked her over as she rushed into the room.

"Advil?" she mumbled, her eyes barely open.

"Night stand. Water too," Rachel replied.

"I see Scrabble got out hand, huh?" Erica popped one of the gel pills into her mouth before polishing off Rachel's water. She rubbed her temples, "I never understood how you slept with the blinds open, especially with the way my head is throbbing." Erica sneered at the windows.

"I'll have you know one of the most prominent yogis in India told me it was good for your internal sleep clock or some other bullshit I can't remember right now," Rachel said yawning. Erica folded her hands into prayer and gave her a little bow, making Rachel giggle.

"Right, ready to face the day, fragile one?" Rachel asked her baby sister. "Let's just all try to stay alive today, okay?"

"Trust me, it's all I want right now. I don't know what else to do with Maggie. It was all so stupid, such a mistake and I just—" she fiddled with the zipper on her onesie.

"I know and I'm sure, deep down, she knows you were just looking out for her. Let's just take the day as it comes, okay?" She linked arms with her sister and they headed into the kitchen. Or was it a war zone? There was spilt milk on the counter and soggy Cheerios floating across the floor. Chloe had yogurt all over her hair, face, and somehow even her feet. Her pajamas were stripped off and lying in a pile beside her. Max was wiping the floor with a paper towel.

"Hey there Max, how's feeding time at the zoo?" Erica chuckled.

"Just living the dream! Apparently, Anna hates Cheerios now, but Abby loves them so they decided to 'share' and I guess you can see the result of that. Mags has taken them into the bath and Chloe won't be far behind."

"Where's Mom and Dad?" Rachel asked.

Max pointed to the patio. She poured a cup of hot coffee and headed out to meet them in the sunshine.

"Morning sweetie! How did you sleep?" Mom chirped. *How was she so perky after all that wine?* Rachel made a mental note to up her drinking game to try and keep up with her mom next time.

"Headache subsiding, this helping," Rachel said holding up her mug.

"You check the itinerary today there, Crick?" Dad chimed in from behind the paper. "You ready to hit the water skis soon?"

"Oh god, before that, I'll definitely need some of your famous bacon and eggs. I didn't see it on the schedule but don't deny me in this state!"

"Was just waiting for my two youngest to finally break the bed and get up! We've had a whole day without you two sleeping beauties."

She glanced at her watch, barely even 7 a.m. Yep, slept the whole day away.

"Ah and here's the baby of the family now!" he boomed, taking advantage of their hungover state.

"Dad, can we just," Erica squeezed her fingers together to motion for him to keep it down. "Whose idea was that third bottle anyway?" she whispered into her coffee mug, still not ready to cast her eyes up into the sunshine.

"That would be the reigning wino of the family…your mother," he said proudly gesturing to his wife. He got up and gave her a peck on the head on his way to start breakfast.

"Hey, I'm just good at judging an audience. They looked parched!" Mom smiled.

"Extra bacon and extra crispy, Pop!" Erica called after their dad.

"You got it, kiddo!" he shouted back. "Probably a good idea to put another pot of coffee on, keep the ladies of the house happy," he said to Max as he started to refill the perk.

"Which then keeps us happy," Max joked as he sent Chloe to the bathtub. "Speaking of these women, what are we going to do about this whole Erica and Maggie situation?"

"Ah son, when you're as old and wise as I am, you'll know how smart it is just to butt out. They'll come around." He cracked another egg onto the pan, and threw the turkey bacon in the oven. His classic hangover cure for the family, with a slight health adjustment that he hoped no one would notice.

"And Rach?" Max whispered looking out at his sister laughing with Mom and Erica. "She seems okay, but there's so much we don't know," he said. The eggs started to sizzle in the pan, the smell wafting up and enveloping the room.

"I think we need to let her be the first to talk about it," he said. "And trust me on that one, kid. She did not like us prying." He raised his eyebrows in warning. "I can tell you one thing, if I ever get the chance to cross paths with Peter again, he'll be walking funny."

"I always knew there was something wrong with that kid. Pretentious asshole," Max muttered, just as Rachel walked in for a refill.

"Who is?" she asked.

"Um, the guy we rented this place from!" Dad said a little too quickly. "Don't host parties, no extra people, be careful with the boat," Dad winked at Max. "Here ya go, darlin, fresh pot just for my favorite."

Rachel put a hand on her hip. "And I'm sure you'll say the same to Mags when she gets out here." She smiled as he put his arm around her.

"Okay, I'm caught out!" he said putting his hands up. "But you're really my favorite," he whispered before going to check on his eggs.

"Mags! Morning sis, another cup of the good stuff?" Rachel handed her a mug as she came up the stairs.

"Thank god for you," she said. "Max, the girls are all clean and playing Barbies in the basement. Rach, wanna have this cup out on the dock with me?"

They walked out the side door and headed for the water. Erica raised an eyebrow as she walked past the table and Rachel gave a shrug. The sun was beaming down, casting everything in a delicious yellow glow. Rachel had so missed family vacations on the lake. It seemed all her favorite summer memories were wrapped in yellows, greens and blues from views just like this.

"Look, I know I've been a fucking brat so far this trip and we aren't even twenty-four hours into it yet," Maggie started as they walked along the grass. The blades tickled their feet, remains of the dew not yet dry.

"Hey, it's fine, I'm the black sheep coming home after a divorce and years of neglect." Rachel forced a laugh.

She smiled, "true, but it's not a competition. To be honest Rach, I don't know what to do. I'm so mad over everything still. But it's not even about Erica."

Rachel stopped short and looked at her older sister. She noticed for the first time how tired she really looked. How these past few years seemed to have taken a toll on her. "No offence sis, but you have a funny way of showing that."

"I know, I know. It's just so much easier to get mad at my younger sister than...*him*," she said, the latest word dripping with disdain.

"Why don't you fill me in a little? I've had some space from everyone and everything. Might be able to provide some perspective."

"Yeah too much," Maggie said, throwing her arm around Rachel's waist.

"Fair point! I hate how we've drifted over the years, I wish I handled things better so you could have come to me. What went so wrong, Mags?" she asked linking her own arm around Maggie.

15

When Maggie first met Pierre, she was barely a year into her Client Relations role at Bank of America following her Business degree. While Maggie was getting started on the smaller accounts, Pierre came in to have a meeting with her boss who handled all the international financiers.

She was walking back from the break room with a hot cup of coffee, desperate after an intense day of training on their new systems. Engrossed with taking her first sip, a delicious smelling man bumped into her in the hall. Annoyed after nearly spilling steaming hot java down her top, she looked up to see who was the cause of this interruption.

"*Oh, pardonnez-moi, mademoiselle! Je suis très très désolé,*" he said, grabbing his hankie and passing it to Maggie. All annoyance drained from Maggie's face as she looked up into his dark almond eyes. His black hair perfectly gelled, not a strand out of place. She quickly scanned his six foot frame, noting his Armani suit that must have been custom made. His rich cologne seemed to wrap around her, the earthy undertones creating a bubble around them.

"Oh, sorry, no, my fault! Just too desperate for coffee I guess!" she mumbled, embarrassed as she made a quick exit. *Don't look back, just keep walking and you can clean yourself up in your office,* she kept thinking. Dammit, she looked back! And as luck would have it, he was still staring after her. He gently waved before being escorted to his meeting.

"Holy hell," she muttered as she closed her door. "Must not sleep with clients..." With this being Maggie's first job after university, she wasn't going to let some silly crush get in the way of that.

By week two, the mysterious Pierre had held three different meetings with her boss. Coming from an avid coffee drinking family, it wasn't at all suspicious that Maggie would get up to refill her cup multiple times a day (even if she hadn't slept in weeks and she had the resting heartrate of a hummingbird lately). And it wasn't entirely coincidental that her boss, Pamela's office was on the way to refill said cup, offering her a sneak peek at Pierre—even if it was only the back of his head.

It was on one of these coffee runs they had a similar encounter. Pierre stepped out to stop Maggie from leaving the kitchen. She had her long blonde hair rolled up into a neat bun. Her new loose fitting royal blue blouse perfectly draped her thin waist and was tucked into her black pencil skirt. His eyes quickly scanned her from the tip of her bun to the soles of her stilettos. "Bonjour," he purred. Dammit why were French accents so irresistible? Maggie practically fell in love with every Frenchman she met during her year in Bordeaux.

Flustered, Maggie set her mug down to avoid any more spills down her blouse. "Oh, hi Pierre, how are the meetings going? Busy-busy it seems!" She hoped he couldn't tell how nervous she felt.

"*Mais oui*, but I'll be leaving for Paris tomorrow. So sad to be going," he said, eyes lingering on hers.

"Well, I hope you accomplished everything you wanted to while in town?" she asked.

"Almost everything," he softly inhaled, "I'd like to have one more meeting before I go though."

"Oh yes, anyone here I can put you in touch with?" she asked.

"*Chérie*, it's you!" he said. "Have dinner with me tonight, please?" his big brown eyes appeared to plead.

"Um, sure I think that can be arranged." She was aiming for calm, cool and collective in her voice.

"*Parfait*, here is my card, I'll send a car to get you, just text me your address." And with a swift kiss on her hand, he was gone.

Maggie watched him exit as Pamela came out of her office. "Oh, I see you've met Pierre" Pamela said. "Makes you realize why the French have the reputation they do! But with his account, I'll tolerate it!"

But Maggie was barely listening as she floated down to her office and counted the hours, until 5 p.m. rolled around.

The next few months passed with Pierre constantly jetting off somewhere else for business, but luckily for Maggie this often brought him into the city. She was staying with an awful roommate in Brooklyn but was able to make use of Pierre's expense account in fancy hotels and restaurants. To say she was smitten would have been an understatement.

"*Ohmigod* Rach, he is unlike any guy I've ever met!!" she squealed on the phone after another fantastic visit with Pierre. "He's had to fly off to Frankfurt for a few days but he's letting me stay at the hotel another night, isn't that so amazing?"

"Sounds so exciting, sis. I'm just on my way to class though so I better run!" Rachel was trying to hang up to get a much needed coffee before her early morning lecture.

"Okay-okay, little one. Just make sure you're at Friday night dinner, okay? I'm going to bring *le Frenchman* for everyone to meet! And please tell everyone to be on their best behaviors. You know we're a lot to handle," Maggie said before the phone clicked. Rachel needed no reminding of that.

16

"I remember you were totally head over heels with Pierre when you first brought him around," Rachel said, sitting cross-legged on the dock, facing her big sister. "There was nothing any of us could have said that would make you think otherwise!"

"We seem to have that in common." Maggie gave her a little nudge. "I don't know, Pierre just totally came in like a whirlwind. I swear he coined that phrase, 'sweep her off her feet' because I lost all footing when we got together."

"But you were happy, right? I mean your whole lifestyle, the girls, the travel—happy, right?"

"For the most part, yes. The part I chose to believe, the parts I wanted everyone to see, that was perfect. But I ignored all the other signs." She stared intently at her finger making circles around the lip of her mug.

"Aww Mags. I'm sorry you've had to go through all of this alone." Rachel wrapped an arm around her shoulder.

"I've really missed having you around, ya know." Maggie wiped a tear away, then wiped one from Rachel's cheek.

"I know, it seems we have a lot of baggage to unpack this weekend," Rachel said looking at the mist rising off the lake.

"Come on, I can smell that bacon from here and we've got all week to cry and talk about our mistakes!" Maggie laughed pulling her little sister up to her feet, "come, I'll go make peace over breakfast."

As they walked into the kitchen, mimosas and Bloody Mary's waiting, Maggie took her chance. "A toast," she said grabbing a mimosa, "to family. No matter how screwed up, mad, annoyed or angry we get, I'm glad to have you in mine." She met Erica's eyes with the last line.

"To the Woods!" Dad exclaimed. "Now dig in, nobody likes cold eggs and we've got an itinerary to stick to!" he smiled down at Mom. And with that, they broke bread.

"Gee Dad, you're right—you'd never know this was turkey bacon and vegetarian sausage" Max said as he made a vomit motion.

Dad just smiled, "it's better on the ticker," he pointed to his heart. "For all of us," he quickly added.

Max barely heard him though as he was making his next move. Feeling particularly bold that morning after fighting through the trenches of breakfast with toddlers, he decided to ask, "So Rach, no warning signs? You just up and left one day?" Mom gave him a kick under the table as Dad let his vegetarian sausage roll off his fork.

"Come on son, go easy…" he whispered.

"No Dad, it's okay, really. I guess I'll have to talk about it at some point, right?" Rachel tried to manage a small smile. Erica topped her mimosa… heavy on the fizz and light on the orange juice. Girl after her own heart right there.

Rachel thought back to that final straw…

17

Rachel woke up and for a moment totally forgot where she was. Her head was pounding from those martinis. She looked around, and eyeing her bags in the corner, she remembered. The fight with Peter, the frantic call to Ellie, the cab over in the middle of the night. Her savior. She may not be family, but it was the closest thing she had in London right now.

She got up and checked her phone. Fifteen missed calls from Peter. She listened to the first voicemail.

"Babe, where are you? I came out of the shower and you were just gone! You're scaring me, call me back." He sounded frantic.

The rest of the messages were similar. Although the latest one from this morning struck a chord. "Honey, I'm so sorry, just come home, we can talk about it, okay? I hate this! I'm so lost without you by my side. I *need* you."

Although ashamed to admit it, the broken baby bird routine still worked. She so badly wanted that nuclear family, she was blind to the cycle they had created.

Ellie peeked around the corner to where Rachel was laying on the fold out sofa in the tiny living room. "Morning sunshine, coffee?" she asked handing her a cup.

"My hero," Rachel said taking the steaming mug from her. "I can't thank you enough," she started.

"Hush no, don't even sweat it, Rach. We girls have got to stick together! Are you going to call him back?" she asked nudging her phone that kept lighting up. "For a guy who works such long hours, he's somehow finding the time to call an awful lot." She gave her shoulder a reassuring tap on her way to the bathroom. Rachel could hear the tap turn on while Ellie let the water get hot. English plumbing left a lot to be desired.

Yeah, Rachel thought, *look at how much of his day he's giving up trying to get in touch with me.* He might not show it in the ways she needed all the time, but she knew he loved her and maybe for now that was enough? *Stupid woman,* she thought, *you're an intelligent, successful woman, and you've watched enough chick flicks to know that isn't always the case.*

Nevertheless, she picked up the phone on the next ring to hear him out.

18

"He let you just walk out?! In the middle of the night?" Max threw down his fork. "What a douche, I always hated that guy!"

"Whoa Mr. Macho, slow your role," Erica said, grabbing a piece of cantaloupe from the beautifully arranged fruit platter their mom had designed.

Rachel burst out laughing. Somehow along the way she had forgotten about this amazing support system. "It really was a blessing—like the wakeup call I needed to move out, get my own place and start following my own dreams again."

"I just can't believe all this was happening and you didn't even tell us, dear. Having to go through all of that on your own, way over there," Mom's soft green eyes draped Rachel in the love only a mother could give.

"Mom, it wasn't like you guys approved of Peter anyway, is it?" Rachel asked.

"Now, it's not that we didn't give the guy a chance there, Cricket, but we can't exactly tell you what to do anymore, you're an adult!" Dad laughed, reaching for another egg before thinking better of it.

"Anyway, change of subject please," Rachel pleaded. She had only provided a brief summary and this was their reaction?

"Huh? That was like one question, Ray Ray! Don't you owe us at least one each?" Max asked, his mouth full of pancake.

"Fine. But not all at once! Blimey, there's not enough alcohol, even for us, in this house for me to rehash everything in one sitting. Especially before 11 a.m. Maxxy, why don't you catch me up on things with Kailey?" Rachel said, putting someone else in the hot seat.

"Kailey, my mommy!" Chloe said across the room where she was playing with her cousins.

"Guess they really are always listening," Erica whispered.

"You haven't filled her in on that one either yet, Max?" Maggie said as she started clearing plates.

"Tell me what?" Rachel asked, feeling more and more left out of her family's lives.

"Come on girls, let's go get our bathing suits on!" Mom called as she took the kids to their rooms.

"Shit, it must be serious if we needed it to be PG," Rachel said. "What the hell is going on?"

"Let me just go show Mom where Chloe's suit is," Max said before bolting from the room.

"I guess it was something I said?" Rachel remarked, loading the dishwasher with Maggie.

"Kailey is M.I.A., sis," Erica whispered. "Has been for about a year now."

19

Max was leaning with his back against the paneled hallway across from the doctor's office door. "You're sure it's positive?" Max asked Kailey.

She exhaled. "Well, the five tests I took at home said positive, and now the doctor has just taken a blood test that says positive so I'd say it's pretty certain."

Life events started flying by in Max's head: become Dean, travel ancient cities, meet the right girl, settle down, start a family. Nowhere in that plan was: fuck up at your little sister's wedding with the girl next door and pay for it for the rest of your life.

"Max? Hello? You've been staring off into space."

"Sorry! So, we're keeping it…?" He didn't let himself suggest the alternative.

"Of course, I'm goddamn keeping it. We're in our thirties now, Max. We're going to do what responsible adults should be doing." She threw her purse over her shoulder and stormed to the elevator.

"Wait! Kailey…I'm sorry, it's just this is all such a shock." He chased her into the elevator just as the doors were closing.

"It is for me too. You act like I planned it all along or something."

"Well, thirty-five years of crushing makes a guy wonder," he joked, trying to lighten the mood.

"Don't flatter yourself too much there, old boy," she said, tapping her foot angrily on the elevator floor. "While I may not have plotted this, you can't deny it's a sweet story. And one day our little baby will grow up to hear their story and be thankful their parents did the right thing." She reached down to give his hand a squeeze.

He squeezed back, "okay, in it together then. We'll figure out the rest later."

"Like telling our parents," Kailey mumbled as the elevator doors opened on the ground floor. They both took a deep breath in; they would definitely need it for that conversation.

～

"Oh my! Another little grandchild to join Maggie's growing brood!" Mom shouted when they told them the news. "I'll grab the champagne! And sparkling cider of course," she assured Kailey.

"Let me help you, Mrs. Woods" Kailey said getting up.

"Darling, you've been our neighbor since you were two and you're now carrying my grandbaby…please do call me Judy."

When the girls were safely out of earshot, Dad pulled Max aside, "You're sure this is legit, son?"

"Yes, Pop, it is. Went to the doc and everything…here's the first ultrasound." He handed over the grainy black and white image.

"Now that's just beautiful, Max. I mean, at thirty-two, it's about time you become a dad, I just want to make sure it's what you want too."

"It wasn't exactly in my plans, especially with Kailey, but here we are. And who exactly am I waiting for? It's been this long, maybe it's all meant to be somehow?" he said, looking up at his dad, as if asking for his permission.

"Well I mean part of that is true enough, she's a good girl, from a good family and has a good job as an architect. I just thought she was kind of a stalker all along." He laughed quietly as the ladies re-entered.

"What's so funny?" Kailey asked, handing out champagne flutes.

"Dad saying we should name the kid John if it's a boy, that's all," Max said reaching for a glass.

Two parents down; two to go.

～

Kailey's parents were less than thrilled. A sheltered only child, they wanted the world for their little girl.

"So, you plan to keep it?" Kailey's father, Ted, asked.

"Daddy! Yes, of course. We're really looking forward to raising this baby together," she said looking over at Max.

"Well, married then of course," Susan, her mother chided.

"Um no, not exactly," Max said. "We've discussed it and since we live so close to each other, we have no reason to marry simply because we're having a baby together. I mean it is the twenty-first century after all…." he shifted uncomfortably in his seat and looked to Kailey for encouragement.

"Pfft, charming words from the guy who knocked our baby girl up," Susan smoothed her skirt and looked out the bay window beside her.

"Look, Mom, it's not like that. Was it a mistake? Yes. But is it also a blessing? We think so."

Realizing they were at a stalemate, Susan went to make some tea to toast the news. Not exactly a warm welcome to the family, but for Max it would have to do. He made the right decision and was growing excited to bring a new little Woods into the family.

Max had just finished his date with Chloe: a trip to her favorite cafe in town, where they shared a banana split for her second birthday. A few days before, they had a big party on the weekend at his parents place with the Conroy's and a few of the little kids from Chloe's daycare to celebrate. Mom had hung little jungle animals throughout the trees, and bought special floaties for the pool. She had a wide array of fruit on skewers and red velvet cupcakes for the kids, with Bloody Mary's and low fat bran muffins for the adults. Relishing her new role as grandma, his mom loved finding new ways to celebrate their birthdays.

"Oh, hi Susan, it's Max. Chloe and I were just wondering if you've heard from Kailey? She was supposed to come by and get her today but I can't seem to get a hold of her." Max hoped she couldn't hear the panic rising in his voice.

"Nope, nothing here, Max. She only just landed from her business trip today though so I'm sure she's just getting unpacked and organized."

"Okay, I'm sure too! Not to worry, Chloe has already fallen asleep for her nap so we'll wait to hear from her."

Max peeked into the tiny room he had created for Chloe in his tiny two bedroom condo. It used to be a modest office but once she arrived, he happily put his desk in his bedroom and a little cot for Chloe soon held pride of place along a wall with unicorn wallpaper wrapped around the tops of the walls. Her little snores reassured him she was still sleeping soundly.

He smiled as he closed the door tight to let her sleep. He walked into the kitchen and switched on the coffee perk. He wanted to put the worst out of his mind—Kailey had been on more and more business trips lately with her Architecture firm, Perkins Designs, each getting longer than the previous. He knew she was set for a big jump in her career but he was worried it was pulling her away from their daughter.

Hours later Kailey finally called. "Hey! Um, can we talk for a minute?" she asked timidly.

He put his documentary on pause and placed his empty scotch glass down. Why did he get the feeling he would be refilling it very soon?

"Sure thing. Are you coming by soon to get Chloe? She's sleeping so I don't mind if you need to come tomorrow instead." He was quite proud of how they had been co-parenting without any extra pressure to be in a relationship.

"That's just the thing. You see, I've been offered this position at my firm. You know that promotion I mentioned?" Kailey asked without waiting for a response, "well they want me to start immediately. And the package is too good to pass up."

"Wow that's great! I know how important it was for you to get back into the swing of things right after Chloe," Max said. "Will the hours change a lot? You sound nervous Kail...."

"Well, it's actually in L.A.," he could hear her nervously tapping her fingers on a table over the phone. "And I've taken it."

Max heard the elevator down the hall ping its arrival. He opened and closed his mouth, willing the words to come out.

"What? I mean, what about Chloe? Shit, Kailey don't you think this is something we should have discussed?" His voice sounded more forceful than he'd intended.

"I knew you would react like this. This is why it wasn't a discussion."

"Kailey I'm not some possessive boyfriend here. We're raising a child together! What's your plan exactly? We fly this toddler back and forth across the country? Summers in one state and school in another? I mean Jesus Christ, how did you expect me to react?" He was pacing around his living room, trying to keep his shouting to a minimum to avoid waking Chloe. The reality crashing: he'd either lose his beautiful little girl, or have to raise her on his own. Both were equally terrifying.

"Look," Kailey started, her voice catching in her throat, "I never wanted this, okay? I mean sure, I thought I always wanted to be a mom at some point but the reality is totally different. I'm trying to make something of myself, reach goals, be my own person and this isn't the way. It's just. It's not what I want, okay? I'm sorry."

Click. Max stared at the blank phone screen. All the scotch in the world wouldn't help him now. A wail from down the hall. Dammit, the yelling must have woken Chloe.

20

"So that's just it?" Rachel asked her family. "What the hell? Why didn't you track her down to L.A., Dad?" She couldn't believe it.

"Now come on, honey, if I was going to go chasing down every little brat that did my kids wrong, I'd be flying all around the world." He finished drying the pans and gave Rachel a knowing look.

"I know but, poor Max," she said sadly. She really had missed so much. She chastised herself again for letting her ego get in the way of her family.

Before she could ask any further questions, Max came running up the stairs from the basement. "Who's ready for the boat?!" he shouted cheerfully.

Rachel did her best to put on a happy face. They walked outside to a cloudless blue sky, the beaming sunshine immediately warming her skin. She didn't know what it was about the water, but just being able to glimpse it, to see the sunshine reflecting back at her, had always managed to calm her down.

Why the hell did she ever think she wanted to live in the city without these views? The green grass seemed so much brighter than the fried little garden they had when they lived in New York. And while London had numerous manicured public parks, the residential gardens left much to the imagination.

Thoughts of London flashed through her mind—had it always been such a grey and ominous place, or had everything with Peter tainted her time there?

"Helllooooooooo earth to Rach," Erica said, giving her bum a tap on the way by. "I said, do you think this is enough beers for the boat ride? I made sure to grab us some light ones too."

Rachel looked over at the massive cooler her sister was wheeling toward the boat. "Ya sis, I think we're good. Only thing is will the boat still float once we put that thing on there?"

"Who's up first?" Dad shouted from the driver's seat as he turned the key in the ignition and the motor gave a little gurgle. He let it idle as everyone made their way onboard.

"Me!" Mom shouted, grabbing the skis on her way down. "If the day continues this way I'll be too drunk to stay afloat, let alone get up." She laughed, already slightly wobbly.

"You sure about that, Mom?" Maggie asked. "We can just go for a cruise too, Dad, can't we?"

"Oh Mags, don't be such a worry wart," Max prodded, "this woman taught us everything she knows! Let her rip, Mom!" he shouted as he cracked a beer.

Dad pushed the put the boat into drive. Rachel winced as she glanced back at her mom on the dock. Looking older than she liked to admit, her mom still flew off the dock, made the landing and was gliding over the calm water, making little cuts with her skis like a skilled chef with her blade.

"Damn she's still got skills!" Erica exclaimed, passing Dad a light beer.

"Thanks, dear, you always were my favorite," he whispered.

"I heard that," Maggie smiled as she lathered the girls with sunscreen.

"Don't worry, babe, you know you're my *real* favorite," he said with a wink. "Who's up next? I reckon we should bring your mother in while we're on a high." He signaled to her that he was going to slow down.

She swam up to the boat and climbed in. "Not bad, huh kids! Mom's still got it. Now, the only thing missing here is…"

"A wine cooler? Got ya right here, mama." Erica passed her mom a can of cold white wine spritzer as she dried off.

"See kids? That's why Erica's the favorite," Dad joked.

"You keeping everyone nice and liquored up huh, sis?" Maggie jeered. The tension hung there, palpable in the air above them like a low hanging cloud.

"Nice new leaf Mags, what was that? Ten minutes?" Max said shooting her a look to chill.

Erica hung her head before setting her unopened light beer down in the tiny cupholder beside her seat. "I'll go next, Pop."

"You're up, superstar!" Dad shouted as Erica jumped in the water.

Rachel was sitting on the bow nursing a beer watching the family dynamics unfold. It was funny how you could practically abandon your family, literally not see anyone for years and then simply slip back into the fold. *Was every family like that?* she wondered.

"You really are in another world today, Ray," Max stated, flopping down on the seat next to her.

"A million miles away," she said.

"At least not for real anymore, right?"

"Absolutely. I think I just got a bit lost," she said, fiddling with the sticker on her beer. Her stomach sank, disgusted with how she behaved before moving away. Thinking she was better than the small town, better than the life her parents bent over backwards to offer them, better than every one of her siblings—thinking she deserved more.

Bullshit.

21

"Here we go!" Peter said, giving her hand a squeeze. She couldn't believe it. Their flight to London was about to take off. A whole new life awaiting in one of the most historically rich and inspiring cities in the world. She planned to channel Shakespeare, Dickens, Rowling...make a name for herself with the greats.

"Are you okay babe?" Peter asked snapping toward the flight attendant for a refill on his champagne. "You want another?" he asked her.

"I'm okay for now, think it's gone straight to my head," she replied, feeling a bit woozy after the first glass. But she knew it wasn't just that. The growing pit in her stomach was there long before the first sip of bubbles had hit her lips. It was a gnawing, gaping hole barreling down into her stomach. She knew that feeling, she had experienced it before when she moved in so quickly with Peter that first summer. Something her parents had balked at.

It was doubt.

"I think I'm just going to try and sleep a bit." She pulled her eye mask out of her bag.

"I don't know how you could...aren't you so fucking excited, babe? I couldn't sleep if you paid me right now," he said, wiping his face with the hot towel from the attendant.

"Just a long few days. It's been such a whirlwind packing everything, saying goodbye to everyone...."

"Yeah," he interrupted, "I know you're going to miss everyone, but look, I know a million girls that would kill for this opportunity. Don't dwell on the small town you're leaving but on the incredible life we're going to create!" He gave her a quick peck on the cheek and popped his headphones in.

Guess that was the end of that conversation. A lone tear escaped as she moved swiftly to pull her eye mask down. She was sure it was just homesickness already and fear of the unknown. It would pass. Peter was right, this opportunity was amazing. She'd have access to more daily and national newspapers than she ever would have imagined at journalism school. She'd be living in one of the most cosmopolitan and culturally diverse cities in the world. It was definitely just nerves.

"So nice to meet you again and really thanks so much for this opportunity," Rachel said, cringing inside at how much it sounded like she was kissing yet another editor's ass.

"It's fine Rachel, thanks for coming in. We'll be in touch. Ta." He was already dialing his phone as he said the last word. "Ta," so London, wasn't it? They didn't even have time to say "goodbye" these days? Too important and self-involved? She clenched her fists as she walked out of the big tower and started to walk along the Thames. She crumpled up the printed CV and cover letter they didn't even want to keep a copy of and threw it into the bin. All around her, men rushed by in slick blue business suits, while ladies power walked in high heels and Burberry trench coats.

She'd managed to arrange—and fail—five interviews since they arrived. The dream was not quite panning out. London, the land of opportunity? Or was that New York?

Who fucking cared?

Before she realized it, she had wandered back to The Anchor in Borough Market. A pub in the sunshine would be the perfect spot to drown her sorrows. If the job interview wasn't stellar, she could at least have a beer to toast sunshine in London, couldn't she?

She grabbed a pint and headed onto the patio. Autumn's first chill had arrived, Rachel pulled her "lucky" NYU scarf from her bag and wrapped it around her shoulders. *Some luck so far,* she thought. She closed her eyes and tilted her head to the sky, letting the sunshine soak into her bones.

Maybe if she stayed like this long enough the sun would slowly shrivel her up and she wouldn't have to worry about finding a job. Raisins didn't need to work, right?

Her phone vibrated in her bag and brought Rachel back to reality. She glanced at the ID: Mom. Oh shit...she couldn't keep dodging her calls and yet she couldn't face admitting there had been no changes since she had checked in last week.

"Hey, Mom!" she put on the cheeriest tone she could muster.

"Darling! About time you picked up...we were worried you were too busy for us with some fabulous new London job!"

Rachel took a long gulp of her beer, "never too busy for you!"

"How's the job hunt going? Did you hear back from that paper, The Night Standard or whatever it's called?"

"The Evening Standard. They called for a second interview, but I'm not sure I want to take such a crummy entry position. I'm holding out on The Times to call me back. I may not have the most experience but I mean, I was Editor of The Washington Square News at NYU, Intern at New York News and Features writer at The Philadelphia Inquirer! That's got to account for something, right?" Rachel realized she was raising her voice. The couple next to her moved one table over.

"Sorry Mom, that wasn't at you, I'm just frustrated I guess."

"Oh hon, these things take time! I'm sure something will come up, how's everything else? How's the 'flat' as they say? And Peter?"

"Oh. He's good. Work is amazing, best move ever, they love him...blah blah blah," she half whispered at the end. "Look, I've gotta go Mom, that's a recruiter beeping in. Bye!"

Rachel flagged down the waitress. "I'll have another pint please. Oh, and a whisky. On the rocks." What the hell, it was Tuesday and she didn't have to be at work in the morning.

～

"How was the interview, babe?" Peter asked when he finally got home after 9 p.m. while Rachel had already taken a nap after her boozy afternoon and was now watching Little Britain reruns. If she was going to live in this country, she was going to try and understand the humor. Market research during unemployment.

"Ugh," she said switching the TV off. "They seemed so interested and really liked my clippings but I felt like I got the brush off at the end."

"Wanna practice your interviewing skills again?" he asked, pouring himself a glass of whiskey, "maybe you could learn something."

Was that comment meant to be patronizing or was she still in a bad mood?

"I'm good, thanks. I was actually just about to head to bed."

"Wanna hear about my day?" he said, without waiting for a response. "It was awesome! My boss, Paul, is already talking about a promotion after the way I handled bringing the new clients over. I've got to go to Moscow next week to schmooze some new big wigs with him!" He finished his tumbler then poured another.

"Wow babe, that's awesome!" Rachel gave him a big hug and kiss. "I knew you'd be great! Glad they're giving you some recognition so quickly," she said holding in her resentment.

"Yeah, I know, right? That's why I'm happy to give you tips on your CV or interview tactics. Guess I might know a thing or two," he smiled as he pulled out his Blackberry to check emails.

With Peter completely absorbed into his phone, Rachel took this as an opportunity to go to bed. She climbed in without brushing her teeth or washing her face. She just wanted the day to be over. Tomorrow she'd start fresh.

22

"I've taken the liberty of working naps into today's itinerary," Mom said cheerily as they docked the boat. "Some of you have jetlag," she nodded toward Rachel, "and some are kids who need to nap."

"For all of our sakes!" Dad chimed in.

Mom smiled. "And some of us want to keep the party going late so you all now have two hours of quiet time."

"Wow, when you plan an event, Mom, you make no room for error, huh?" Max asked. "However, I will not complain! This one's ahead of schedule it seems," he said nodding down to a sleeping Chloe in his arms.

"Wanna spoon?" Erica whispered as they walked inside.

"You know it!" Rachel said as she went to get changed out of her wet bathing suit.

When Rachel walked back into the room Erica had a sly look on her face.

"What's that about?" she asked laughing at Erica. "It's me, I look like shit, right? I know I've aged, I'm old and divorced." She was trying to sound light but the frown said otherwise as she flopped on the bed.

"Shit, now I'm even more glad I packed this then…you need it more than I do," Erica said as she passed her sister the little joint she had tucked into her bag.

"No way! Oh my god I haven't done that in years," Rachel sat up staring at her sister, "Peter hated it."

"Add it to the list," Erica said laughing as she lit a match.

"Hey Rach, here's that book you asked about," Max said opening their door. The girls looked up trying to hide the joint behind them. Rachel exhaled a puff of smoke and started giggling.

"You little weasels!" he said closing the door. "Good thing Mom and

Dad's room is on the other side of the house. Pass it here."

"Does the Good Professor want in?" Erica giggled and handed it over.

"It can be very enlightening you know," he said chuckling.

"Knock, Knock," it was Maggie.

"Oh god, here we go!" Max said as he ducked down along the other side of the bed.

"What's all the noise in here? Thank god the girls passed out," Maggie said opening the door. "What's that smoke over there? Did you guys drop a candle?" She peered around, sounding more and more like Mom.

"Oh, it's just, um…steam," Erica said, curling her lip as she realized how stupid that sounded. She burst out laughing.

"Oh my god! Max where did you find that?" she asked as he sheepishly rose from his hiding spot.

"Oh our little sisters—the new druggies in the fam. Come on sis, what do you say?" Max said holding it out to her.

"The kids are here! I haven't done that since before Pierre…he did it so much it annoyed me."

"Don't worry, Mags, it's not for everyone," Erica said reaching out to take it from Max.

"Excuuuuse me, but I think you might remember who gave you your first toke," Mags said intercepting her and grabbing it for herself. She took a long inhale.

"Wow, that takes me back," Maggie said, once the coughing subsided. "As a mother I could use this—fuck wine."

"Mom and Dad are definitely asleep, right? I'm already the divorcée who has shunned her family for years, I don't need to be the pothead too." Rachel passed the joint to Erica.

"Oh, come on, Rach, no one thinks that," Erica said putting her arm around her. "We just think it was temporary insanity brought on by a third party."

"Ditch the modeling Ernie, clearly therapy is your true path," Max said as he threw the finished joint out the window.

Rachel was feeling brave as the high hit her. "Tell me, how bad is it? Which one is sick? Why are they tired all the time? Why do people get old? I can't have them die." Her heart was starting to race as she envisioned her parents in failing health.

"Whoa whoa, I forgot how paranoid she gets when stoned," Maggie said, "lie back, I'll tickle your arm."

Rachel did as she was told and closed her eyes listening to her siblings.

"We don't know anything more than you. Dad is looking a bit thinner these days but then again, he's always trying to kick a few pounds. Maybe something stuck?" Erica said.

"Yeah, and why didn't he waterski? He loves waterskiing!" Rachel said.

"I still remember when he taught me and then all of you. God, we were so young then," Max said, lying back on the floor.

"Well come on, they are almost 70...even the fittest people can't be cutting across water and doing jumps at their age; they're ripe for breaking a hip or something," Maggie said, the voice of reason.

The door opened and they all jumped up. "Geez, don't worry, kids, just your mom," she said peeking in, seeing the kids all lying together. "Well, isn't this sweet? This is all a mother could want!"

"Oh Mom…" Erica rolled over on the bed to see her mom standing there smiling wide.

"You kids sleep well" she blew them a kiss before closing the door again.

As soon as the door closed they couldn't contain their laughter. Maggie threw a pillow at Max before his loud hyena laugh nearly woke the kids.

Rachel woke to the sound of country music blasting from the patio. Dad's subtle alarm clock.

"Guess it was a while since we did that, huh?" Maggie said lifting Erica's arm off her face. Everyone looked completely disheveled after their not-so-short power nap.

"Forgot how tired that can make you," Max said getting up from the floor. "Or how god damn old I feel crashing on the floor." He stretched his back.

"Did someone say chips?" Erica said rolling over, "I could go for some chips."

Everyone burst out laughing as they headed for the deck. "Oh my god, is that Mom's famous taco dip?" Erica asked all but running over the kids to get to the chips and dip.

"Guess that swimming and skiing took a lot out of you, huh, Ernie?" Dad asked Erica.

"Yeah Dad, what a workout!" she said playfully, scooping up a generous serving of dip.

"Anyone smell that skunk when we came in? I hope there isn't some decaying carcass under the deck that's gonna follow us all week," Mom said on her way into the kitchen.

"Nah Mom, just an herbal remedy," Erica snorted.

"I told you it was your kids up to no good Jude!" Dad said laughing as he closed his newspaper. "That takes me back to the seventies. Your mom and pop could really get down on the grass back in the day."

Before his reminiscing could go any further, Max tried to change the subject.

There was a sheet of paper on the table next to Dad's beer. "Hey, Dad pass us that itinerary will you?" Max asked popping a straw into a juice box for Chloe.

"Where's the laminated ones I left in the rooms for y'all?" Mom asked from the kitchen, carrying a tray of drinks.

"Oh god, what's this surprise dinner guest you have written here for this evening?" Maggie asked reading over his shoulder.

"Just an old family friend, they said they'd be visiting the area this weekend so I said they should stop in for a glass of wine," Mom said, evading the real question.

"Oh, so no one we would know right, Mom?" Erica asked suspiciously.

"Well you used to play with their kids I guess...remember Josh and Devon?" she asked.

"You mean the people who came to every Christmas party of ours and we all attended each other's weddings?" Rachel asked sarcastically. "Yeah, I think we remember them. Thank god it's just the parents," she said grabbing a glass of wine from her mom's tray.

"Well, she did say the boys might come." Mom hustled back into the kitchen, "forgot the rest of the snacks!"

"Bullshit," Erica took a big gulp of her wine.

"You know, Josh went through his own divorce a year or two ago," Dad said, aiming his gaze at Rachel but speaking to no one in particular.

"Oh yes, and he's an incredibly successful psychologist these days!" Mom said returning from the kitchen. "Last I heard poor Devon still hasn't found the right girl...chasing his dreams in New York I guess."

"Well isn't this sweet, girls?" Maggie said. "Looks like your mom and dad arranged a little meet-cute for you both!" She almost slid off her chair in a fit of giggles. Mostly relieved it wasn't her they had thrown under the bus.

"You cannot be serious!" Rachel squealed, "I haven't seen you guys in years and all of a sudden I have to sit here awkwardly while you try to set up the divorced kids?" She was trying to remain cool but the remaining weed in her system made her paranoid that she sounded crazy.

"Dear, it's not like that," Mom started, "Margot called me last week to see if we wanted to come by for dinner. When I told her where we rented the cottage she said they have a place just on the other side of the lake. What could I do?" she asked tucking Rachel's hair behind her ear.

"Now, let's eat this dip before it becomes a soggy mess!" Dad said, polishing off his light beer. Before he could grab another, Judy gave a little shake of her head. "Damn diet," he muttered.

Rachel grabbed her wine and turned to leave. "Where are you goin', Rach?" Erica asked following her out.

"Seeing as this is a blatant hook-up, I'd rather not look like the thirty-year old divorcée I am, and try to look somewhat decent," Rachel shook her head at the thought.

"Come, we can both get cleaned up, take a shot or two, and we can laugh about it all tonight. I brought more of that sleep remedy so we can sneak off later to medicate if need be," Erica gave her a little push toward the bathroom.

Erica put on a folk playlist and plugged in her pink hair straightener. Rachel took a long, slow sip of wine and looked at her reflection in the mirror. She hoped whatever she had in her makeup bag would help cover up the stress lines on her face. She pulled out her mascara and as she applied the little wand to her lashes, took a deep breath and decided to try and go with the flow this week.

When the divorce process started, she realized she had started to lose pieces of herself. Likely, she had started losing pieces of herself a long time before that. The more Peter seemed to fly (first-class) towards his dreams, the more hers seem to diminish, until she felt like a little shadow of the person she once was.

To escape that terrible web, she started to say 'yes'. Yes to meeting new people; yes to trying new things; yes to doing the scary things; and yes to a life she wanted to be proud of.

"There ya are, little one," Dad said, poking his head around the bathroom door where the girls were finishing their hair. "Mom's just getting some champagne. Now, I know what you're thinking and this is not a set up. Just enjoy yourself alright?"

"Sure Dad, just needed to clear my head a bit. Plus, you guys know champagne is my weakness so if it's here, so am I," she said with a laugh.

"That's my girl!"

As Erica and Rachel made their way back out onto the patio, as if on cue, Mom whispered, "they've just pulled up!"

Here we go.

"Judy this place is an absolute dream!" Margot said as they walked through the front door. She slid off her leather jacket and let her shoulder length black hair fall onto her white blouse.

"Hey John, here's a nice bottle we picked up in Napa last year, make sure you leave it to air a bit," Frank said before they shook hands at the door. He adjusted his chino's and ran his large hands through his thick grey hair.

"Oh please, come in! You didn't have to bring anything," Mom said, "it's just so lovely to see you guys out this way!"

"Jude, it's our pleasure! Oh, and here come the boys—you remember Josh and Devon?" Frank asked ushering the boys inside. Josh seemed to take after Margot with soft hazel eyes and sandy brown hair he kept clean and cropped. Devon was the wild child with a thick head of jet black hair and inability to stay in one spot too long.

"I should think so!" Mom laughed before giving both boys a kiss on the cheek.

"Yes, thanks so much for letting us tag along, just like old times," Josh joked.

Mom closed the door behind them. "Well come on, the kids are having drinks out back. And you should see the grandkids, they're just growing so quick!"

"We'd love to see them! We're still waiting on our own these days...." Margot said with a little nudge to the boys.

"So it begins," Rachel whispered to Erica as she heard voices inside.

Everyone come say hi to the Mackie's," Dad motioned to the kids to leave the safety of their bar cart and come around to the other side of the patio.

With a collective long gulp of their drinks, the kids headed around the large wooden table. "Keep the bonfire warm for us kids!" Max shouted over his shoulder to the kids sitting around the bonfire pit on the grass.

"Hello darlings, so good to see you all again!" Margot said as she gave everyone a hug. Frank wasn't far behind kissing the girls and shaking Max's hand. After exchanging pleasantries, Rachel led the exodus back to the drinks.

"So, this must be the big kids table?" Josh said following her to the bar cart.

Max handed him a scotch on the rocks. "Trust me, bud, you're gonna need it. And hey Devon, good to see you man, how's New York treating you?"

"Not bad. I'm feeling more like a rat living with a bunch of roommates, making no money, trying to break into the advertising world. Just living the dream!" he raised his glass up in triumph.

"Sounds like our little Erica," Maggie said, grabbing some more champagne, "isn't that right, Ernie?"

"Yep, living in the Big Apple is totally glam, right?" she said, munching on a carrot stick.

"Oh, you're there too?" Devon asked seeming more interested. "Whereabouts?"

"Brooklyn. Cliché I know but the rent is good, my roommates aren't complete weirdos, and I had to keep the Woods tradition alive with every child paying their dues in the borough."

"Ya, I know what you mean. I'm actually in Dumbo, so not far from you probably. We're in the building with the pizza place down below."

"Um maybe try and be more specific." Erica laughed. "What building doesn't in New York?"

"True! We're in the one with Gino's, got a guy with a handlebar mustache and red cap on the logo?"

"Oh yeah! That isn't far at all, they've got the best greasy stuff after a late night out. Not great before callbacks though." She giggled.

"Oh ya, you're still doing the modeling thing?" Devon asked.

"Trying to!" she said.

"She's done some amazing work!" Rachel said thankful to participate in a conversation instead of watching the sweat drip off her glass of champagne.

"Anything we'd have seen you in?" Josh asked.

"You know that H&M campaign from winter? The one with the hot twenty somethings in winter gear and igloos in the background? Erica is one of the bundled-up models!" Rachel exclaimed.

"Wow, not bad!" Devon exclaimed.

"And how about you, Rachel? My parents said you were living abroad but just came home?" Josh's gaze was fixated on her, his hazel eyes looking expectantly at her. She felt a flutter in her tummy. Must be the champagne—or lack thereof. "How about a top up there, big brother?" her eyes pleaded to Max who had just done a lap for refills.

"Yeah, you know the drill—girl has big dreams, girl moves to a big city, girl meets guy, girl leaves guy, girl moves back. It's your classic eighties rom-com, no?" she tried to laugh but nearly choked on her champagne.

"Ah yes, the divorce. Well hey, all of us black sheep meet once a month to commiserate and get drunk together. Membership is pretty cheap and it's a pretty sad bunch but you're one of us now!" Josh laughed.

"Is that supposed to be funny?" Rachel asked with a sly smile, "cause I kinda think that sounds like fun."

"Well, not yet but we can set up a chapter," he smiled.

"Everyone, dinner is ready!" Mom called from the other side of the table. "I've taken the liberty of assigning us place settings tonight," she said with a cheeky grin. "Why not make it a little more formal affair?"

"We can still get pissed drunk though, right?" Devon whispered across to Erica.

"I'm halfway there, buddy—do catch up," she said before taking another long sip of the cold bubbles.

They took their seats complete with calligraphy name cards and a little sprig of rosemary tied around each napkin. Somehow their mother had even managed to find table chargers, unchipped plates and formal dining cutlery in a log cabin on the lake.

"I've got red and white on the table," Dad said. "We may be formal but we ain't fancy so eat the steak with whatever poison you like!"

"Rach, what can I get you?" Josh asked beside her. Was he being extra attentive or was she just extra lonely lately?

"Oh um, what goes with Bloody Mary's at brunch, beer all day, champagne before dinner and the tequila shots Erica and I took while getting ready?" Did she sound as drunk as she felt?

"I'd say this red should be a good mellower," Josh said. He threw the white cloth napkin over his arm like a waiter and filled her glass.

"Not sure that's the right context, but I guess I have to trust my sommelier," Rachel said with a hiccup. "But maybe some water first."

"How do you know? Ah yes of course, the globe-trotting journalist," he smiled. "I still think I'm right though, remind me to challenge you if we play Scrabble later."

Josh was looking straight into her eyes again. His eyes were focused on her with a slight gap between his soft pink lips, the moon making a little halo around his head. Why was she finding this so unnerving? She hiccupped again.

"Don't worry, if it keeps up, I promise to scare you," he said with a playful touch of her leg.

"I um—I need to use the restroom," Rachel said abruptly. She suddenly felt the need for air.

"Erica, weren't you going to get extra butter for Mom?" she practically hissed as she walked by Erica, deep in conversation with Devon about the best place to get martinis in Manhattan.

Erica looked at the two full plates of butter, but thankfully got the hint and followed Rachel inside.

"Yo Crick, smooth moves…" she said as they closed the door behind them.

"Shit, I am so not good at this!" She was pacing in the living room, away from the gaze of the dinner party.

"Look, just chill, you've just practically met the guy again. It's not like you're moving in together or getting married. God you're not even splitting a cab in midtown together, it's no big deal!"

"It's just been awhile since I've really dated. And a really loooooong while since someone was so attentive. In the half hour they've been here, I've felt more looked after than my entire relationship with Peter," she drifted off.

"Oh hey, come on, want one of my valiums? Might help you just chill and enjoy the night instead of overthinking every goddamn thing," she said laughing as they padded into Erica's room.

"Fuck it, yeah, give me one. The red wine will be a good chaser for that, right?" she said already feeling herself relax as she gulped the pill down. "You realize we all packed our own stash for the weekend? What does that say about us?" she sighed.

"Now come on, Devon is actually pretty cute…and seems impressed with my piddly modeling portfolio. Maybe we could both get lucky."

"Oh god don't even...I think I need carbs to settle my stomach," Rachel whispered, feeling her stomach somersault again.

"Got the butter sorted then?" Devon asked with a knowing smile.

"Ah yes just had to, umm, let the backup thaw...you know, can't be too prepared!" Erica quickly put her napkin back over her lap and reached for the salad.

"Hey Rach, hope you don't mind, I picked you a steak as it went by. Your dad warned me you'd be pissed if you didn't get a good hunk of meat," he said as he grabbed some baby potatoes.

"Gee thanks, Dad," Rachel glared over at him. He raised his arms in surrender.

"I'd like to make a quick toast before we get all tucked in, if I may Mr. and Mrs. Woods?" Josh asked.

They all raised their glasses in anticipation.

"I just wanted to say thank you so much for opening your cottage—even if it is a rental, to us. It's so nice to reconnect with people from the past. To new, mellower beginnings," he smiled down at Rachel on the last line.

"Cheers!" they shouted in unison.

Dinner was filled with the usual: layered conversations, details missed from one revisited hours later for clarification. But it was everything Rachel had missed. The chaos, the laughter, even the, dare she call it, flirting? She wasn't sure if it was the alcohol, the valium, or the high of the night, but she felt like she was floating as everyone said goodnight.

"Night kids!" Mom and Dad shouted as they headed for bed, it was nearly 1 a.m. and long past their bedtime.

"Night guys!" Erica yelled. As they finished tidying up the kitchen, she looked to her siblings. "Anyone want to have a night cap around the bonfire?"

"I'm out," Maggie said, "those girls are going to have me up in five hours and at my age, you're desperate for beauty sleep." She hugged Rachel, Max and even Erica before heading to her room. Seemed like progress.

"Me too, girls, maybe tomorrow." He stifled a yawn and followed Maggie out, knowing Chloe would have him up early as well.

"Guess it's just me and you then?" Erica said with a presumptuous grin. "Besides, I want details on why Josh had your phone earlier? Putting a number in perhaps?"

"Only if you explain why you had Devon's cell hmm?"

"Deal."

"I've got the tunes," Rachel said. "I want it to be mellower out there." She smiled to herself. They walked across the large patio, the small twinkling lights their dad had hung earlier still cast a beautiful warm glow across the property.

"Mellower? That doesn't even sound like a real word," Erica said as they sat down.

The ashes crackled as Rachel threw another log on the fire and wisps of smoke climbed up into the night air. The lake was so peaceful this time of night, just the crickets and Ray Lamontagne to keep the girls company.

23

Not long after Rachel left for London, John finally lamented to Judy's prodding to go see the doctor following his second fainting spell in as many months. "Stop jiggling your leg John, people are going to think you've got something contagious," Judy said looking around the waiting room. She always hated doctor's offices. As a mother of four it often meant one of them had broken an arm, or burst an appendix, and the hours spent around drab white offices melded into one. What was it about doctor's offices? Why couldn't they paint it a nice neutral grey instead of the standard white? Something about it had to scream sterile so people didn't freak out?

"Did you hear what I said, Jude?" John asked.

"Sorry, in my own world," she said. "What was that, dear?"

"I just said this is a colossal waste of time. I'm the picture of health, they always tell me that!" John said, clearly annoyed with having to spend a sunny afternoon stuck in a colorless office.

"Darling that was years ago when you last came for a check-up, after that bout of pneumonia, remember? Besides, I'd like to get ahead of anything just in case. We're not as young as we used to be, ya know," she said giving him a little jab.

"At this rate, the only thing that's going to get to me is a broken heart. I hate this distance between Rachel and us," he said quietly. Rachel had only been gone a few months but everyone was still struggling with how things ended.

"Oh John, don't start or you know I'll break down. She's just following her dreams right now. She'll come back to us, don't worry," she said more to herself than her husband.

"I just wonder if it's her dream she's chasing though—" he said before the receptionist cut him off.

"Mr. Woods? The doctor will see you now." Judy grabbed her purse and slipped her hand into John's. He may be taller than her but she knew when he needed to lean on her. He gave her hand a little squeeze as they walked through the doctor's office door.

"Hi Doc, thanks for seeing us. I was just telling Judy I'm the picture of health, right?!" he said shaking Doctor Miller's hand.

"Well she was right to bring you in John. To be honest, I don't like what I've heard from your wife when she booked the appointment. I know we put you on a diet a few years back and you've stepped up your exercise but I think it's time we take a few more in depth tests. With your history of high cholesterol, blood pressure and these new fainting spells Judy mentioned, I think we need to act sooner than later. You're still taking your cholesterol pills, right?" John looked at Judy, noting her betrayal.

"Of course. Come on doc, nothing too serious. I just stood up too fast a few times! That's just old age!" he said hopefully.

"Well, John, that's only the couple I knew about. No harm in getting some scans done, is there?" she asked the doctor.

"Precisely, let's get you in ASAP for some more tests. I want to make sure that ticker stays nice and strong for years to come," the doctor said sternly before turning to leave. "Book an appointment at reception for next week. Prolonged hypertension can lead us to heart failure. And I think we'd all like to avoid heading in that direction John."

John and Judy lagged behind, the weight of every word pulling them closer to the ground. Heart failure. As in, your heart stops working. As in, you'll never see your wife or children again. As in, goner. Dr. Miller gave them a wave and handed them back over to the receptionist. With the appointment booked in for next week, John left armed with strict instructions on fasting before blood work, notes on sleep habits, and more homework than he had since high school.

"Geez, that sounds serious," he said to Judy as they headed back out into the brisk November afternoon.

"I'm sure he's just being cautious, dear. Come on, we'll go get a coffee and we can walk around the hardware store. I know how much you love that," she said giving his arm a squeeze.

"Mom? What's going on? Where are you and Dad? I've been calling all day," Maggie sounded frantic when Judy finally picked up her cell phone.

"Fine, just at a few appointments sweetie," Judy answered while John shot her a death stare she understood to mean: don't you dare say a word to the kids.

"What is it? Who's sick?" she sounded panicked now.

"No one, honey, just a check-up, come on! What's up?"

"Okay, if you're sure. I wanted to see if you guys could watch the girls this weekend? Pierre is going to Paris with work and I want to go and surprise him!" she said excitedly.

"Oh hon, that sounds excellent! Just what you two need." It had been no secret they were struggling to work things out since Rachel's wedding.

"Great! I'll call you back with arrangements, Abby's got the scissors dangerously close to her hair though so I better go!"

"Well a good test for your heart will be watching the girls this weekend," Judy said with a laugh as John pulled out of the parking lot.

Maggie had barely spoken to Pierre since the fiasco at Rachel's wedding. She was so humiliated. And contrary to the way she had been behaving to Erica, it wasn't because of her, but him. How could he so blatantly philander in front of her own family and friends? She had been stupid for long enough. Playing the innocent housewife while her husband flirted his way through one conference after the next. The biggest thing holding her back was the girls but enough was enough.

The first time she caught him, she thought it was just a blip. A one-time thing, a man being a man and blowing off steam. He was always so flirtatious, even when they met. For God's sake, he was dating someone else when he picked her up—he confessed a few months into their relationship! She just assumed she was different, that he'd never do it to her, right? He'd been away in Moscow for weeks on and off and incredibly stressed. They had just moved in together and she was so happy they'd have all this extra time together between his crazy travel schedule. He had a tight turnaround between coming home for meetings, and packing the next day to return and meet clients on a skiing trip in the Alps. Maggie had begged to join him, she felt they were drifting and it could be good for them. He shot her down, only too quickly and made her feel like an idiot for even asking.

"This isn't some romantic tryst I'm going on without you, Chérie. Mon Dieu! This is my job. How would I look showing up in the chalet with some American on my arm?" he said as he threw his suit across the chair (expecting her to take it to the dry cleaners no doubt). He had stripped down to only his Armani boxers, which helped him look like he'd just walked out of a Vogue catalogue. "Now, I am going to shower and we will be done with this conversation, oui?" he said as he huffed away.

Maggie was near tears. She just wanted to spend some time with her boyfriend. Shouldn't he be thrilled she wanted him close for more than a day? She picked up his suit to put in the front closet with the other clothes for the cleaner. His Blackberry fell out and when she bent to pick it up she saw a number of messages flashing. Anita. Who the fuck was Anita? His secretary? No, that was Celeste. If no one at work, why would they need to reach him so urgently? She knew she shouldn't read them, she'd never been the type to snoop. But fuck it, no one was here to have to lie to. She entered his PIN and started reading. She knew she could click 'mark unread' as soon as she got a bit of background.

Can't wait to see you.

Hope home isn't too stressful.

You deserve this getaway so much!
Are you picking up the champagne or should I?

Maggie's eyes welled with tears and her cheeks flushed. But she couldn't help herself, her hands were shaking as she kept scrolling. As she was about to click on the next string of texts, she heard the shower stop.

Fuck.

She gave her eyes a wipe and quickly marked the messages unread, threw the Blackberry on the floor where the suit had fallen and ran to the hallway. Trying to catch her breath and act as natural as possible, she hung the suit in the closet.

"Chérie? Sorry I was rude before," Pierre said walking into the kitchen with nothing but a towel on, his hair perfectly tousled from the shower, little water beads dripping down his abs.

She hated him right now. She pretended to wash up a cup in the sink with her back to him, buying time on how to confront him.

"Come on, let's go to bed. I've missed you." He came up behind her and whispered in her ear. She could feel his hot breath on her neck. She almost felt herself giving in.

"I actually don't feel very well, sweetie," she lied. "I think I'm coming down with the flu—one of the girls in the office was sick. I'd hate to infect you before such a big important trip like this," she said, as she screamed inside her head to turn around and confront him. *You lying pig! How could you?! How long has this been going on?! Anything!* She willed herself to open her mouth and just say something.

Pierre gave her a quick peck on the back of the head. "Good point darling, can't drop the ball on this one!" He squeezed her side before going to bed.

The irony was not lost on her. She looked up at her reflection in the microwave. *You total and utter coward.*

24

Rachel was the first one up and headed for the kitchen to put the coffee on. In her family, they were only somewhat addicted to caffeine—okay, they'd probably create a shiv out of the hollowed out coffee canister if someone left it empty, but that was just a healthy appreciation, right?—So the rule was always first one up puts the coffee on and for god's sakes, put on another pot if you've finished the last one!

"Morning dear, how did you guys sleep? It was so sweet seeing you all cuddled up in that bedroom yesterday! Everything a mama could want," Mom said giving her daughter a hug. In a family of six it was easy to feel left out, but her mom always made her feel extra special, like she really was the favorite (no surprise there).

"I forgot how nice it was to sit around with them—we spent so many years hating each other it's really nice to be stuck with them now," Rachel smiled.

The coffee perk clicked into life and soon the sweet aroma of coffee drifted throughout the house. Like a spell creeping its way along the floorboards and around the corners, breathing life into the rest of the house.

"I can't believe the girls are still sleeping," Maggie was the first one to join them. "God, I needed a coffee, thanks sis," she said taking a mug from Rachel.

"I guess you kids stayed up drinking after us oldies went to sleep!" Mom laughed.

"I can't believe Dad's not up yet; did he finally learn how to sleep in, Mom?" Rachel asked.

"I wish! That man still tosses and turns all night, especially now waking up to pee every hour," she said then sipped her coffee.

"TMI Mom," Erica said, grabbing a scone from the counter. "Yum, peach?" she asked.

"Yes, we had so many to eat up at home and I know they're Ray Ray's fave," she said smiling at Rachel. Yep, definitely the favorite.

"So, what's the deal? Is he more tired these days for a reason, Mom?" Rachel fished for answers.

"Don't bother, Rach," Maggie chimed in, "they claim everything is fine."

"That's because everything *is* fine!" Mom declared. "Now I'm going to take your father his coffee. Why don't you make some toast for everyone?" She asked no one in particular and rushed off before anyone could press further.

Rachel looked at her sisters as their mom disappeared down the hallway.

"So, what is nobody telling me?"

"Well we don't know much either to be honest," Maggie started. "Remember after the wedding, the ahem, unfortunate incident? I took the kids over to Mom and Dad's for the weekend. Ya know, to surprise Pierre in Paris."

"Oh yeah, you never did share how that went," Erica said. "I only heard about it from them," she said looking down, careful not to start any new fights.

"Yeah well anyway, they were coming back from the doctor and then seemed preoccupied when I picked them back up the following week. I think they've had a few 'check-ups' but won't say if we need to worry," Maggie finished.

"So of course, we do," Max said as he walked in and grabbed a cup of coffee. "Ah sweet java, who made this pot? It's strong, just the way I like it."

"Same here, glad you like it," Rachel said, raising her mug to his. "Ok so he had a few check-ups a few years ago and that's all we know?"

"Well, not exactly everything," Max whispered, barely audible with a mouth full of scone.

"What the hell?" the sisters said in unison as they turned to face Max.

"Look I didn't want to worry you girls, okay, but he just had me help update his will. I pressed them for answers at the time, but they said they were only being careful and prepared." He put his palms up, declaring his innocence.

"His will? *Ohmigod*," Maggie said near tears. "Why would he want to do that if everything was fine? When was that?"

"Um, just a year or two ago…he said everything was fine but just so he had things in order. Guess he wanted the eldest to help," he shrugged.

"But why do it now out of the blue?" Erica wondered.

"Fuck, there was one other thing but he bloody swore me to secrecy so it'll be my balls in a vice if he finds out I said anything," Max's face was all business. "It's his heart, one of the ventricles is stressed or something. Just years of high blood pressure I think, but he's on meds and it should be absolutely fine. Apparently it's why he gets a bit more rest these days, cut the cigars and eats all these low fat foods," Max said in a hurry.

Rachel was softly crying. "A weak heart? Shouldn't that be something we're all privy too?" she claimed.

"How's that toast coming kids?" Mom shouted down the hall.

Everyone took a breath and started busying themselves around the kitchen. Maggie threw some toast in the toaster, Max started pouring orange juice, Rachel was making a fresh pot of coffee and Erica grabbed the first thing she could find—a potato masher.

"Honey, I don't think we'll need that this morning," Mom said, taking the masher from her hands. "So tell me…what did we think of dinner last night?"

"It was really nice Mom. I know I moaned about it, but thanks for organizing it." Rachel gave her mom a peck on the cheek, holding herself close a second longer, imagining the private pain she'd been carrying around.

"Yeah Mom, kudos on the agenda, really!" Erica said handing her a glass of juice. "Are we turning these into mimosas or staying clear headed for one morning?" Erica said, now uncertain of what everyone's health concerns would allow.

"Kiddo, who do you think you're talking to?" Dad said as he walked in the room. "Fill 'er up!" he said grabbing a bottle of prosecco from the fridge.

"Morning Pop," Rachel said going over and giving her dad a hug. Maybe if she pulled tight enough, she could get the last three years back.

"Hey Crick!" He said giving her a squeeze. "Miss your old man that much overnight?" He gave her a kiss on the head before grabbing the paper.

"I'll take that mimosa outside son," he said to Max. They all stared as he walked away, sharing an unspoken lucidity.

"Hello...earth to my children," Mom said, breaking their silence. "I said, should we do breakfast outside today since it's so beautiful?"

"Sure thing Mom, I'll help set the table," Rachel volunteered.

<h1 style="text-align:center">25</h1>

Peter and Rachel were sitting in their small but bright apartment in West Philadelphia, surrounded by unpacked boxes and clothes stacked on the kitchen table. "I think we're really gonna love it here Rach," Peter said as he unpacked his precious school trophies to place on the mantle.

They had only been in Philadelphia for one night and already Rachel wasn't so sure. Unfortunately, New York News wasn't very keen on letting such a newbie work remotely, even when she offered to commute into New York twice a week.

Alas, her big dreams of working at a daily in the city were side tracked. She had the summer experience but just as her internship was about to end, they offered her the incredible opportunity of staying on as a junior researcher. A role every intern to walk through the threshold of the New York News could only dream about. Of the thousands of interns that apply, only fifty get chosen. Of those fifty, usually only two or three can even think about getting offered something more long term.

In fact, when Rachel got offered the position, her mom nearly passed out. Not an avid reader of the NY News, she knew how competitive it was. Dad started mapping out Rachel's world domination. "First the News, then the White House, babe!" he shouted popping a bottle of actual champagne. Not one for splashing on the good stuff, Rachel knew it must mean a lot to them.

"What do you mean you're not taking the job, Ray?" He had asked her when they had coffee in the city one day. "I thought it was your dream?"

"Yeah, well dreams change Daddy. Philly could be a great opportunity for both Peter and me," she started, not sure she bought her own story as she was saying it. "At News, I'd be one of thousands. In Philly, I could probably get a writing job ASAP, not just a research position."

"Yeah, that's true enough, little one," he replied, taking a bite of his low fat bran muffin. "I just want you to be happy. Is this going to make you happy?"

"Yes Pop, I'm happy." She tore off a piece of his muffin and smiled at him.

Peter's company sent a moving company to box everything up the following week and she was headed to a new home. A new city, a new job (hopefully), new friends, new shops, new restaurants. It was all so… exciting? Sure, she tried to tell herself that. She always wanted to travel and see the world, right? But was Philly that much of a change?

"Hey, Rach, you here or what?" Peter asked as she sat staring off into the distance. "I said, we're going to be really happy here, just wait and see."

"No doubt, babe," she said. "I'm going to hit the pavement tomorrow, start calling up newspapers and see who's hiring," she said, pulling out her stack of clippings. She smiled looking down at her university writing career. Was that going to be her highlight? Her smile started to fade.

"Yeah, you better jump on it, babe, I bet a lot of people have settled into roles after the summer," he said walking into the kitchen. He grabbed a beer and turned on the baseball game.

Gee, thanks for the vote of confidence, she thought. How did he have this way of blaming her for something he created?

"I've already spruced up the CV and have a great reference from NYN so I'm pretty hopeful." She puffed up her chest, willing herself to sound more confident than she felt.

Rachel's phone vibrated on the table. "Hey babe, ya mind taking it somewhere else?" he yelled from the other room. She was pretty sure the neighbors four blocks over could hear the TV.

"Oh hey, Mom! Yes settling in fine thanks!" she said. Peter shot her a look. "Hang on, let me go somewhere quieter." She crossed the hall into their new room where there was not a thing on the walls, nothing but muted white paint and stacks of boxes to keep her company. Rachel wished she could just reach through the phone and get a hug from her mom.

26

"Did Rachel say if they're coming home for Christmas, Mom?" Erica asked as she came down for dinner. "They missed Thanksgiving because Peter had to work and the poor baby apparently couldn't be alone," she said grabbing some of the carrots her mom had chopped. It was only two days before Christmas and everyone's schedules were up in the air.

"Now, now don't be like that," Mom said as she put the salmon in the oven.

"I'm sure if you were living with someone who had to work late over the holidays, you'd want to be there with them to celebrate too," Mom said pouring a glass of wine. She gestured to Erica.

"Like you need to ask," she said sliding a glass over to be filled. "I'd totally buy that, Mom, if I didn't know for a fact that Rach was sitting around eating that sad little chicken she bought on her own because he worked till one in the morning again." Erica looked out the back window at the snow dusting the backyard. The pool was well under a few inches of snow now and the maple trees had shed their leaves weeks ago.

"So that's when I think they're going to come," Mom finished. "Did you catch that, Ernie?"

"Yeah, uh Christmas day, right?" she lied.

"Christmas Eve. Rachel is hoping they can get the five o'clock train so they're here for dinner. Peter is meant to only work in the morning but let's see. Have you heard from Maggie lately?"

"Last I heard she was extending her little Euro trip with Pierre," Erica said in a mock French accent. "Zee petite Franchman has quite zee hold on Margaretttte it seems."

"Yeah, it does seem that way! I'm just glad we finally got to meet him! I was beginning to think this high flying client of hers was imagined," Dad said passing by with a jumbled set of Christmas lights.

"Let's hope that's just a fling," Mom said laying her Christmas themed plates out on the table adorned with a large Poinsettia. "I'm sure he is quite successful but there's just something about him. He seems too *experienced* for our Maggie."

Her cell phone rang. "It's Maggie!" she shouted.

"Hi sweetie! I hope you're calling to say you'll be home for the holidays." No one did guilt trips like a mother.

"*Ohmigosh*, Mom, yes we're on our way now! We've just landed and will be bringing some macarons and champagne for everyone from Paris. There's going to be a little something extra to toast!" She could hear Maggie giggling before the line went dead.

"Mom, is everything alright? You look like someone just let the air out of your tires."

"Oh sorry!" she said with a shake of her head. "Yes, they're at the airport. John, you better go get them!" she shouted outside. "The lights can wait. They've already been delayed three weeks this year, another couple hours won't kill us," she said under her breath.

Erica headed upstairs to give Rachel a call. "Bitch better be coming," she said as it rang.

"And Merry Christmas to you too, Ernie," Rachel said laughing as she picked up.

"Ha, whoops! Just want to make sure you're not leaving me alone with this insane family of ours for *another* holiday."

"Fear not, my dramatic younger sister, I am on a train as we speak!" Rachel was so excited. It had been months since she had seen her family. Four to be exact and it was the longest she had gone without seeing any of them. When she was at school in the city, someone was always passing through for an appointment, or to hit a show or the shops. No one seemed as excited by Philadelphia. She couldn't even tempt them with the cheesesteaks or cream cheese (to be honest, she wasn't a fan of either herself).

"Oh, thank the good Lord! Mom said you weren't coming until tomorrow!" Erica cried through the phone. "Wait, you said 'I' not 'we', where is Peter?" Erica asked.

"Closing some big merger," Rachel said exhausted. "He's hoping to drive up tomorrow morning so we can have Christmas Eve together."

Actually, it was an all-out screaming match when she tried to put her foot down about Christmas. She had felt so alone in Philly these past few months and just wanted the comforts of home. Peter accused her of being a horrible girlfriend who needed lessons in how to support her hard-working partner. In return, she smashed one of their new wine glasses on the floor asking for the same emotional support he expected of her. She cried for days trying to convince him to come with her. She had wanted to come last week and compromised. Couldn't he do the same?

Now he was so pissed when she bought her ticket, he threatened to 'see her in the New Year' and was going to go to Aspen to ski with the partners. She managed to patch things up a bit. She had to cut him slack, she knew that. He struggled so much not having much family around for the holidays. It wasn't his fault.

So, she'd have Christmas with her family and then head to Aspen with him. She wasn't much of a skier, but was looking forward to a few days reconnecting with Peter in a cozy cabin away from all the stresses of home.

"Okay I'm picking you up at the train station, text me your arrival and we'll have a good ol' gossip on the drive home."

"Ah Rach!! God it's so good to see you. I'm not sure you know this. But our family is kind of nuts and I've been locked up in the mental ward alone for months!" Erica shouted in her ear hugging her. Their cheeks were red with the cold as they hurried through the terminal and to the parking lot.

"Oh, thank god, is that coffee?" Rachel asked grabbing her sister's mug. "Ernie! Did you by any chance make this coffee Irish?" she said barely tasting the coffee.

"It's the holidays! Roadies are allowed...in fact, encouraged," she said grabbing it back to take a swig before starting the car.

"Alright, alright, so what's the drama now? I know it's hard to believe this, but someday you will finally fly the nest and you'll actually miss the noise and drama," Rachel said looking longingly out the window.

"If you're that depressed, sis, just move back. I'm sure Peter can survive and do a bit of long distance. I mean, he's this high-powered businessman, right? Surely he can manage."

"It's not that easy, we're a partnership. Me and him against the world," Rachel said as she looked out the window at the passing buildings. The bowling alley she had her twelfth birthday at, the dank and dingy Chinese buffet their parents used to treat them to. Rachel was starving for the familiarity and nostalgia of home.

"Ok 'nough said. Mom has the bubbles on ice so let's get this shit unloaded and get toasted!" Erica said pulling up in front of the house.

"Hey guys!" Rachel cheered as she walked into the house.

"Ray Ray! John, our girl is home!" Mom said running to the door. "This is officially the longest you've ever been away!" She was still hugging her daughter tight when Dad walked by with the Christmas lights.

"Cricket! Champagne is being poured as we speak...you might want to head in to see your sister and Pierre." He raised an eyebrow and deposited the lights on the floor before following the girls down the hall to the kitchen.

Rachel shot a quizzical look at Erica. She shrugged. Maggie let out the loudest squeal from the kitchen as she thrust her left hand into the girls faces.

"Check out this rock!"

"Oh, wow!!!" Rachel shrieked. "Congrats Mags!"

Pierre leaned in and gave both Rachel, Erica, and even their mom a kiss on the lips to thank them for their well wishes.

"Oh my, I'm afraid I'll never get used to that European way of greeting…" Mom said flustered.

Erica made a sick gesture as she reached for glasses.

Ouf my head, Rachel thought, using her hand to prop it up right as she wandered down into the kitchen the next morning. It was Christmas Eve day and she knew it would rush by in one big blur of Christmas music, last minute gift wrapping and a constant flow of alcohol. But it usually started with sampling some of Mom's cookies, washed down with Irish coffee for breakfast.

"Good morning sunshine, little hair of the dog to kick the holidays off, right?" Erica said handing Rachel the coffee liqueur to splash into her coffee.

"Thanks, I'm definitely going to need it. Where are the lovebirds?"

"They booked a hotel so I'm sure they will be enjoying a nice relaxing sleep before the chaos!" Mom said bringing in more cookies from the freezer in the garage.

"God Mom, expecting an army for the holidays, are we?" Rachel teased as she gave her mom a hug. She missed being able to just sit around and talk about nothing and a million things all at once with the women in her family.

"Well I wasn't going to do much, but then thought I had to at least make everyone's favorites! So here we are…rushing out the final batches."

"Well that is the tradition isn't it, Mom?" Erica blew her mom a kiss. "Tell us what to do to help."

"Yes! Erica, you can finish these gingerbread men and Rachel you can help me whip up the punch for tonight. Then we can at least get the table set so it's all done and out of the way. Do you know what time Peter is coming, honey?" she asked.

"Uh, no not yet. I'm sure he'll text me soon." She bit the head of another poor unsuspecting gingerbread man.

"I call bullshit," Erica said as Mom rushed off to tick another item off her list.

"And what exactly does that mean?" Rachel said trying to act normal. She was surprised she hadn't heard from Peter yet. She had texted him good night and received nothing in return. And now, still no word.

"Okay, let's keep pretending then, big sis. Whatever you want." Erica teased.

"I just haven't heard anything yet, nothing new to report!" She gulped down the last of her coffee. "What time do mimosas start?"

"Ah, now there's a conversation we can both enjoy," Erica exclaimed.

As the girls finished the cookies and got the table set for Christmas Eve canapés with the Mackie's, Rachel finally felt able to confide in Erica.

"We had this horrible fight right before I left, Ernie" she said, as Erica topped up their mimosas.

The girls were sitting around the Christmas tree, Dad still busy fiddling with lights (was it his way of staying sane surrounded by the women in his life?). Mom had passed by in a blur of red and green on her way to the market to pick up last minute groceries.

"About what? You know you don't have to bullshit here."

"Yeah, I'm not pretending, it's just he's so damn busy these days. I barely see him, I miss him. I love the holidays and he knows how important Christmas is to me. But lately it just seems like he doesn't have time or space in his life, even for me…" Rachel picked at a thread in the old beige sofa.

"Yeah, but I'm sure it's just a phase. How are things otherwise? In Philly?"

"It's um, not bad, it's just different. I'm not settling in like I thought I would I guess."

"Heeeeey girls!" Maggie bounced through the door, her smile threatening to split her face in two. "Tucking into some mimosas already?! Guess I better catch up!" She poured herself a glass. "Pierre had to run to the store for some last minute present for me…guess he thought this beauty wasn't enough!" She shrieked holding her finger out to let her ring sparkle in the light from the Christmas tree.

Erica gave Rachel a look to say *to be continued* and the girls shifted focus.

"So, tell us all about the engagement, Mags!" Rachel said excitedly. "I didn't catch the whole story last night with so much going on."

"Oh god, Rach, it was so incredibly romantic—champagne on top of the Eiffel Tower, he even paid one of the staff to be involved and everything!" Maggie gushed.

"*Ohmigod!*" Max shrieked in the hallway. "Tell me you girls aren't still going all googly-eyed." He laughed. "Erica don't be cheap with the mimosas, help your big brother out!" he said grabbing a glass from the kitchen.

"Should we switch off the girly topics, Max? What do you think of your soon to be brother-in-law Pierre?" Maggie asked.

Max looked up and saw three pairs of eyes fixed on him as his sisters waited. He took a long sip of his drink to buy himself some time. "Yeah, I mean he's great! He's not that into hockey and I think soccer is the worst sport on the planet, but I'm sure we'll find something in common!"

Rachel's phone rang. "Oh, it's Peter! I'll be right back." She stood to take the call in the dining room. "Hey babe! Are you on your way? What time can I pick you up at the station or are you driving? It's such a bad snowstorm right now I wasn't sure you'd wanna drive," Rachel barely paused for a breath, worried about him cancelling again.

"Uh yeah, babe, it looks like I won't be able to make it," Peter said, distractedly.

"What do you mean?" she said, disappointment and anger seeping through. "You promised Peter! And it's Christmas…c'mon…" she chided.

"Well we gotta finish all the paperwork on this big merger before everyone heads up to Aspen. Richards is now coming along so it would look pretty fucking stupid if we hadn't settled all of the numbers before bringing the client along." His tone was sharp, although Rachel knew it wasn't directed at her.

"Oh, yeah," she grumbled, "sorry I just was looking forward to celebrating Christmas with you obviously."

"Aww baby, I know. Sorry if I was short, they're working us like mad to get this all sorted. I didn't even go home last night. I worked till three a.m. and then slept in one of the pods here. I'd say it was pretty cool if I wasn't so sick of this place right now."

"Okay, so what about tomorrow? Will you have to work Christmas day too? Or any chance you can make it then?" she asked hopefully.

"I'll try my best, babe, okay? I want to see you too. Worst case, you'll fly to Aspen on the twenty-seventh, right? We can celebrate then."

She could hear voices in the background. "I guess you better go, just let me know about tomorrow, 'k? I'd hate to think you'd have to be alone on Christmas."

"I'm a big boy, Rach, call you later. Love you, baby." He clicked off before she could say goodbye. She angrily threw her phone on the dining chair next to her.

She turned back into the living room and saw her siblings poorly trying to cover their eavesdropping.

"And that is what the class syllabus looks like this semester!" Max said, failing at acting natural.

"Wow that is so interesting," Erica said with only the faintest sarcasm.

"Okay, so everyone heard then," Rachel said, motioning for her mimosa to be refilled.

"Hey it's fine! At least you're here, right?" Maggie said slinging her arm around her sister.

"I'm sure he'll be able to come tomorrow," Erica said reassuringly. "I mean it is Christmas after all."

"Hey, why so glum in here?" Dad asked, coming in from outside. "Getting a head start before the company comes tonight huh? Not a bad idea," he said heading for the bar.

"Throw a little water on that scotch," Mom said with a gentle nudge as she joined them in the living room. "Oh, and a mimosa for me? Thanks, dear," she said giving him a kiss as he handed her a glass.

"Now before all the significant others and company come around, can we have a little toast, just the Woods?" he proposed.

Everyone stood with their glass.

"I know Christmas has never been the splashiest of holidays for this little brood," he started, taking his time to look around the room at each and every one of his kids. "But I just want y'all to know, that I'm the richest man alive looking around this room," he finished, his eyes glistening.

"Way to start it off light old man!" Erica said wiping away her own tear.

"To family!" Mom smiled as she raised her glass.

"Hear-hear!" they all shouted.

The doorbell rang. The annual Woods Christmas Eve party was about to begin.

"So why am I so short of breath these days, doc?" John was at a checkup just before Christmas. Rachel was due home from her first few months living in Philadelphia, Maggie had been away more and more with Pierre, and the rest of the kids would be home for the holidays—it was not a good time to go see the doctor.

"John, I'm sure it's fine," Judy said patting his leg.

"Well, it might be, Judy, but we'd also like to run a few more tests. Just to rule anything out," Dr. Miller explained.

"Like what doc?" John asked, trying to remain calm.

"Well, a man of your age with stress and lack of activity—could be heart disease, blocked arteries, etc. You've maintained a decent weight most of your life but these things happen with age; then add in the alcohol and cigars you enjoy and it's a bit of a greyer area."

"Okay so what do we need to do?" Judy asked.

"Let's get you booked in sometime in the new year—a full work up, physical, I want to run some more tests on your heart as I think that's what is causing the shortness in breath. And in case you haven't done so, cut the cigars and just watch the alcohol over the holidays. Nothing too high in sugar or fat," he recommended.

"Well geez, Dr. Miller, that doesn't sound like much of a Christmas," he said trying, but failing to hide his grumpiness.

"It's just a precaution, John. Try for me, will ya? Here, I think you should take this prescription for cholesterol pills as a preventative in the meantime." He handed over the white piece of paper before showing them to the door.

"This is bullshit!" John said, as he angrily shoved the key into the ignition. "How the hell do you cut all the good stuff out of Christmas and still say Merry Christmas on the way out? I'll cut the cigars but he can forget about the drinks!"

"Oh, John, it isn't for long. We can do it together," she said, holding his hand.

"No way, you work hard all year, we've got the kids and everyone around. Just act normal and I'll limit the sugars like he said. Whiskey is low-carb right?" he asked with a smile.

"Should we say anything to the kids?"

"No way, there's no need to worry them," he said as they pulled up to the house. "I'm gonna fix those lights, you just see when everyone is gonna be home. And what's keeping Maggie in Paris longer than intended."

Judy knew when to give her husband space. Fixing the lights became his code over the years for just that.

"Heeeeey, Rachel, good to see ya!" Josh said heading over to Rachel and Erica. "This is my fiancée Diana," he said gesturing to the beautiful brunette to his right.

"Nice to meet you," Rachel said, shaking her hand. "Congrats on the engagement by the way."

"Thank you soooo much, that's so sweet" Diana purred, twirling a perfectly curled lock of hair around her index finger. Her light brown eyes peeked out through her big bangs hanging down in front of them.

"Yeah, I can't believe little Joshy next door is going to be a husband," Erica said.

"No one calls me that anymore, just like no one calls you Brace Face anymore." Josh said teased.

"Fair enough!" Erica said. "Congrats to you both."

"Hey, it's Brace Face!" Devon exclaimed, overhearing the exchange.

"How are you, Doodie? I mean, Devon?" Erica asked.

"Yeah good, cheers to another Christmas party," he said raising his glass. "Hey Rachel, where's this infamous Peter?"

"He had to work, believe it or not. Closing a big deal so couldn't really be away," she said, pouring herself more eggnog. She hated always having to make excuses.

"Shame, would have been nice to meet the man that whisked our little Cricket away," Josh smiled with a longing look at Rachel.

That was weird, she thought. Erica excused them and pulled Rachel into the kitchen.

"Whoa, was it hot in there or just you guys?" Erica asked, grabbing some more prosecco from the fridge. "Did you catch that, Rach, or have you been out of the market too long to take notice?"

"Thank you very much, I am not that old. But yes, that was weird, right?" Rachel asked.

"Talk about sexual tension," Erica teased. "That look was next level."

"It doesn't matter, I'm madly in love with Peter. I just wish he could be here," she said, staring down at the table. She started to pick the icing off one of the sugar cookies her mom had laid out. She hated this fighting, particularly around the holidays.

"Don't worry, sis, I'm sure it's just this big client he's got to deal with and once that's settled, he'll come up for air and it'll all be great!" Erica said rubbing her back. "Time to switch back to the fun stuff?" She raised her prosecco.

"Definitely, let me just check in on Peter and I'll be right back. Why don't you go ask Devon about his three months in Tibet?" Rachel said trying to play matchmaker.

"Yeah, I'll ask if he's showered at all in the past three months," Erica said walking away, clearly uninterested in the do-gooder next door.

Rachel pulled out her cell phone and dialed Peter. After five rings she was about to hang up when he answered.

"Hey babe! You'll have to speak up! It's so loud in here!"

"Hey! So, sounds like you're all done? Does that mean you'll be coming out tonight? The party is just getting started, you can still make it!" she said excitedly.

"No babe, I can't really hear you, but we're out with Richards and his team to celebrate. We did it all, babe! Done, dusted, and now we celebrate!"

"*More sake here please!*" She heard someone shout in the background.

"Okay, so tomorrow morning, then? Or...what are you thinking?" she asked, trying and failing to hide the frustration in her voice.

"I'm going to try my best, Rach, okay? The night is young here and these old boys can drink but I have your Christmas present and I'd like to give it to you before Aspen...oh god, they just ordered another bottle of sake so I better go, don't want to be rude, love ya babe."

He didn't even wait for her to respond before he clicked off. She sat staring at her phone but didn't hear the footsteps behind her.

"Hey, everything alright there, Ray Ray?"

She turned to see Josh looking at her across the island, his soft eyes scanning her face to see what upset her.

His smile softened, "What's wrong?"

"Oh nothing, sorry, just taking a quick call with Peter! What can I help you with?" she asked trying to match his calm demeanor.

"John sent me in for more prosecco, seems the bottle Erica brought went faster than the last piece of pie at Thanksgiving."

She let out a little laugh.

"Seriously, everything okay?" he asked, giving her arm a squeeze. It felt awkward and yet, like a tiny frisson of electricity.

"Yes, don't worry!" she said moving away to grab a few bottles from the fridge. "He was just trying to get here for Christmas Eve but now he can't make that either. Surprise, surprise," she said under her breath.

"That happen a lot? The broken promises?"

"Look, Josh, I know you mean well but please don't use the psychobabble bullshit tonight okay? Be a friend, and pop that bottle."

"Hey, 'nough said! Miss Cricket." He popped the top on another bottle, "May I offer you a top up?" He said in his best British accent.

"Why, yes sir, that would be simply maaaaahvelous." She played along.

"Joshua?" Diana walked into the kitchen looking for him. "I've been wondering where you ran off to. Rachel, where's this boyfriend of yours?" she asked, looping her arm with Josh.

No need to go pissing all over him, she thought.

"Good news is: he landed his big fish, bad news: he's got to sit around and fry it up all night," she said.

Josh laughed.

"I don't get it," Diana said, "he's a fisherman? I thought he was some big stockbroker?"

Rachel tried to hide a snort behind her glass.

"Um, see you lovebirds back in there," she said as she exited through the opposite door. She searched for a friendly face in the crowd and found Erica pinned with Devon. Her 'rescue me' eyes pleaded from across the room.

"Hey Erica, can you help me find that wrapping paper? I have a last minute gift wrapping emergency," Rachel lied.

"That's pretty last minute, Rach" Devon said. "You know, when I was in Tibet, they had this way of—"

"Sorry Devon, tell me later?" Erica cut him off.

"Jesus, how fucking long does it take to get some rescue out there?" she said to Rachel as they walked down to the basement. "And lame excuse, you've gotten rusty all around in Philly. Too much cheesesteak in the brain?" She was laughing as they tumbled down the stairs.

"I got you out, didn't I?" she smiled. "Oh, thank god for this quiet hideout of the basement." She sunk into the tattered red bean bag chair that had been around longer than any of them. "I can't believe this still has stuffing."

"I can't believe we're still doing these 'block parties,'" Erica said grabbing the ottoman across from her.

"You love this party every year, don't lie," Rachel said. "Tickle my arm?" she asked her little sister.

"Fine, but you're not getting out of doing me when I'm done!" she replied.

"So, Josh has grown up a bit. What the hell does he see in that puppet?" Rachel said.

"Meeeeeow!" Erica joked. "If I didn't know better, I'd think someone had a teensy crush on Dr. Mackie."

"Oh god, grow up," she said jokingly. "She just seems really..."

"Fake like a plastic Barbie doll on her way to Skipper's junior prom party?" Erica finished.

They both burst out laughing.

"What's so funny down here?" Maggie said coming down.

"Mags!" they cheered.

"Pull up a chair, we're gossiping about boys," Erica said.

"Oh yes! Is Peter coming tonight?!" Maggie asked.

"No, he's still with the client so maybe tomorrow...we'll see I guess. He did say he wanted to give me my Christmas present so one can hope."

Pop!

Maggie and Rachel looked over to Erica who made the noise. "Oh, I always carry supplies." She walked around and topped up everyone's fizz.

"And this is why we love you," Maggie said. "Pierre has gone back to the hotel too—something about calling Hong Kong when it's their morning since everyone works through Christmas? Blah, blah, blah, I didn't bother listening." She burst out laughing. "I was too busy telling everyone the proposal story—he'll be back in the morning."

"So, you're sleeping here then, Mags?" Rach asked excitedly.

"Yep! Old school slumber parrrrrrty!" she shouted as she jumped up on the old floral sofa.

"Oh god, she's gonna start dancing, isn't she?" Max asked as he came down the stairs.

"Yeah, put on some fucking tunes, Maxxy!" Maggie shouted. She was swinging her hair around, one big blonde blur against the old wood paneled walls of the basement.

"Oh god, you know what would be awesome right now?" Maggie asked.

"A little herbal refreshment?" Max asked, pulling a joint out of his tweed jacket pocket.

"*Ohmigod,* I knew those pockets were for something!" Erica squealed.

"First things first," Max said, "someone turn that diffuser on...those oldies are getting pretty hammered but let's not get crazy now." He laughed.

"This is why I miss living nearby," Rachel sighed, letting herself sink further into the bean bag chair.

"What? Getting high with your siblings in a basement that hasn't changed since the '80's?" Erica said, passing the joint along.

"No, just all this family time. Philly is so...so lonely," she mumbled.

"Ah yes, but, it's just temporary!" Maggie said. "Like me and Pierre, right? We had to do long distance for ages and finally we're looking at places in Connecticut! I mean it's the dream, right? He can commute to New York, and it's a great place to raise a family." She smiled looking down at her ring.

Erica rolled her eyes at Rachel. "So, what's the deal with Joshy?" she cooed, batting her eyelashes.

"What did I miss?" Maggie asked, snapping her head up to look at Rachel.

"There better be no deal!" Max said, putting on his best over-protective brother tone. "He's engaged and you basically are too," he stated matter-of-factly to Rachel.

"Geez, let's all just relax here," Rachel said. "He just wanted to make sure I was okay after Peter bailed."

"Yet again," Erica added.

"Hey, it's not all the time." Rachel suddenly got defensive.

"Sorry, Rach, it's fine! I just thought you said that earlier..."

"He's just busy now. I'm sure Aspen will make everything better, allow us some time to reconnect," Rachel said, already feeling better herself.

"Exactly, to the other happy couple!" Maggie said raising her glass.

27

"Rach? What do you think?" Dad asked.

"What? Sorry, Dad, I missed that one," Rachel said, snapping back to the cottage. The family was all there. She was divorced, her dad was sick, but how sick? Maggie's marriage was also on the rocks. She felt like a patient recovering from temporary memory loss with all of the flashbacks the reunion seemed to be bringing up.

"Yeah, seriously, Crick, you're like a million miles away," Max said across the table. "What's up?"

Rachel, tired of not letting her family in, decided to be honest. "I'm thinking of that first Christmas I was in Philly and came home without Peter," she said.

A wasp was circling the remaining orange juice and pieces of toast from breakfast. Mom shooed it away and looked at Rachel, willing her to go on.

"Just, how stupid I could be." She shook her head. "Listening to Peter promise time after time that he'd finally show up for me."

"Oh honey, I know you think that now," Mom started, "but that Christmas was a one-off. He had that first big client to snare, and he just got whisked away with it all."

"Pretty dick move not even showing up or calling on Christmas Day though," Max said quietly across the table.

"Right!" she said sitting up in her chair. "He bails on Christmas Eve, promises Christmas and then blip, nothing—nada. And I chased him all the way to Aspen as soon as the first flight left on Boxing Day." It wasn't just anger at Peter, it was the realization that her dad had most likely been struggling with his health and she had chosen Peter over her own family. "Sorry, excuse me," she stood up abruptly and headed into the bathroom.

"I got this one guys," Dad said as he followed his middle daughter out.

"Cricket? Come on out now, dear." He tapped on the bathroom door.

"Daddy, I'm fine," she said fighting the tears through the door.

"Now Ray Ray, I've known you since you were a little seed in your mommy's tummy, there's no use lying to me here," he coaxed softly.

She opened the door and rushed into him for a hug. "I'm so sorry, Dad," she whispered into his chest, careful not to give too much away after promising Max they wouldn't ask their parents anything more on the subject of his health.

"Hey hey, come on now. Hindsight is twenty-twenty, right? What's important is, you're here now and if that little bastard comes anywhere near you or us again, I'm going to finally dig that shotgun out and figure out how to use it. Deal?"

She laughed into his chest. "Sure, Pop, good deal." She wiped her tears. "Ugh, so silly. I know, can we go for that hike now?" she asked, trying to snap out of her bad mood.

"Anyone that asks to go for a hike after mimosas for breakfast, must surely be my kid. Come on, let's go get the others," he said walking with his arm around her on the way back out to the patio.

"Your third born has informed me she'd like to go for a hike up Mount Mansfield, Mrs. Woods," he said to Mom.

Erica nearly dropped the plates she was carrying. "Girl, I'm like, four mimosas deep, you're killing me here."

"I'll put a pot of coffee on," Max said. "Be good to get the girls out of the house for a bit!"

Twenty minutes later they were loaded up into two cars: Max and Maggie with all the kids in her Mercedes G-Class, and the others with Rachel.

"Love the British wheels kiddo!" Dad said, as he folded himself into the tiny front seat.

"Remember when we used to all spend the summers around this area?" Rachel said, pricked with nostalgia.

"Yes, and how you all complained majority of the time." Mom laughed.

"How do you deal with kids?" Erica moaned from the back seat. "Such ungrateful brats."

"Now come on, Ernie, we were kids once too, that's how you can deal with it," Dad said, trying his best to turn around and look at Erica in the tiny space.

"I was probably the worst," Rachel said quietly. Clearly still upset from the morning, she knew once she started down this path, it would be hard to snap out of this mood.

"Pity party, group of one," Erica said from behind her, giving Rachel's arm a squeeze. "Come on Rach, we were all colossal brats. The fact we're all back together now, not killing each other is a goddamn miracle."

"Rach, you just always had big dreams and our small town was never going to fit you. We never held it against you," Mom said. "In fact, it's all we could want as parents, to see our kids grow and follow their dreams."

"Look! We're here," Dad exclaimed. "Let's not dwell on the past, my little daughter. Onward and upward!" He ungracefully turned to lift large frame out of the tiny car.

"Do you think Dad will be okay with this hike?" Erica whispered to Rachel as they got out.

"Shit, what am I thinking?" Rachel started to panic. "Hey Max, come check out this feature on my new wheels," she shouted.

Erica raised her eyebrows at Rachel. She responded with a weak shrug.

"Sweet AC unit, sis" Max joked when he got to the car.

"I'm such an idiot, can Dad even do this hike?" Rachel asked him. "Quickly, or we're going to need an out."

"We'll just stick to one of the smaller trails, and if he seems to be struggling, I'll throw one of you girls down the trail so we have a broken ankle excuse." He laughed, proud of his quick wit.

"How about this trail?" Max asked pointing to one of the smaller ones on the map. "I'm worried about the little ones keeping up." He gave a reassuring glance to Rachel.

"Good plan, without Pierre, I cannot handle carrying both girls around when they inevitably get exhausted," Maggie said smearing the girls with sunscreen.

"Last one to the start has to cook dinner!" Dad said taking off at a jog.

"Every time!" Max said running after him.

"Here, Mags, let me help you with Abby," Rachel said looping her hand through Maggie's youngest.

"Ah thanks, after all this is your fault," she joked.

"Yeah me and big mouth." Rachel smiled. "I figure we can earn back some beer points for later right?"

"Yeah and to be honest, I was worried there might be a murder if we stayed cooped up too long." Maggie laughed.

Erica came running back and scooped up Anna. "Piggy back time!" she cried as they went running off. Anna was laughing hysterically as they went.

"It's nice to see them playing," Maggie said, pulling her long pony tail through the back of her ball cap.

"Guess these past few years have been a bit hard on everyone."

Maggie squinted up into the sun. "You could fucking say that again," she said with a sigh.

Rachel threw her arm over Maggie's shoulder, allowing her older sister to lean on her for a change.

"Still no word from Pierre. Can you believe that?" Maggie asked.

"I'm sure he's just taking some time and space. It's good for everyone."

"Yeah, too much can't be good though."

"Look at me, Mags. I wish I took space when I needed it, who knows, maybe Peter and I would still be together if I took a moment to step back and focus on me a little. I'm sure Pierre just wants to be there one hundred percent for you and the girls," Rachel said.

"He's fucking his executive assistant, Rach. I'm not an idiot," Maggie said surrendering to the truth.

"Now we don't know that for sure."

"Oh yes we do, the last big fight we had before he left was about more texts I found between them. I was never this crazy jealous housewife until he created it, you know? And I got a call from a hotel a few months ago that the card on file was declined from our—and I quote—'romantic weekend away'. I felt like such a colossal fool I couldn't tell the fucking concierge it sounded lovely but I must have lost the invite to that romantic getaway." Maggie wiped a tear off her cheek.

"Oh Mags, I'm so sorry." Rachel stopped and turned to her older sister. "We're gonna get through it. Together, you're not in it alone."

"You're home for two days and act as though we're the Brady Bunch," Maggie said. Yet the small smile she let creep out told Rachel she appreciated it.

"I missed too much; I've been sick over this week if you wanna know the truth," Rachel said sliding her backpack off her shoulder and opening the small zipper on the front. "Valium—I've been chewing these like Poprocks for the past few months what with the divorce, and having to face everyone."

Before Rachel could finish, Maggie grabbed the bottle and popped two in her mouth. No time for water.

"Genius, this will definitely help, sis, thanks!" Maggie said.

They caught up to the rest of the family as Dad was teaching Chloe all about the scat they were finding on the trail. "Could even be a mountain lion!" he said with a low growl.

"Hey Pop, let's not give the kid nightmares, more than likely, it's from that dog up ahead kiddo," Max said pointing to the adorable golden retriever down the trail.

"He looks just like our old dog Champ!" Rachel said, sounding like a schoolgirl. "God, I miss having pets. No one in London has dogs. No time, no patience, no room. Ugh," she said in disgust, remembering how empty her new flat felt without Peter or even a pet to welcome her home at night.

"Guess he likes you too, heads up!" Dad shouted as the dog came bounding toward Rachel.

"Hey little guy, oh my god you are sooo cute! What's your name, fella?" she asked scratching his ears.

"Woody! Come here boy!" she heard around the corner. That voice sounded familiar. Then she saw him. Josh walked through the trees. Jesus, home for two days and she kept running into this guy.

"Hey! Woodses!" Josh exclaimed. "Sorry about Woody, he just loves being around people. See, he's got good taste," he said looking at Rachel.

Erica was behind him making googly-eyes. *What are we, six again?* Rachel thought, although cognizant of the little flip in her stomach. What was that? She had been in a relationship for so long she forgot what this stage was like. The banter, the flirtation, the…

"Uh Rachel?" Josh asked. Rachel snapped back to reality. "I promise we can all walk together, you just gotta give me my dog back." He grinned.

Rachel looked down and realized she was still holding on to Woody's collar as he was itching to go after a nearby squirrel. "Sorry! Must be a side effect of this morning's mimosas," she said blushing.

"Joshy, are your parents around?" Mom asked. Rachel cringed when she still insisted on calling him by his childhood nickname.

"Sorry Mrs. W, my parents aren't, but it's okay, I asked permission before heading out for a walk on my own." He laughed. "I just wanted to get out for a run with Woody here before the day got away from us."

"Well, if you guys are still around this week, we must get together again soon!" she said looping her arm with Josh.

"I'm sure they'd love that," he said turning to look back at Rachel once more. "I better fly though before he actually catches something and we've got another dead carcass on our hands." Josh took off after the dog. "I'll tell my mom to give you a call," he shouted back. "Woody, here bud!"

Just as quickly as he came, he disappeared down the trail.

"Well, I don't know about you guys, but watching Josh run has got me feeling wiped!" Max said, noticing Dad was slowing down a bit. "Beers on the dock?" he asked everyone.

"You read my mind, son!" Dad cheered. "Last one to the car needs to do the beer run!"

"Every damn time!" Max said taking off again after their father.

28

"I can't believe you're getting married today, sis!" Erica shrieked as they applied a third layer of makeup onto Maggie's face.

"I know, right? God it feels like only yesterday we got engaged."

"Six months isn't very long to pull off this big extravagant wedding," Rachel said. "But somehow you did it with ease, girl!"

"Our wedding planner was amazing—how she booked us the Plaza in June during high season on short notice, I'll never know, but then again, we paid her to avoid the tiny details, right?" Maggie smiled.

"You must be most excited about the honeymoon though," Erica said grabbing some fruit off the room service tray. "You know what goes great with strawberries? Champagne." She grabbed the bottle from the ice bucket.

"Ooooh, yes, I cannot wait! Quick layover in Paris so Pierre can finalize a bit of work before two blissful weeks laying on the beach in Bali." Maggie was staring off into space, already daydreaming.

"Yeah, this time tomorrow, you'll be married and on your flight!" Rachel said. "A toast! To our beautiful sister and the first Woods to tie the knot!"

"Cheers!" the girls shouted.

Rachel's phone buzzed from her purse. Probably Peter, he was of course running late and was making his own way over from Philadelphia.

Made the train! Will get taxi to venue and see you at 4. XO

Thank god for that. After the fiasco at Christmas, Rachel wasn't sure she'd be able to handle him bailing on another big family gathering, not to mention a completely ostentatious wedding.

Her phone buzzed again. Max.

We can't find Pierre!! Bachelor party was crazy. Woke up this morning and he wasn't in his hotel room. Call now. Emergency. 911!!

"Um, I'm just going to go see how Mom and Dad are getting on," Rachel said, excusing herself.

"Remind Mom her hair appointment is at noon! I don't want her to be late," Maggie said staring at herself in the mirror.

"Hey, it's me, what do you mean you can't find him?" Rachel whispered into her phone down the corridor, away from Maggie's suite.

"Oh Jesus, Rachel, not so loud. Definitely gonna need an aspirin chaser this morning to get going," Max whimpered into the phone.

"I'm serious! Did he come home with you guys?"

"We all came back here for more drinks. There were a bunch of girls hanging around and last I remember, Pierre was ordering everyone rounds. I'm sure he didn't come back up to the room with us though." He took a big gulp of water, his mouth was so dry.

Just then Rachel could see Pierre walking toward her from the elevator. He looked like the cat that ate the canary with that smug smile on his face.

"I see him, call ya back. And have a shower!"

"Pierre!"

"*Bonjour ma soeur*" he cooed. "*Comment ça va?*"

"Hey, yeah all good. So, Max says you didn't go back up to the room with them last night?" Rachel said crossing her arms.

"He was, euh, so drunk, Raquel."

She hated the way he said her name.

"I had to pay the tab then I made a few calls to Europe, it was morning time there, *tu sais*," he said, fixing his cufflinks.

"Wait, so you never went to bed? This is you on no sleep?" she asked annoyed at how good he still looked.

"You flatter me," he said touching her arm. She quickly pulled away.

"I took the extra suite we had booked, all the groomsmen in one room like that? *Non*, I needed my beauty sleep for this big day!" He smiled. "Pardon, I see my parents there."

"*Maman, ici!*" He smiled as he glided down the hallway.

Smug bastard. Rachel wasn't sure if she was just constantly suspicious of him because she had a reason to be, or whether it was simply his French ways that seemed out of place here.

"Rach, come on! You're up, and Mags is not having anyone screw up her schedule," Erica said from behind. "Everything okay?"

"Yeah, Max is so hungover." She laughed.

"A little hair of the dog and I'm sure he'll be fine!" Erica rushed her older sister back to the suite for her hair appointment.

Maggie and Pierre were wed under a beautiful arch filled with enough flowers to easily fill a large greenhouse. White and pink peonies tumbled down and wove themselves around thousands of tiny twinkling lights, flooding the flooring all the way down the aisle. They swung open the oversized white and gold doors to the cocktail reception amid high tables with white gloved waiters, trays of ice cold glasses of Dom Pérignon waiting.

"Such a beautiful ceremony!" Mom shrieked. "Absolutely stunning!"

"Max looked a little worse for wear, though," Dad said. "Guess the bachelor party got a little of hand, is that right, son?" he asked as Max hobbled over.

Thankfully for Maggie, Max had managed to hold himself together for the reception. Immediately following however, he had rushed for the first canapé tray he could find, sweat beading across his forehead. "Oh god, these mini sliders—best idea ever," he said scarfing one down.

"Anyone see Peter yet?" Rachel asked. "I saw him sneak in while we were up on the altar, but I just haven't been able to find him yet. How the hell they knew enough people to invite five hundred guests is beyond me."

"Champagne anyone?" It was Peter!

"Oh, thank god! I hadn't seen you and I was worried something happened," Rachel said throwing her arms around him, her sleek strapless black bridesmaid dress trailing behind her as he swung her around.

"I snuck in the back—too many people and I didn't want to offend the wrong person!" He chuckled. "Congrats Mags," he said to Maggie and Pierre who had just approached, both looking beautiful and every bit the happy couple. "Excuse me," Peter said as his phone started to ring.

Rachel glared at him. "I thought you were offline today?"

"Just a quick one, babe, grab me a shrimp puff when they come 'round again, will ya?" He kissed her on the cheek before disappearing into the crowd.

"That's one of the hardest working guys I know," Dad said. Rachel couldn't tell if his tone implied pride or annoyance.

"Hey, Rachel." It was Josh approaching now. "I thought we might actually be able to meet this mystery man of yours?"

"Hey guys, so glad you could make it!" Maggie said, blowing air kisses to Josh and Diana.

"Congrats!" Josh said shaking Pierre's hand. "I might need your advice when we take the plunge at Christmas."

"A Christmas wedding? That's what you guys decided?" Rachel asked.

"It's just the most beautiful time of the year, plus it will be the anniversary of our engagement," Diana beamed up at Josh.

"How's business, Josh?" Erica decided to change the subject.

"Yeah, getting there!" he said. "I got on at a great practice in the city, so even though New York rental space is through the roof, at least it's got the clientele!"

"Oooh, my Joshy is doing so well! I'm so super proud of him," Diana said, clinging to his arm.

"I bet." Rachel smiled. "What are you up to these days Diana? Still nursing at the hospital?"

"Oh, god no! With those hours? I'm starting to sell my jewelry online! It is, like, so popular right now to do things on the computer. I have so many new requests from all over!" she gushed.

Erica faked a yawn behind Diana, while Rachel stifled a laugh.

"Oh wow, I bet that keeps you busy. Do you make all the jewelry yourself?" Rachel asked, feigning interest.

"Uh, yeah like, for now it's good, but I dunno. Maybe when I make it real big, I'll need to have help, but for now, it's great! I work from home and get to make Joshy a nice dinner every night." She nuzzled into his neck.

"Good to hear the Joshy nickname is making a comeback," Rachel smiled.

"Um, just Dee, I'm afraid," Josh said blushing. He hated the baby talk, especially in public.

Maggie and Pierre went off to mingle with their guests leaving the five of them stranded.

"Right, Rachel, while you've been left unattended, how about a top up? You too Erica?" Devon asked the girls.

"Yes, that would be great!" Erica said, surprisingly enthusiastic. Damn weddings and their tendency to tug on the heartstrings and make the most stoic of people become a pile of mashed potatoes.

"So, you came stag, huh?" Rachel asked Devon. Why not stir the pot?

"Yeah, I'm off again next week to Haiti so have been a little preoccupied I guess," Devon said as they walked across the ballroom.

"Wow, Haiti! What's the plan when you're done saving the world, Superman?" Rachel asked as they found a spare spot at the bar.

"Three champagnes please," Devon asked the tuxedoed bartender. "Well, it looks good on my Master's applications to have some charitable work. I'm not sure what I'll do once I'm accepted and actually get it, though."

"Not much need for Humanitarian Aid grads?" Erica asked, scanning the room for eligible bachelors.

"Well, the Master's program is actually for an MBA. I figure if I can get that maybe I can still help from the inside out…be part of the movement from one location, not running from one war torn country to the next.

Don't get me wrong, it's incredibly fulfilling," he said noticing he was losing Erica's attention.

"Oh, I see Peter! I'm going to go catch him for this dance. Thanks for the champers Dev!" she shouted behind her.

"Yeah, that or get into advertising," he finished.

"Advertising? What does that have to do with helping people?" Erica asked suddenly slightly more interested.

"Well, a lot of the problems start because the message isn't shown to the masses. Without the right marketing campaigns around these aid projects, they can really struggle trying to find funding or people to get involved."

"That makes sense. Haiti huh? Is it safe there?"

"Safe enough, you're not worried about me, are you?" he asked, moving his chocolate brown eyes up to meet hers.

"Pfft, hardly. Just not sure your New England ass will be able to handle it." She gave him a playful shove.

"So, what's next for you? You graduate next year too, right? Going to go to grad school?"

She shook her head. "Not likely. I mostly went to college to appease the parents. Something about not spoiling opportunities and appreciating what I have versus what they had."

"Yeah, I know what you mean. So, you'll get a job in fashion? That's your degree, right?" he asked, polishing off his glass of champagne. He signaled to the bartender for two more noticing Erica's was also empty.

"God no, I want to wear the fashion, not make my fingers bleed designing it," she said with an air of arrogance. "I've booked some gigs over the past couple years, and now that I'm done, I'll get an agent, make it big and forget this place." She laughed.

"Hey, it hasn't been that bad, has it?" he asked.

"Yeah, look, I'll check you later, okay Devon?" Erica said, spying a few of Pierre's French friends on the dance floor.

"Sure thing, see ya on the dance floor!" he said, sad to see her go.

"Baby, come on I'm dying for a dance!" Rachel said when she found Peter. Upon closer look, she couldn't read his expression. "Everything alright, babe?"

"Everything is fucking awesome, Rach," he said now smiling. "That was my boss—they were so impressed by the new accounts I took on this year, I just got a huge promotion! We can move out of that dinky apartment and even better…" Peter took a deep breath and placed one knee on the floor.

"*Ohmigod*," Rachel said, her hands covering her face. Was he actually going to propose? Here? Now? At her sister's wedding?

She suddenly realized the music had stopped, and the entire room was staring at them.

"Rachel Mary Woods, would you make me the happiest man alive and be my wife?" Peter asked beaming from ear to ear.

"Yes, yes, *yes!*" she shrieked, throwing her arms around him.

"Ladies and gentlemen, love is definitely in the air tonight!" the DJ screamed as he pumped the music back up with "I Wanna Dance with Somebody" by Whitney Houston.

"Holy shit," Erica whispered giving Rachel a big hug. "Maggie is gonna kill you," she joked.

"Aaaaah!!! Little sis!" Maggie ran through the crowd. "Just think, you guys will always have the memory of this proposal at *my* wedding!" she shouted.

"On second thought, maybe the champagne has softened the blow." Erica laughed.

Rachel was still in shock as everyone came up to congratulate them.

"A toast to our little Cricket," Dad said raising his glass to the happy couple.

Rachel looked down at the giant solitaire diamond sitting on her left hand. She had such a mix of emotions, happiness, excitement, and yet a big pit in her stomach. That was normal though, right?

"John honey, how are you doing? Hope you're watching the drink count…" Judy asked finding her husband sitting at the bar with a scotch in his hands.

"Oh, Jude don't worry about me. Just taking a break—between all the Frenchies, and the sheer number of people here, I decided it would be easier to make friends with the bartender here. A glass of chardonnay for my wife please, Jack."

"Thanks, darling. You really should do the rounds though," she said, remaining standing beside him and leaning in to put her arm around his shoulder. "You're feeling okay, right?" She had to admit he did look worn out. Although weddings had that effect on most people.

"Yes, dear, I am fine, okay. Took my meds this morning, see?" He pulled out a little vial of pills from his inside pocket.

"I wasn't checking up on you! Just making sure nothing got forgotten on such a hectic day. I can't believe our little Margaret got married today." She sipped her wine.

"Seems like just yesterday she was dressing up in that big sheet of hers and playing bride with poor Max forced into being the groom." He laughed.

Judy smiled. "They used to play so well together, didn't they?"

"Yeah, I think it became a numbers game after the other two came along," John said. "Had to get better at playing defense than offense."

"And little Rach getting engaged tonight! Can you believe it?"

John was twirling his glass on the bar. A ring of water pooling around the glass, keeping his mind occupied.

"John, you're happy for her, right?" Judy checked.

"Yeah, I mean she seems happy, right?" he asked, looking for reassurance.

"Well, he seems to be able to take care of her…he really is going places. And they seem generally happy I think. I mean, look at us when we first got together. They have so much more available nowadays."

"That sounds like a roundabout way of saying you're not sure either." John laughed. He leaned in to give her a kiss on the cheek. "Come on, you can get me another drink—I promise I'll water mine down with soda," he said as both their glasses sat empty. Jack sensed their needs before John could ask for another.

Judy smiled, letting her own words sink in. "Can you believe we've been married over 30 years ourselves? When did we get so old?"

"It's been 33 wonderful years I'll have you know," John said wrapping his arms around his wife's waist.

"I just hope the girls can say the same thing three decades from now," Judy said before taking a sip of her replenished wine. "Come on, Mr. Woods, I'd like one more dance with you before we turn into a couple of old pumpkins," she said grabbing his arm and pulling him to the dance floor. "I promise to go easy on the old ticker, no tango tonight."

29

Back at the cottage, it was time to hit the water. "Righto Pop, gonna fire up the boat? I restocked the beer fridges and we're ready to roll!" Max said coming through to the deck.

"Ah son, maybe in a bit, I might have a little lie down," Dad said looking tired after their hike earlier that morning.

"Yeah, sure thing. Anything I can get you?" Max asked, concerned.

"I'm good, son, don't worry."

"Taking your pills every day?" Max asked.

"Ah shit son, you sound like your mother now. I'm the picture of health I keep telling her. And the doctors for that matter! I'm just not twenty-five anymore," he said, giving him a reassuring pat on the arm.

"Hey Dad, race ya to the boat?" Rachel said with a smile when she found the boys out back.

"Give me an hour or so and you're on!" he said as he turned back into the house.

"Everything okay with him?" she asked Max.

"Just a bit tired, nothing to worry about!" he replied.

"I somehow doubt that…" Rachel trailed off.

"Well, I can still race you!" Max shouted before giving her a shove and running toward the dock.

"You shit! Always with the cheating!" She puffed behind him trying to catch up.

As they got to the dock they heard a boat approaching. Rachel looked up from untying the lines and recognized Woody sitting on the bow.

"Quite the bow babe you got there, Mackie," Max shouted to Josh in the driver's seat.

"He knows it, trust me! Where you guys off to?" Josh asked, throwing them a line.

Max grabbed the line and pulled them in. Woody was off the boat, jumping up and slathering Rachel with kisses in seconds.

"Man, he really does love you," Josh said. "Wish he took to Diana like that when I first rescued him."

Rachel's tummy flip flopped. She really wished that would stop happening. "We were thinking about firing up the engine and grabbing the waterskis, you in?" she asked.

"I could be persuaded. I'm trying to get some rest from all the family time." He laughed.

"Oh please, you guys are like a monastery compared to this zoo," Rachel said.

"Hey, I love all that action. It was always so quiet at our place. Coming to yours was like free live television," he joked.

"Trade ya man," Max quipped. "I'll go 'round up the troops and see who else is keen for some action," he said leaving Rachel alone with Josh.

Fuck. She forgot how this all worked. Why was she so damn nervous?

"How about a beer?" she asked.

"Sure thing, but let me grab them, you look pretty content there with Woody on your lap." He smiled.

"Yeah, I didn't realize retrievers were known for being lap dogs." She laughed reaching for her beer. Their fingers touched. It was electric. *Was it always like this? Or am I just out of practice?* No, he definitely lingered longer than he should have.

"You never got a dog of your own? God, I remember how puppy sick you were back in the day," Josh said, grabbing a seat beside her and dipping his feet in the water.

"Oh, I wish. Peter was allergic. Should have been my first warning sign, huh? Plus, we were never really settled, you know? And then life in London was totally different—small flats, long days. It wouldn't really be fair to a dog."

"I get that. I think I brought Woody home trying to fix the hole in my own marriage," he said, looking down at the little ripples his feet were making in the water. He took a long swing of his cold beer. "As a therapist, I should have realized adding more components into the equation is never a good idea!"

"I suppose we're all just trying to survive and do the right thing in the moment, hindsight is twenty-twenty," she said squinting into the sun, repeating her dad's earlier comment.

"Isn't that just the writer coming out," he said looking toward her. "To doing more than surviving," he said reaching his beer out to her.

"Agreed," she said as their bottles touched.

"Well, isn't this cute?" Devon said swimming up to the dock.

"Shit Dev! Did you just swim from your place?" Rachel squealed. "That's gotta be…a good couple of miles?"

"Hope so. I've been slacking on this vacation so had to get out," he said. "Plus, can't be without the big bro for longer than twenty minutes or we spontaneously combust." He reached up and pulled himself onto the dock.

"Here man, you need this more than we do," Josh said handing him a beer.

"Having a party without me?" Erica asked, walking down the small stone steps to the dock. She caught sight of Devon's glistening abs as she got closer. "Devon, have one too many?"

"This crazy lunatic just *swam* from their place," Rachel said. "He deserves a freaking Olympic medal."

"Jesus, don't you guys have cable over there?" she asked, grabbing a Diet Coke from the cooler.

"I'm realizing that would have been a better idea. I think I'm gonna puke." Devon mocked dry-heaving onto the dock.

"So, Max said something about getting the skis out for a run. Will you boys be joining us?" Erica asked.

"I call spotter for the first few rounds," Devon said still out of breath. He leaned over to take a sip of his beer. "This is helping," he smiled.

Erica took a seat in one of the big Adirondack chairs on the dock. The sun was sitting high in the sky making the day almost unbearably hot. Thank god, they had the lake.

"I have so missed summers like this," Rachel said, leaning back onto her arms to let as much vitamin D soak up into her skin as possible without disturbing Woody on her lap. "I feel like I lived under a cloud the whole time I was in London."

"Oh, come on, living in one of the world's biggest and most cosmopolitan cities? The history, the architecture? Sounds ideal to me," Devon said.

"Some of us can find that down the road in New York," Josh said grabbing another beer from the cooler. He grabbed some of the melting ice and threw it onto Rachel. The beads landed right near her navel above her coral bikini bottoms.

"Ah you little weasel!" Rachel said jumping up, causing poor Woody to somersault off her lap. Josh was too busy laughing to notice how quickly she was in front of him. She mustered as much confidence as she could as she stared intently into his eyes.

"Thanks for cooling me down. Only fair I do the same for you." She shoved him into the water as Woody ran to the edge and barked.

"Hey bud, I'm fine!" Josh said laughing as he resurfaced. Taking that as an invitation, Woody jumped in to keep him company.

Everyone was laughing on the dock as Max came down.

"Looks like the parentals are tucked in for a nap, and Maggie is watching a movie with the girls, so looks like it'll just be us gang!" Max said. "Wait, are we swimming or skiing?" he asked seeing Josh dripping on the dock as a very wet Woody leaned up against him.

"Nah, your sis just thought I looked a bit warm and helped me cool down," he shot Rachel a cheeky grin.

She looked at Erica who was hiding her own smile behind her Coke can. *She is enjoying this a little too much*, Rachel thought.

"Cool, I'll fire up the boat," Max said. "You boys joining us?"

"Yeah, we're down. Dev is gonna sit the first runs out—he *swam* here," Erica said, clearly impressed.

"Shit man, you've got my respect," Max said giving him a pat on the back. "The life of a professor leaves much to be desired in the fitness department."

"No, Max has just annoyingly been blessed with good genes the girls all missed," Erica said giving him a shove. "He eats whatever, whenever, and has been the same size since tenth grade."

"Ahem, twelfth, I had a final growth spurt in grade eleven. And you're one to talk Miss Model—drink like a fish and still show up to casting calls."

She stuck her tongue out at him.

"Yeah, you should be shooing the girls away with a stick," Josh said. "No, Mrs. Woods on the horizon?"

"Oh god, is he sounding like a therapist right now? Or is it my own avoidance?" Max joked.

"Chloe is Max's only girl right now," Erica stepped in. "He's had his fair share of crazy for now."

"Yeah but if you know of any ladies that are into single dads on tenure, you send my way! I can bust out my finest tweed for any date." He stood up and adjusted his imaginary bow tie.

"Enough with the dating talk," Rachel said, grabbing the bowlines. "Let's hit the water! Josh, you can grab your cooler since I think this next round is on you?" She threw her long blonde hair up into a bun without looking back. She was finding her confidence again and liked the way that felt.

"Yes, boss! That sister of yours runs a tight ship," he said to Erica as she climbed in behind Woody.

"Oh yeah, maybe Ms. Bossy pants would like to be first up on the skis?" Erica asked Rachel.

"Oh god, it's been awhile. But probably a good idea before too many more of these," she said putting her beer down. "What the hell, let me suit up!"

As the boat drifted away from the dock, Rachel gave a final adjustment to her skis. Her foot was tapping within the ski, making little waves in the water. She waited for the line to go taut before she would be flung forward and pulled around the crystal clear lake. She loved waterskiing but it had been years since she had been for a spin.

Shit, the line was lifting out of the water.

No time to be a chicken shit.

Here we go!

And with that, she was up and off—just like riding a bike.

"John, dear? Everything alright?" Judy turned in bed to face him after she heard the boat roar away. She had pretended to be asleep when Max knocked on the door. John had passed out as soon as they got in from their hike. She checked his cholesterol pills and knew he had way too many in there. Was it possible he was not taking them all? She counted them out most days but leading up to this trip, and with so much going on at the cottage, it had been harder with the kids around. She wanted to stay close to talk to him about it.

"John!" she said louder than intended.

"Huh, uh what is it, dear?" he asked groggily.

"I just wanted to know if you took your heart pills today?"

"Ah geez hon, can't a guy take a mid-afternoon nap when he's on vacation anymore?"

"I know, I know. I just want to make sure you didn't miss a day, there's so much going on with everyone around and it's easy to forget," she started to trail off knowing she sounded like a nag.

"I'll take it when I get up, okay?" He reassured her, but he sounded short of breath. And had looked pale on the walk.

"I'll just grab some water for you now. Then I won't forget either!" She tried to sound light but knew she failed. She went into the kitchen, and glimpsed the kids across the lake. It made her so happy to see Rachel flying behind the boat on skis, she didn't think it was just her mother's intuition that knew she was happy to be home. She could see it plastered on her daughter's face right now.

Thud.

It came from their room. Judy ran back to find John slumped on the floor. "John!" she shouted dropping the glass of water she was carrying. The glass splintered on the floor and sent water splashing up around Judy's ankles.

A moment later, Maggie came running through the living room. "What's going on? I heard a bang and it sounded like something broke." She barged through the door and saw her mom leaning across John and shouting his name.

"*Ohmigod*, what's happened?" she asked rushing over. "Dad! Daddy!"

Tears flowed down Judy's cheeks as she yelled his name louder and louder.

"Mom, call 911. I'll start CPR," Maggie said. Judy ran out into the living room to grab her cell phone and call an ambulance.

"What's going on? What's all the commotion?" John asked, coming to.

"Thank god. Daddy, you passed out! Do you remember what happened before you wound up on the floor?" she quizzed.

Tiny beads of sweat were starting to form on John's forehead. "I, I think I just stood up too fast." His voice was shaking as he looked around the room. There were lots of little black dots dancing in front of his eyes. He blinked a few times to try and make them go away.

"Ambulance is on its way," Judy said running back into the room. "Oh, thank god!" she cried and ran over to give John a big hug. "You scared the shit out of me!"

"Oh Jude, don't over-exaggerate. I just told your oldest daughter here, I got up too fast to take a leak. Wait, did you say you called an ambulance? Oh, Jesus Judy...call them back and cancel," he said trying to get up. Feeling weak he slid back down the side of the bed.

"No way Dad, just let them come check on you, there's no harm in that," Maggie said. She left to grab a broom in the kitchen and sweep up the glass.

"She's right, dear. Please, just relax. I'll grab you a new water glass," Judy said heading back into the kitchen.

She and Maggie met in the hallway, Judy still shaken and Maggie in tears. Maggie scooped her mom into a hug. Judy could recall countless times she had done the same for their kids when they were sad or needed comforting.

How the roles had reversed.

"So, who's next?" Max asked slowing the boat down as Josh jumped back onboard.

"I haven't done one ski in a while, that was a bit choppy!" he said, grabbing a towel from the seat cushion.

"Someone's being modest," Erica said. "I'm happy I managed to stay up for a lap of the lake, I'm suddenly feeling very old and, well, a bit buzzed." She laughed.

"Maybe if you ate some carbs, you'd have something to soak up that booze," Rachel teased.

"Plus, you're the youngest here, Ernie, don't start playing the age card," Max said putting the boat in neutral.

"Oh Ernie! I remember that nickname!" Devon said with a laugh. "I'm so glad it's still in circulation. If we're gonna chill here for a minute, I'm gonna cool off. That cool Max?"

"Be my guest," he replied. "The bow is calling my name with a cold beer and some hot sun to warm this pasty dad bod."

Josh and Devon jumped in the lake. Erica smiled coyly at her sister, they both knew what the other was thinking. It was going to be a nice gossip session around the campfire tonight.

"Hey girls, you joining us, or what?" Josh said, splashing the side of the boat.

"We're working on a crucial part of the cottage vacation—day drinking. It's like normal drinking, but with a tan," Erica said, pulling her sunglasses down over her eyes.

Rachel went to grab her hat on the other side of the boat. She could see red flashing lights in the distance.

"Hey guys, doesn't that look like it's coming from our place?" she asked, trying to peer into the distance. "Oh my god, I think those are ambulance lights!"

"Here, let me grab the binoculars," Max said, walking to the back of the boat. "Shit, it is our place. Party's over, guys!" But the boys were already climbing back into the boat.

"Floor it Max, what the hell?" Rachel said in a panic.

Max sped across the lake, trying not to let his imagination run away with him.

Seconds ago, the hot sun beating down on them was a welcome feeling. Now, Rachel felt smothered by the heat and blinded by the reflection off the water. She just wanted to get her feet on dry land.

"You guys run up, we'll tie everything off," Josh said. Before he could finish Max, Erica and Rachel were scrambling up the steps and toward the backyard.

Rachel got there first. Panting and tears already falling freely down her face, she watched as paramedics came down the back steps with their dad in a stretcher. "Dad!" she cried, "what's going on?"

"Oh Cricket, don't worry, dear, come on I'm totally fine," he said, untucking a hand from the sheet to give his daughter a pat on the arm. "This is just a silly precaution. I told your mother, and these fine medics, that I feel one hundred percent! Waste of these fine EMT's time is what this is."

She wiped her eye and chuckled softly. "Even in a gurney, you can still rant like the best of them." She put her hand over his arm.

"Mom? What happened?" Erica asked as she and Maggie followed behind. Their eyes were red but had seemingly stopped crying. She took that as a sign that things were under control.

"Pop? What do you need?" Max asked, putting his arm around Rachel.

"Kids, don't worry," Mom said. "Your dad just had the tiniest fainting spell, but we just want to be sure everything is okay." She looked to her husband, her eyes asking for permission to fill the rest of the kids in on his heart. He nodded. "With his condition, maybe he needs to adjust his meds is all."

"Condition?" Erica asked, looking for final confirmation that his health was in fact, fading, as Max had alluded to previously.

"Ma'am, will you be joining us?" asked a paramedic with the name *Laura* scrawled across her nametag.

"Yes, kids I'll text you how we're doing." She jumped into the back of the ambulance.

"Where are you going? We'll follow you," Max said.

"Absolutely not. Over my dead body," Dad said.

The kids all looked at each other. Rachel wrapped her now soaked towel tighter around her as she leaned into Max.

"Kids, that was a joke! I don't want anyone else wasting their time at the hospital. I'll be home for dinner…save me a steak and a glass of wine," he whispered with a wink to Erica.

"Love you, Dad," they all said as the doors closed. And with that, their towering, strong, indestructible father was being driven away in the back of an ambulance.

"Hey, it's gonna be alright, girls," Max reassured them, wrapping his arms in a big group hug. "I'm sure he just wasn't taking his cholesterol pills like he should."

"He never could follow rules very well," Maggie said with a small laugh.

"Remember when he had laryngitis and the doctor told him no talking whatsoever and it took about three follow-ups to ER before he finally listened?" Rachel said, even though she was smiling, a small tear rolled down her cheek.

"And Mom got him that stupid whistle to blow anytime he needed something." Erica laughed.

"I was so happy when that thing disappeared," Maggie said.

"You're welcome guys," Max said with an impish grin.

"No way!" Maggie shouted.

"I saw an opportunity, and took it—it was that, or poke out my own eardrums. That just seemed easier."

They all laughed.

"Ahem." They turned around on the deck to see Josh and Devon, their arms laden with everything hauled off the boat.

"Everything okay, guys?" Josh asked.

"You know our old man," Max said, "was moaning the whole way into the truck so I'm sure he'll be back to normal in no time."

"Good to hear it. You'll let us know the latest though?" Devon asked.

"Course, thanks guys," Max said, shaking both their hands.

"Good. Come on Woody, let's go home," he said, trying to lure Woody away from Rachel's side.

"Fickle dog, he seems to want a new owner!" Josh laughed.

"Therapy dogs are legit," said Rachel, scratching him behind the ears. "I didn't realize how soothing this was." Woody was contently staring up at her with his tongue hanging out.

"Tell ya what, why don't you watch him this afternoon?" Josh said to Rachel. "If you're feeling up for it, we can swing by later for a bonfire and pick him back up?"

Was that a date? She shifted in her place.

"Um that's really kind, but we have no idea what's going on with my dad, and I can't just take your dog," she was stumbling, wishing she had something more on than a bikini and damp towel.

"Look, no pressure. I'm gonna walk away. If Woody doesn't come, enjoy the snuggles—he's a great listener. Just text me when you want me to come get him. You've got my number," he said with a little nod.

"Thank you," Rachel mouthed as he turned to walk away. Woody did seem pretty content sitting on her feet, nuzzling in for more ear scratches.

Josh threw a thumbs up and with that, he and Devon climbed down the steps and into their boat before heading back down the lake.

Max left the girls on the deck to go in and check on the kids inside. Miraculously all three had slept through the entire ambulance ordeal.

"Who needs a fucking drink?" Maggie asked.

"Hear-hear!" Erica said following her inside. Rachel stood watching the boat get smaller and smaller. She was struggling to remember the last time she felt so taken care of with such a small gesture. She turned to pad back into the house with Woody following right on her heels.

30

"Good morning, soon to be Mrs. Mitchell," Peter said, as he gave Rachel a peck on the cheek.

It was almost a week after Maggie's wedding and Rachel was still getting used to how that sounded.

"Good morning yourself," she purred. She pulled back the duvet and padded into the kitchen to make coffee.

"Ah thanks, babe, I'd love a latte too, please," Peter said as he went into the bathroom and turned the shower on. *Somehow it never seemed like his turn to make the coffee*, she thought before her ring caught the light and she watched the sparkle dance around the room. She stared at it—it really was beautiful. Growing up with such happily married parents, she always thought she'd get married one day but she had a career in mind first and foremost. She wanted to accomplish all of her goals and then settle down with a husband and family. Could she say she had really achieved that?

"It's early, I haven't had my coffee," she mumbled to herself reaching up for her favorite NYU mug.

"What's that, babe?" Peter yelled from the bedroom.

"Nothing, dear, just excited for coffee," she said, powering up their espresso machine. It had been a Christmas gift from Peter. Yes, she loved her coffee but she was sure it was more for him than her. Give her an urn and kettle and she'd be just fine. Hell, anything but instant and she was happy. Oh, who was she kidding? As a poor student, she lived off instant coffee.

"So, dinner with my folks tonight to celebrate, right?" he asked, tying his tie.

"Yep, that's what they tell me," she said. "My parents are really looking forward to it."

"Yeah, it'll be good for the in-laws to meet. Just make sure your old man keeps the sarcasm to a minimum. Mr. and Mrs. Mitchell are a bit more... um," he struggled for the right word.

"Refined? Is that what you were going to say?" She couldn't help but be annoyed.

"Of course not, Rach, they're just different people. My dad is white collar, your dad is…a bit more blue. But those are your dad's words, not mine," he said, putting his hands up.

He grabbed his latte in the tumbler Rachel held out for him. "Thanks babe, see ya tonight, make sure they're not late either, my dad hates that," he called as he opened the front door.

No, "thanks for the coffee, babe!" or "sorry my parents are so much better than yours." She frowned as she heard the elevator ping at the end of the hall.

"I just need my coffee," she said to herself again before selecting her shot. It was a double shot kind of day and it was just after six in the morning.

"Mom, Dad, I'd like to introduce you to Mr. and Mrs. Mitchell." Rachel said, as the hostess brought them to their table.

"Wow, such an exclusive table! Way to go, Peter!" Dad said, shaking his soon-to-be son-in-law's hand.

"Oh please, do call us Eugene and Miriam," Miriam said, leaning into her mom with a double kiss on each cheek.

"Oh my, lovely to meet you both, and please call us Judy and John," she replied.

"I can't believe it's taken this long for us to all get together!" Dad shouted, wrapping Miriam up in a big bear hug. Her eyes nearly popped out of her head at the intrusion of personal space. Rachel hid a smile behind her napkin. Mom noticed and gave her a wink.

"Yes, well my schedule leaves me little time for play these days I'm afraid," Eugene said snapping for the waiter. A man dressed in head to toe black arrived. "A bottle of the 2006 Dom Pérignon, please. We're celebrating tonight."

"Right away sir, and may we say, it's lovely to see you back at The Ritz," the waiter said with a nod.

"Yes, and I'll have another scotch while we wait on the Dom. Anyone else? Place your orders."

"Two gin and tonics please," Dad asked for Mom and himself.

"Make it three," Rachel concurred.

"I'll have whatever scotch the old man has please, and keep the martinis coming for my mother," Peter said.

Miriam finished the last of her cocktail and smiled at her son. "Always looking after me. Do you know how lucky you are?" she asked turning to Rachel. "This boy is going places and that ring! My god," she said reaching out for Rachel's hand.

"Yes, we're very happy," Rachel beamed at Peter.

"I think these kids are both pretty lucky to have found each other in today's crazy world," Dad said, feeling a burst of protectiveness for his daughter.

"All these phones and apps and nonsense, crazy anyone can get together today!" Mom said as the waiter placed their drinks onto the table.

"Yes, well, it's not like it was back in our time is it?" Eugene said. "I practically married Miriam out of high school before leaving my bride at home in Connecticut to put in my time over in London with Barclays. Best business decision I ever made," he said raising his glass to...his own success? Rachel wasn't sure.

"Yes, and look at us now!" Miriam said, already sounding quite tipsy.

Rachel wasn't sure what their future looked like but she hoped to god it didn't look like this in twenty years.

"Ah, the champagne. A toast," Dad said, holding out his glass. "To the union of these two great families!" He received a polite smile from Peter's family as they raised their glasses up.

Happily, the night progressed with little incident, aside from Dad's gasp when he first opened the menu. However, it didn't take Eugene long to insist the night was on him.

When they arrived home later that night Rachel slipped off her heels and rubbed her foot. "Well, I think that was relatively painless."

"Yeah, I'm surprised your Dad didn't offer to pay their share though," Peter said as he carefully hung up his suit. "Not that it was expected of course."

"What are you talking about? He offered repeatedly," she said, her face growing hot.

"Oh, did he? Sorry, I must have missed that," he said nonchalantly. "Either way, I'd chalk it up to a success!" He kissed her before climbing into bed. "Now we've just got to sort out our move to the new condo. God, that'll be good!"

"Yeah, very exciting!" Rachel said deciding to not dwell on his earlier comment. "When are you away in London again?" she asked taking her makeup off in the bathroom.

"Monday for two weeks. So, hate to say it, babe, but you'll have to do a lot of the packing while I'm away."

She let the tap run as she stared at her reflection.

Woo-fricking-hoo.

"Seriously? Can't we bump it by a week?"

"No can do, babe, the lease is up and we gotta get into the new place. Come on, aren't you happy my work is covering the costs and most of the rent every month? Can't be ungrateful and spit in their face," he said plugging in his Blackberry beside him. She swore he cuddled that thing more than her each night. "Mind closing the door, babe? I'm exhausted." He clicked the lamp off and she stood staring through the light in the bathroom. She slammed the door and aggressively started scrubbing her makeup off with a face cloth.

Rachel didn't want to seem ungrateful. Sure, she had supposed much of the packing would fall to her. And how hard would it be, his closet consisted mostly of suits, and the new place would come furnished. Thank god, they could leave their ratty student furniture behind.

"Not like I work full time either or anything," she mumbled, squirting toothpaste onto her electric toothbrush. She let the buzzing quiet her mind and then spat out the remains. She climbed into bed next to him and tossed and turned.

She was sure this was just a transitional period and they'd be back to golden in no time.

31

Maggie took the lead in being the matriarch while their parents were away. She commanded the kitchen as though she were a top chef in a five star restaurant. Before anyone could wallow, she had assigned them each their own tasks. Now the air was filled with the scent of fresh lobster on the grill and roasted potatoes.

"Way to go, Mags, this spread looks fit for a king!" Erica said setting the table on the patio.

"Honestly, it just helps to keep my hands and mind busy. I'd be a mess if I stopped," she said, grabbing a chilled sauvignon blanc from the fridge.

"Trust me, when Peter and I first split, I threw myself into so many different things. Did I tell you girls I tried baton twirling?" Rachel asked her sisters.

Erica nearly choked on her wine. "Um, you definitely did not."

"Ellie asked me to join after work and I thought, what the hell do I have to go home to?"

"I hate picturing you over there all on your own, going home to some dingy London flat. Like a scene out of Oliver Twist or something," Maggie said drizzling balsamic over the fresh caprese salad.

"Or, sipping cosmos with her girlfriends at some fabulous London bar," Erica said filling everyone's wine glass, plopping an ice cube into each.

"I would say it was something in between the two. Yes, once I left Peter and had to get my own place, I wouldn't say the flat in Clapham was super glam, but you know what? It was mine. It was my first real place, I paid the rent every month and every item hung or put on a shelf was mine and for that, it was perfect."

Rachel didn't mean to sound blunt but she was damn proud of how things turned out as of late. No, it wasn't the opulent two bedroom flat in

Hyde Park she shared with Peter but it was hers and she had much greater pride in it as a result.

"Sorry, Crick, I didn't mean anything by it," Maggie said frowning.

"Oh god, no, I know, Mags don't worry. I guess I'm still sensitive about it all," she said raising her wine glass and passing one to Maggie. "Cheers, to the sisterhood."

Erica bit her lip and fidgeted with the stem of her wine glass. Things had been going well with Maggie but she was still aware of their distance.

"Hear-hear!" Maggie said clinking glasses before shooting Erica a reassuring smile.

Let the healing begin.

"Alright, these lobsters are turning a real nice color for us!" Max said walking in on the girls sharing a moment. "Am I missing some bonding time?" He poured himself a glass of wine.

The girls laughed at their effeminate brother. They loved how he always wanted to be one of the girls.

"Come on in here, big brother," Rachel said opening her arms to him. "Cheers to the children of the Woods!"

"Now, this is exactly what my old heart needs," a voice said from behind.

"Dad!" Erica said running over to him.

"How are you feeling? How did it go?" Rachel asked Mom before letting her old man wrap her up in his arms.

"I'm fine," Dad said cutting them off. "Just like I knew I was. These doctors today are just so worried about lawsuits. Gotta check everything and anything to make sure no stone is unturned."

"Oh, I am so thrilled to hear that!" Maggie said giving him a kiss on the cheek. "Don't know what we'd do without our Papa Bear," she said giving her mom a hug.

Max connected eyes with their mom. She looked down to the floor and pretended to be enamored with the dust on the counter. He knew why she wasn't making eye contact.

"Come on, Pop, the grandkids were asking after you. They want to hear all about the big ride in the ambulance!" he said setting Dad up in one of the Adirondack chairs on the patio. "Go easy, girls, Grandpa has had a bit of a long journey," he said with a smile as the three girls climbed onto his lap. Nobody wanted to be left out.

"Well, first, they asked if I wanted the sirens on, and of course I said *yes!*" he said animatedly. As though mere hours ago he wasn't on the floor giving everyone the fright of their lives.

Max walked back into the kitchen to find Mom pouring herself a scotch. "Mom, the sauvignon-b just isn't cutting it tonight?"

"Just a little to take the edge off. I hated that whole experience." She wiped her eyes.

The girls stopped what they were doing to have a good look at their mom. Rachel couldn't believe that she somehow looked even smaller right now than when she walked through the door only days ago. Maggie put her arm around their mother. Her tiny shoulders relaxed and a tear slowly rolled down her cheek.

"Oh mom," Rachel said placing her arm around her mom's other shoulder.

"I'm so sorry kids," she said wiping her cheek. "I just hate those damn hospitals," she said with a weak smile. "Okay, Max, I'm ready for that wine now!"

"How about the old man, they just discharged him without any further follow up?" Max said pouring their mom a cold glass of wine.

"The doctor told him off for not taking his cholesterol medication seriously. He's got a new prescription for a stronger Beta-blocker. But that's it for now. Let's enjoy the rest of our time together!" She clapped her hands together. "I can't believe how late it is. Maybe someone could see what he'd like to drink with dinner?"

"I'll do it!" Erica volunteered. "I assume booze is a no go?" she asked looking into the fridge. Shame, as they were heavy on the booze and light on the soft drinks. "Tap water perhaps?"

"I'm sure a light beer would be fine, but just *one*—no matter what he says. No red meat either, just to give his system a break."

"You got it, light beer, on its way!" Erica said and went to find him out on the patio alone, the girls having gone to chase fireflies around the backyard. "Hey Pop, how about a cold one?"

"You read my mind, Ernie." Erica handed him his beer and gave his shoulder a squeeze.

"Thanks, kiddo…surprised you guys weren't in there clearing the fridge of all the fun stuff." He took a small sip as he got up from his chair. "Ya know this light beer ain't so bad, is it?"

"So seriously, you're okay?" Erica said looking up at her dad. No matter how much she grew as a kid, she knew she'd always be looking up to him.

"Hey, of course I am! Picture of health the doc said. I just gotta be more careful with that—" he made bunny ears—"'fun stuff!'. No major adjustments. And anyway, it'll keep your mother happy. God help me if she buys one of those day-of-the-week pill containers at the hospital pharmacy." He put his arm around his youngest daughter.

"You're officially old then?"

"So it would seem! I hope I didn't scare you kids tonight," he said softly.

"Ah, just a little but you know how much we love the drama around here."

Just then, Woody, tired from another swim in the lake, came up to the house to join everyone.

"How long was I at the hospital? Did we get a dog while I was gone?" he asked, squinting into the dark.

"Oh no, Josh left Woody here for our little Ray Ray," Erica said teasingly.

"Is that so? And what do we think his intentions are exactly?" Dad laughed.

"Hard to say, could be something there but still not sure Rach is ready for it, ya know? There's still so much we don't know about how things unraveled with her and Peter. I'm just happy she's here."

"Me too kiddo, me too."

"You too what?" Rachel asked as she walked out with a glass of wine for herself and Erica before taking a seat.

"Just that we're both pretty happy with the dog you stole for the family, it's just what we've been missing since Champ passed away," Dad said.

"Aww Champ! He was the best, wasn't he?" Rachel said. "And for the record, I did not steal Woody." At the sound of his name, Woody ran over to her side and laid his head in her lap. "You can't steal something that came of its own accord, can you?" she said smiling down at his big brown puppy dog eyes. "I should text Josh and get him to come pick him up, I feel a tad guilty I've had him all afternoon!"

"Brilliant idea!" Dad exclaimed. "Why doesn't he join us for dinner? Hell, extend to the whole family," Dad gave Woody a pat and headed inside. "I'll go tell Jude to set a few more places."

"Whoa dad, slow down, you need to rest. And I haven't even written him yet!" Rachel urged.

But it was too late, he was already inside grabbing Rachel's phone for her.

"So, this is my thirties? My dad playing matchmaker for me?" Rachel said as she leaned back in her chair and took a long slow sip of sauvignon blanc.

Erica laughed. "Hey, if only we had let him meddle more as teens, maybe things would have turned out a lot differently."

Rachel looked up at the pink and purple skyline as the sun began to set. She couldn't believe how crazy today had been and they hadn't even eaten dinner yet. But as she sat with the quiet sounds of the crickets and gentle lapping of the water, she felt a stillness she hadn't experienced in months... maybe even years.

"Gotta throw a few more lobsters on the grill," Max said interrupting Rachel's thoughts.

"How many more exactly, dear brother?" Erica asked.

"Just two, seems the Mackie's are out for dinner with their neighbors across the lake. Looks like it's just the boys! I hear someone wants to retrieve their retriever," he said, letting Woody give his fingers a lick.

"How convenient," Rachel mumbled. "I suppose you and Dad texted from my phone too? It better not have been overly mushy with a bunch of emojis," she said narrowing her eyes at him.

"Cheers girls!" Max said clinking glasses with his sisters. He seemed to be enjoying all of this just a little too much.

"Hey, don't the Mackie's still hang out with Lucinda's parents? Maybe we should really try and arrange a lunch with them one day?" Erica smirked.

"You know, I think they just might!" Rachel said chiming in.

"Ha! That girl was batshit crazy at school. Thank god someone else married her and took her to Tucson. So, nice try but she's off the market." He stuck his tongue out at them.

"Girls, I hear we have two more for dinner, come help set the table please," Mom said as she fixed her lipstick from the back door.

"Shouldn't we be the ones getting all dolled up?" Erica whispered as they walked back inside.

"I'll put some more wine in the fridge. You look great, mom," Rachel said.

"Thanks, dear. I think a bit of company is just what we need!" she said selecting a playlist on Erica's iPod. "What's that one you had on the other night dear? I just loved it!" she said handing the iPod to Erica.

You'd never have known she'd spent time at the hospital today.

"Mom, are you sure having people over is the best idea?" Maggie asked.

"Dad might be a bit tired…" she started.

"Nonsense. Look, your father is fine. And the more we tiptoe around him or act like he's a delicate little flower, the worse it will be. Trust me. You don't spend more than half your life with someone and not learn a thing or two about what they need."

"You better not be talking about me," Dad said, coming back into the kitchen after a quick shower. "I had to get that awful hospital smell off me," he said grabbing an asparagus spear off the stove.

"Nope, just choosing the music for tonight's soirée!" Erica said. "How about this one, Pop? It's called 'Dad's Playlist', all the classics from a million family road trips. Sound good?"

"Wonderful!" Mom said giving Erica a peck on the cheek before freshening up the flowers on the table. The girls all took a cue from their mother: if she was confident everything was fine, then so were they.

"Knock, knock," Josh said through the screen door on the patio.

"Oh boys, come in!" Mom said greeting them at the door.

"Thanks for the invite, Mrs. Woods. It seems our parents stranded us." Devon laughed.

"Wow, mommy and daddy left you two alone for the night? No big party then?" Erica teased.

"Nah, they prefer us to take our parties elsewhere these days, so here we are!" he said, handing over a bottle of chardonnay to Rachel.

"I'll just pop this in the fridge," she said, letting her eyes catch Josh's. "Oh um, I was wondering about Woody, he's had quite the afternoon of snacks thanks to vacuuming up after the girls, but I was wondering if he needs something for dinner?" she said awkwardly, suddenly feeling everyone's eyes on her.

"Oh no, just a lobster should suit him fine." Josh joked. "He can eat later when we get home, hope he was good company? A total gentleman?"

"The best, thank you so much," she said, feeling her cheeks grow hotter.

"Right! Who wants a glass of white?" Erica said swooping in.

"Make it two, please," Devon said. "I'll help you," he said moving closer to Erica.

"Think I can manage," she said. "Why don't you go check on those lobsters with Max?"

"Alright boys outside, girls inside—we get it," Josh teased.

"Wait for me guys, I've had enough of this estrogen for over thirty years. You catch on quick that the safest spot is usually anywhere else." Dad whispered on his way out the door.

"Amazing, isn't it? You'd never know he spent the afternoon in the hospital," Maggie said watching them from the other side of the kitchen.

"He really is indestructible, isn't he?" Erica said.

"Let's hope so," Rachel whispered.

<h1 style="text-align:center">32</h1>

The winter following Rachel's wedding, Erica found herself at a Starbucks in Midtown waiting for her dad to show up for their coffee date.

"Hey Kiddo!" he said as he came in from the cold. The January sun was already starting to set and it wasn't even 4 p.m. yet, giving an extra chill to the already frigid temperatures.

"So, have you talked to Maggie lately?" he asked her after grabbing his Americano at the bar. Erica had been struggling with her modeling lately. She was sure the terrible mess at Rachel's wedding didn't help with matters.

"No, Pop. Nothing yet," she said shortly, pouring a bit of cream into her coffee. She used to love these family dates but more and more she was feeling like the family outcast. Especially without Rachel nearby, or even speaking to her. Rachel seemed to still be punishing everyone for the wedding fiasco.

"I can't stand all this tension between my kids," he said staring down at his untouched bagel. "It's bad for an old man's ticker."

"Dad, it's not for lack of trying, she wants me dead. And to be honest, I'd want the same seeing how humiliated she was. But she won't even let me explain…I was just trying to look out for her. I swear *nothing* happened!" Erica said as she looked down sadly at the coffee still swirling in her mug.

"I know that dear. And come on now, everything is fixable, right? Your mother is working on her too. Maggie and Pierre are off again in Paris, I think they needed a little time and space to decompress too." Dad placed his hand on his youngest daughter's hand. "It's only because we love you guys, ya know."

Were those tears welling up in his eyes? Shit, Erica could not handle this without a full coffee in her system, or hell, some hard liquor.

"Oh Dad, I'm sure you're right, it will all blow over, ya? Mags and I got really close while Rach was in Philly and I hate that we don't have that same relationship anymore but I just don't know how to fix it. Her husband hasn't exactly made it easy either…"

She knew her dad was taking it hard since he had such a tough upbringing himself. They never did meet their paternal grandfather, he had taken off when their dad was only two, and showed no interest in getting to know his kids. He didn't speak much to his older siblings; he felt they somehow blamed him for their dad leaving. He always wanted that nuclear family and wasn't about to have it explode now.

"Well when they get back, your mother has invited them over for dinner so we'll work on it, Scout's honor," he said holding up his fingers in the Scout symbol.

"Sure thing, Pop, thanks."

"Now, onto sister number two…"

Erica pinched her eyes closed and took a deep breath. "No contact there either, Dad—hell, I don't even know her new U.K. phone number."

"Here, put it in your phone, she at least sent us that," he said handing her over his cell phone. "We know our Ray Ray and she'll come around; it's hard being a newlywed, moving overseas and the timing of everything else was just awful," he said ripping off a chunk of his bagel. He gestured to Erica but she shook her head. While she wasn't booking modeling gigs, she sure as hell wasn't going to let her weight go up.

"Okay, little one, I should get back to the country. This old man can only take so much of the big city these days." He stood up and pulled her in for a big hug.

Erica felt like she could collapse into his embrace. Life was a whole new level of shit at the moment and without her sisters' support she was feeling more lost than ever.

"Bye, my youngest," he said then pecked her on the cheek.

Erica watched her dad walk out onto busy 42nd Avenue where Midtown swallowed him up. She felt totally alone.

Seeing Rachel's number in her phone, she took a chance and sent her a text.

Hey! It's your favorite sister. Finally tracked your number down. The Daily Mail published it this morning xo

She hoped laughter was the quickest way back into her sister's heart. For the next twenty-five minutes, she stared at her phone while finishing her coffee.

Nothing.

Erica threw her untouched fat-free muffin into the garbage. She was delaying going back to her tiny cramped apartment in Brooklyn with three roommates. Even in a busy house where you were practically on top of one another, she felt all alone.

Totally alone.

33

The next morning at the cottage, Rachel arose to a beautiful sunrise peeking out over the lake. As she walked across the living room, she could just see the top of Erica's head leaning back into one of deck chairs, looking out over the water.

"Oh my god...that coffee smells amazing, sis!" Rachel said, finding Erica texting away. "I'm gonna grab a cup and join you, unless I'm interrupting something?" she asked seeing Erica turn her phone over.

"Hardly! Just some work stuff."

"Suuuuuure," she said walking back into the kitchen to grab her coffee.

"How is work is anyway?" she asked Erica, coming back outside, mug in hand and a small bowl of fruit for them to snack on.

"The modeling is slow to be honest with you. I'll have bursts of amazing bookings and then nothing for a few months. I may be only twenty-four but I swear to god, at some bookings I am ancient," she said, grabbing a strawberry from the bowl.

"Don't make me spit coffee on you, okay? You're talking to a thirty-year-old divorcée who has to start all over again in another new city. I feel like I'm about ninety-years-old sometimes."

"Well, don't say anything, but I'm considering a bit of a career change. Maybe," Erica confided.

"Oh really? Do tell!"

"Well, maybe revisiting my fashion degree, get behind the scenes, or something? I haven't fully thought it through yet."

Rachel was smiling.

"And just what is so entertaining in that?" Erica asked.

"I just find it interesting you fought it for so long and here comes Devilish Devon raving about your style and brilliance in the field and now we're thinking career change. Hmm okay, surely a coincidence," Rachel said spearing another piece of cantaloupe.

"Oh puh-lease! As if I care what Brace-Face Devon has to say about my career movements," Erica said, hiding her blushing face behind her coffee mug. "Besides, let's not start throwing stones in our glass house, okay, dear sister?"

"Excuse me?" she said with a laugh.

"Oh Joshy…thank you so muuuuch for letting me cuddle your dog all day! Next time I want it to be your hot body next to me insteaaaaaad," Erica said batting her eyelashes.

Laughing, Rachel threw a grape at Erica's head.

"What's going on out here then?" Max asked, joining them on the deck with the paper.

"How are the girls still sleeping? Did someone slip them something last night?" Maggie came out with a hot cup of coffee in hand. "I'm not even mad, just want to know so I can get more supplies for later." She giggled.

"I had fun last night and think it was all harmless—just neighbors catching up with neighbors," Rachel said grabbing the World Events section from Max.

"Anyone know how Dad is doing today? Can't believe he's not up yet," Maggie said grabbing the Arts section from Max.

"He did turn in kind of early, but I mean, he did spend some time in the hospital yesterday, I'm sure he was just exhausted," Erica said grabbing the Fashion section from Max.

"Guess I'll read…Sports?" He tilted his head.

"Do you guys think we should be more worried?" Rachel whispered. "I feel like they're not telling us the whole story."

"He's on his meds, and they said he just needs to take it easy, right?" Erica asked.

"That sounds a little naive to me," Maggie said. "No offence, I want to believe it too, but heart conditions are no joke." She grabbed a scone from the table and started to butter it. "But he's a tough guy, I can't imagine him not being the big strong dad we've always known and looked up to."

This made everyone pause. Of course, parents don't live forever, but no one was ready for an expiration date.

"Kids? Oh, there you are!" Mom said interrupting their thoughts. "Sorry we had to cut last night short, it was a long day for everyone," she said, bringing her coffee outside to join the kids.

"Mom, please, it was a great night!" Rachel said, a little too enthusiastically.

"How great, sis?" Maggie asked with a smile.

"What are we, five?" Rachel said to the table.

"I could feel that sexual tension, even as an oldie!" Mom tittered, wrapping her robe up extra tight in the cool morning air.

"Oh my god, let's just leave it as the night was fine, okay?" Rachel said grabbing a scone herself. If nothing else, to keep her hands and mind busy.

"Only teasing, Cricket. Those boys are so nice though…barely ate a thing, did all the cleaning for us, and then I turned around and they were gone!" Mom said. "Was it something we said?"

"I think they just didn't want to intrude, they know it was a long day for everyone." Erica folded down the corner of her newspaper to scan her mom's face.

"Yes, while your father is still asleep I wanted to have a word with everyone," Mom said, very businesslike.

"Oh god mom, it's bad, isn't it?" Maggie asked panicking.

"Good Lord, no, no. I was just going to say, don't treat your dad like he's some frail old man you have to tiptoe around. He would absolutely hate that," she said grabbing one of her scones.

"So, he's as healthy as he says?" Rachel asked.

Mom put down her scone and looked at her children. Mothers liked to pretend they always had the right answers. And always just knew the right thing to say. But as she looked around the table at her children, all grown, and every bit their father, she faltered. "We just need to start taking better care of ourselves. We aren't your ages anymore!" She forced a laugh but let her mind drift to the events of yesterday…

She couldn't deny the concern she heard in the doctor's voice yesterday. Dr. Lee seemed concerned. Based on the records they had of John's previous visits with Dr. Miller, his cholesterol was climbing, even with the pills. She was going to immediately change their menu for the rest of the week. Over the years as the trips to Dr. Miller became more frequent, Judy stopped placating her husband when he argued about having an extra glass of wine at dinner or gave her a cheeky glance as he took a third serving of bacon. Gone were the days when she'd simply laugh him off and say, *"Oh, John, you really must watch what you eat dear."* After his last check up this spring when the doctor said if he didn't maintain the exercise program, diet and medications, he was heading for a heart attack, they both knew it was time to change their approach.

"We'll just take it a bit easy today, yeah?" Max asked. "I can take the girls into town to give dad a bit of a break from the grandkids, and we'll just hang around the lake today."

"That sounds great, Max, count me in," Maggie volunteered. "I should try to get a reliable signal and call Pierre in town."

Nobody moved. Maggie had hardly mentioned Pierre since they arrived.

"It's okay, guys, you can all exhale," Maggie said noticing the tension. "He is the father of my kids after all."

Dad, always with impeccable timing, chose then to walk through the patio door. "Here's my beautiful family!" he said grabbing a seat at the head of the table—right where he belonged. "Where are my granddaughters?"

"Believe it or not, still asleep!" Max said.

"That whiskey did the trick then?" He grinned.

"No! Dad, did you really?" Maggie asked.

"God no! I haven't done that since you were kids, I'm sure the sun and excitement is catching up to them." He grabbed the Sports pages from Max, leaving him without so much as an advertising leaflet.

"Well on that note, I guess I'll get some breakfast going," Max said. "Hope everyone likes semi-burnt toast." He joked as he walked to the kitchen.

"Think I'll head to the dock and finally crack my book," Dad said helping to put away the breakfast dishes. "Then this afternoon, let's tackle water skiing again. Who's in?"

"We thought we'd just take it easy today Dad," Erica said, giving the counters a wipe down.

"Geez guys, come on! The doctor said I am fine. Fine, good, better than good, picture of health. Period, end of sentence, finito. Capeesh?" He put his hand down on the counter, signaling the end of the discussion.

"Got it." Erica smiled. "Then count me in, need to regain my title before this week is up."

"Pfft, I think all those years of too much hairspray are catching up to you," Max said. "The only title that existed was thanks to your big bro," he said flexing his biceps.

"If only that was supposed to prove something," Erica said raising an eyebrow.

"Fighting words! Guess we will have to see once and for all this afternoon. Have fun in town kids," Dad said waving goodbye to Maggie and Max then kissing each of his grandkids on the cheek.

"So, guess it's just us three this afternoon?" Rachel turned to Erica and Mom.

"Wish I could girls! Margot and I are going to get our nails done in town, you should come!"

"Count us in!" Erica said, reading Rachel's mind.

"Absolutely mom! We should make sure Mags knows, she hates being left out." Rachel ran out front to let Maggie know the details.

"But wait, is Dad going to be alright here on his own?" Erica whispered hesitatingly to Mom.

"Dear, I know you think you're older and wiser, but believe it or not, we've been on this planet a bit longer than you guys." She gave Erica a kiss and a squeeze. "Honestly, I'm sure this quiet time will do him a world of good and this afternoon all will be back to normal! Promise."

"Mags is in! Max offered to take the girls to the theater in town, seems that brother of ours is a saint," Rachel said. "Let me grab a quick change and we can take my car. This is just what I needed—a girly day out!" She skipped off to her room to change.

"Mags will meet us there, I assume it's the only salon in this town?" Rachel asked returning to the kitchen. "She really wants to call Pierre first. On her own."

Erica looked down. "Do you think we'll ever get to a place where this isn't such a big deal anymore? Where we're all just normal again?" Erica asked her big sister after their mom walked off to get ready.

"I'm sure it will, these things have a way of blowing over. What was it mom used to always say? It will all come out in the wash?" Rachel asked.

"Oh god, I haven't heard that one in a while." Erica smiled but tears were starting to well in her eyes.

"Oh, E! Come here." Rachel wrapped her sister in her arms. It felt so good to be back in this space herself.

"Look at me. Surely I deserve the award for worst sister slash daughter slash aunt," Rachel said holding her sister's shoulders so she could look into her cobalt blue eyes. "I totally bailed on everyone when, as it turns out, they were just telling the truth!"

"Yeah, but I totally humiliated my sister, one of my best friends. For all I know, I'm the reason their marriage is on the rocks."

"I doubt that very much. I know you've tried to mend fences over the years, but have you ever really sat down and explained your side?" Rachel tried.

"That journalist hat doesn't come off much, does it?" Erica said wiping her face as Mom was making her way to the patio door.

"Girls, Margot just called and I'll head in with her—looks like Frank is going to come by and keep your father company so we'll meet you there!"

The girls headed to Rachel's car. She still wasn't sure what she thought about the Mini Cooper. After years of seeing them whizz around London, she decided she'd bring a little piece of her European life home with her. Following her divorce and decision to move back to the U.S., she discovered a fight inside she hadn't known was there. She called every newspaper and magazine company she'd ever dreamt of working in while she was at university. She was floored by the offers that came in. Turned out, she was in demand! Apparently, not as useless as Peter had led her to believe. He had simply been too big of a coward to let her soar in his presence; he had to be the star.

In celebration of her new role at The New York Times (and a sizeable signing bonus), she figured she should treat herself for once with something cute, although Mr. Bean like, but also able to get around the busy streets of Manhattan.

"I love how it feels like we're Mr. Bean climbing into this thing, don't you think?" Erica said.

"Oh my god, you are literally inside my head," Rachel said as she started the engine. "I was just remembering why I bought this car, definitely a splurge but you know what, I'm worth it." She laughed and gave a flip of her blonde hair.

"I don't doubt that for a second," Erica said seriously. "It's gonna take a few more bottles of wine before we get the full backstory with Peter but to see how you came out the other side is, well it's inspirational, sis," she said looking at Rachel.

Rachel's heart swelled. "Shit, that's nice…but you can't change the subject so easily," she said with a smile. "Maybe if you walk me through everything that happened, it will be easier to talk to Maggie about it?"

"Perhaps one day in a land far, far away when we're both shitfaced out of our minds?"

"No…one day soon. We're all not getting any younger. Dad's health thing really shook me," she said as she put the car in drive and merged onto the narrow laneway that took them down to the main road.

"True. I don't even know, Rach. Matteo and I had just broken up. I found out he was sleeping with my two roommates. You know Kristina and Kelly who booked almost every job I went for? I was at such a low point. And you know how Pierre is, watching him hit on every girl at your wedding. Finding him with Leslie in the coat check room, just made me so angry at all the men like them. After what I went through, I thought Maggie would want to know and I tried to confront Pierre…"

"Wait, you found him with Leslie?! How come nobody knows this?"

"I've said too much, it's not even my story to tell! I just wish her loser husband would speak to her so we can all move on," she shrugged as she fiddled with the radio. Landing on a country station, she sat back and looked out the window.

"Well that just isn't going to cut it in my books. And why the hell has no one ever confronted Pierre?!" Rachel asked, her hands gripping the wheel tighter as she felt a sudden burst of protectiveness over her sisters.

"Please, Rach, let's leave it for now," she pleaded. "You don't know the whole story and I'd really rather not share it right now. I know Maggie somehow blames me for their marriage falling apart, but we're in a nice grey area right now that I know how to navigate. Let's just go get our nails done, okay?"

Rachel rolled to a stop at the red light and looked at her sister beside her. She hated to see her hurting but had to follow her wishes, "sure thing Ernie." She gave her knee a little nudge before turning Shania Twain up on the radio.

"Hey girls! I'm so glad this worked out," Margot said giving each girl two kisses on the cheek.

"Yes, thanks for letting us crash your girly day with Mom." Rachel smiled.

"Oh please! This is the drawback to only having boys, I don't get any girl time! Well the first few years, I got away with dressing them and even letting their hair grow a bit, but after that, no way!" She giggled.

"Alright, Mrs. Mackie, I see you changed the reservation to five, correct? Are we missing one?" the receptionist asked.

"Maggie will be coming by in a bit," Rachel explained.

"Great, let's get you girls in the chairs and you can pick your colors!" the esthetician exclaimed. "Champagne anyone?"

"Thank god for that. Make it four and keep it coming," Erica said. "What will you girls be having?"

Everyone laughed. Erica was already feeling better as the cold bubbles made their way down her throat.

"So, dear, tell me, what did you think of having ol' Woody stay yesterday?" Margot asked Rachel.

"News travels fast in small towns, huh," Rachel mumbled over to Erica, before turning back over to Margot. "Oh good! Was really nice of Josh to do that. It was a bit of a crazy day," she rubbed the nail samples across her thumbs.

"Yes, Judy you must fill me in. Is everything okay? How is John today?"

Margot and Mom quickly got lost in their own conversation, leaving Rachel and Erica to themselves. The girls looked at each other and clinked their glasses.

"Room for one more?" Maggie asked finding the girls at the back. She grabbed a glass and helped herself to the champagne. She topped a flute and took a long gulp. She topped it again before going to sit beside Erica.

"So, uh, how did the call go, Mags?" Rachel whispered over Erica. Their mom and Margot were in another world.

"Well he couldn't give a shit about his fucking kids. I asked him when he planned on coming home and he said business in Geneva was taking longer than expected. I'm sure it has nothing to do with his PA staying with him there," she said as she threw her purse down beside her. She leaned back in her chair and let the esthetician place her feet in the warm soapy water.

Erica kept looking down at her hands.

"Anyway, I'm not ruining this, I'm basically a single mother and don't get chances to indulge like this so, here, I'll take this red please, mani and pedi. I deserve it," she said signalling to one of the other girls to top up their glasses.

"Anyone mind if I put my headphones in?" Erica asked quietly. She just wanted to escape for a bit.

"Go for it, just don't tune us out the whole time," Rachel said with a squeeze across to her arm. Maggie was already engrossed in a tabloid magazine, a million miles away.

"So, you want to talk about it Mags?" Rachel tried.

"Nope, I do not. Cheers," she said raising her glass without looking up from her magazine.

Rachel turned to her mom and Margot; they were talking about some old family friend who had recently divorced. Looks like she would be entertaining herself.

She pulled out her cell phone. Thus far she had made an effort to avoid checking it daily. The New York Times were incredibly cool with her delaying her start until the end of her vacation so she knew work wouldn't be piling up. What was she expecting to see on her phone every time she opened it then?

Since the papers were signed, she'd heard nothing from Peter. She preferred it that way. The months that followed her moving out were so emotionally heavy, she had to find things to throw herself into, or risk lying in bed with the blinds drawn all day.

There was that brief relationship with her colleague, Matt, which, although a total fling and rebound, was probably exactly what she needed. For the first time in her life she was getting attention she enjoyed—and she had a choice. Before Peter it was all about school and landing the right job after grad school. She wouldn't have known if someone was into her unless they smacked her in the face. But now that she was home, surrounded by her parents, married for decades, her siblings with their own lives, and while they all had their own issues, she still felt a little…left out? Or was it behind? Something wasn't sitting right. Being back here, surrounded by familial love she still felt something was missing.

She was just about to put her phone away when she felt it vibrate.

Hope my mom isn't regaling you with stories about us in diapers x

Josh. The butterfly unfurled in her stomach again.

She looked around. Erica was half asleep with her headphones in, Maggie was engrossed trying to find out what celebrity was caught cheating, Mom and Margot were still talking a mile a minute. She let herself smile as she started to type a reply.

Sadly, haven't seen the old baby photos yet…besides I couldn't get a word in edgewise between her and my mom

She left her finger hovering over the send. He sent a kiss at the end, should she? What if he hadn't meant to and she sent one—would he think she was some crazy stalker? What if he did mean to and she didn't? She didn't want him to think she was cold.

Jesus, when did flirting become so complicated? She was thirty fucking years old.

Sadly, haven't seen the old baby photos yet…besides I couldn't get a word in edgewise between her and my mom, haha x

There, totally playing it cool. She sat back feeling smug, waiting.

Three dots appeared on the screen—he was typing.

"Miss? Please can you stop tapping like that? It's quite hard to paint your toenails evenly like that," her esthetician, Sammy, said bringing her back to reality.

"Oh god, yes sorry!" She chewed her lip as she waited for his reply.

Well, I'm off for a run with Woody—hope you girls have fun. I told them to keep the champagne flowing ;) x

She looked up as she heard a brand new bottle being put on ice.

"Perrrrfect timing!" Margot purred.

"Girls, how's it going?" Mom asked turning to her daughters.

Rachel shoved her phone back into her purse. She had become completely distracted formulating a witty reply. She was a writer for god sakes, how hard could it be?

"Look at you all! In your own little worlds." She laughed before turning back to Margot.

Rachel grabbed her phone.

Clearly you know the way to a girl's heart ;) x

She hit send but felt a lump in her throat, was that too suggestive?

I may not be a pro journalist like you Ms. Woods, but I can be investigative when I want x

She felt her cheeks flush red. Was it hot in here, or just the champagne?

"Geez Rach, you looking at porn or what?" Erica asked reaching for her glass.

She was so engrossed in her phone she didn't notice Erica had taken her headphones off and rejoined their world.

"Huh, or no, uh, just checking work emails, and um, the weather for the rest of the week." A pathetic cover.

"Mhmm, so you won't mind me just having a look at the...uh, weather, right?" Erica said grabbing her phone before Rachel could stash it away.

Erica's eyes grew wide. "My, my, our little Ray Ray is growing up it seems," she whispered.

"Huh? What's this all about?" Maggie asked, bored with her gossip mag.

"Oh, just our little Cricket flirting with a booooooy," Erica cooed.

"Let's see it then!" Maggie grabbed the phone from Erica.

Fuck, this was causing flashbacks to her childhood.

"Oh my," Maggie fanned her cheeks.

The girls started laughing as she threw Rachel her phone back. She quickly turned to her mom and Margot, oblivious to anyone else in the room.

"Chat about it later?" she whispered. Then smiled conspiratorially.

Erica and Maggie were joking about what the kids' names would be, helping to keep everything civil. Fine, if it took jokes at her expense to keep the peace right now, Rachel was fine with that.

"And don't write anything back," Erica whispered, reading Rachel's mind.

"Really? I thought it seemed rude."

"Oh god, no, always leave them wanting more, Ray," Maggie said matter-of-factly.

With great restraint, Rachel put away her phone and let the sounds of the women around her drown out her thoughts.

34

"I can't believe he's splashing out so much. Don't get me wrong, Jude, if anyone is worth it, it's our little Rachel, but I don't know…I just don't trust him or something," John said one Sunday morning after they had just hung up with Rachel. She had gushed to Judy about another extraordinary date with her new boyfriend Peter, involving renting a boat to cruise around New York harbor with a champagne picnic.

"Hmm…I know what you mean. Although, I wouldn't say no to a picnic on a private yacht or renting out an entire movie theater to screen my favorite movie with just you," she said with a little nudge. She stood to refill their coffee cups. She didn't want to say anything to Rachel, or even out loud, but she had her own concerns. Rachel was never a big dater in high school and she worried she was being swept away. *Time would tell,* was the only thing she could think. Besides, her own mother was always trying to control her every movement as a teen and into her early twenties before marrying John. She knew the rebellion that could ensue!

"We'll meet him soon enough. Thanksgiving, right?" John asked.

"Exactly," Judy said, placing a fresh mug of coffee down on his paper.

"Don't forget, we have your check up later," Judy said as John put his dishes in the dishwasher. She didn't even have to turn around to know the annoyed look that crept across his face.

"It's just a normal check-up, dear. No need to stress. I had mine last week and I'm perfectly healthy for a menopausal woman of my age," she said mocking her doctor. "Sounded a little condescending but at least it's done for another year." She took the last gulp of her juice and met John by the island. She leaned in for one of his big bear hugs. She hated to admit that as they grew older, she had her own reservations about the doctor. She inhaled his classic Old Spice as he leaned down and gave her a peck on top of her head.

"Okay, okay, let me have a quick shower. And they better not tell me to lay off the wine and cigars! I'm outta there if that's the case," he said running up the stairs.

Judy smiled as she wiped the counters down. She was sure it would all be fine anyway, just one of a million things she had to do today.

After the nurse took his blood pressure in the doctor's office, John was waiting impatiently for Dr. Miller to come in. "I'm not liking these numbers I'm seeing John," the doctor said as he took a seat at his desk.

"Oh yeah, I'm always trying to shift a couple pounds, you know that, doc. Too many years working long hours and eating crappy food."

"While I admit, the weight is still a little concern, but we can fix that easy enough. It's your cholesterol and blood pressure I'm concerned with. What's your weekly alcohol consumption?"

John looked at Judy who nodded to tell the truth.

"Well, that's gonna be a bit like the diet there, doc. We enjoy our wine and socializing over cocktails but I don't see how that could be a problem..." he started.

"Well a little isn't a problem, it's when it becomes more often, and we couple it with stress, diet, and cigars, you're not still smoking are you?" He asked looking up from the chart.

"You know, just special occasions...here and there," John mumbled.

"Okay, well I prefer not to prescribe meds until we've tried some other things. Let's cut back on the booze." He saw John's smile fade. "I'm not saying completely. Let's just scale it back. Cigars are a no-no, at least until we get these numbers under control. As for the diet, just less saturated fats, more whole grains and veggies, you know the drill now! A nice brisk walk a few times a week would do wonders as well."

"Gee thanks, doc, we'll definitely get working on those," John said, shaking his hand.

"Great, see you back here in six months then."

"Six months? Isn't this an annual thing?" John whispered to Judy as they walked back through reception.

"He just wants to check how you're doing, I'll be right there with you, dear, don't worry." Judy gave him a kiss before booking in their next appointment.

"This is why I hate going to the doctors. They take all the fun out of things," John said when they got back to the car.

35

"Whoa, I'm a bit tipsy!" Mom exclaimed as they left the nail salon.

"Yeah, who's driving home?" Rachel asked looking from one to the next. All of them had definitely had too much champagne to drive home.

"Did someone call for a ride?" Josh was leaning against his Prius smiling at the girls.

Rachel's cheeks flooded with color. She was sure everyone could tell, so started to fake a coughing fit.

"Oh Rachel, there there," Erica gave her a pat on the back, playing along.

"I called in some reinforcements," he said as Max pulled up.

"Alright, drunkies, who's coming home with whom? I've got room for one in Maggie's car," he said popping open the front seat like a well-trained limo driver.

"I'll hop in with you, Max—should check on the girls!" Maggie said, popping open the back door to give her girls a kiss before settling into the front seat.

Rachel was happy to see Maggie had the chance to relax over the last couple of hours. But damn her for shot gunning the ride with Max!

"Guess the rest of you lucky ladies are with me!" Josh said popping the trunk for their bags.

"It'll be a tight squeeze, but we're all friends here, right?" He winked at Rachel.

There were those damn butterflies again.

"Rachel, why don't you sit up front, dear?" Margot said giving her a little push toward Josh. Was it a push, or did she imagine that?

She shot a look at Erica pleading for help.

"Great idea, Mrs. M." Erica smiled.

"M'lady," Josh said in his best British accent, opening her door.

"Is that the best you could do?" She asked with a giggle.

"I didn't think it was too bad." He laughed. "But it could use some work, how's yours? Maybe you can tutor me," he said, leaning over her to help with her seatbelt.

Her cheeks must surely be on fire by now.

When she looked into the back she saw Erica regaling Margot, and their mother with stories about life as a single twenty-something in New York. Damn her and her good story telling, wasn't she the writer of the family? Why was she drawing a total blank for conversation?

"I don't think you'd want to hear my accent," she said as Josh jumped into the driver's seat.

"I bet you're better than you think you are. I even catch a bit of it when you talk sometimes," he said looking at her before pulling out into traffic.

Air, she needed air. She rolled her window down. "Sorry, I feel we must stink of chemicals."

"Don't worry, Mom made sure we were well accustomed to it growing up," he joked.

"You better not be gossiping about me, Joshy dear," Margot said from the back.

"Just saying how it sounds like you girls enjoyed that champagne at the salon!"

"Yes, son you didn't need to keep it coming like that!" She gave his shoulder a squeeze. "Isn't he just so thoughtful?" she asked Rachel. She was sitting in the middle seat and right next to Rachel's face.

"Yes, very kind. Thanks, Joshy." Rachel nudged his arm with her elbow.

"Anytime," he said, without correcting her on the nickname.

"Oh, I love this song! Crank it," Mom shouted from the back, apparently a fan of the latest Katy Perry song. This had to be the most random drive Rachel had ever experienced. But it felt so good.

"Thanks again for the lift, Josh! You must let us repay you," Mom was saying as he dropped them off at the cottage.

"No, no, honestly, I'm just glad you ladies got to enjoy a bit of time away from the men in your lives! I know we're hard to manage sometimes," he said with a little wave to Rachel.

She smiled as she watched them drive away. Erica gave her a pinch. "Well that was a hot car ride." She laughed as she signaled to Rachel to hang back a bit.

"It was a little hot, right?" Rachel asked. "To be honest, I'm so rusty, I feel like I've been in a nunnery for years or something."

"You and Peter were always pretty flirtatious…wait, weren't you?" Erica asked, realizing she hadn't actually spent that much time around the two of them. Come to think of it, she couldn't even really remember them showing much PDA or hanging out with the family to make a real statement on it at all.

"Yes and no…at the beginning. I was so blind by all the grand gestures that I kind of didn't realize what was missing until, well, until it was too late," she said sadly. "But ouf, I think the champagne has just hit me."

"Say no more, the bed is calling my name and I just want a nap before Dad remembers we had a waterskiing date." She yawned and turned to head inside, nearly bumping into their father on his way out.

"Guess the old man has to go recover a certain car that was left behind after a drunk nail salon date!"

"Oh my god, my car!" Rachel laughed. "I didn't even think about that. Thanks, Pop!"

"Yeah, it was all a big ruse to ditch the boys for the morning, totally get it, kiddo. Here's Max, I'll jump in with him to head back into town. When I get back, we're hitting the water, right?"

He was already hopping in after letting Maggie and the girls out. They all looked ready for a nap, with Abby already passed out in Maggie's arms.

"You have to admit, he does look much better than yesterday, no?" Rachel asked, more so willing it to be true than necessarily knowing it as a fact.

"Totally," Maggie said walking past them into the house. "I'm off to sleep off this champagne. This mama can't party like she used to. Thanks for the fun morning, girls!" She kissed Rachel and even Erica on the cheek on her way.

Erica looked bewildered as Maggie walked inside. "She must be toasted."

Rachel laughed and slung her arm over Erica's shoulder as they headed inside.

When they walked in, Mom was leaning over her laptop, intently clicking away at the keys.

"Gee mom, what's all this?" Erica asked thumbing through the versions of her mom's schedule for the week. "Not messing with the itinerary, are we?"

"Margot and I had a brilliant idea at the salon!" She jumped up to grab a cup of coffee. "Want one? I already put a fresh batch on."

Their mom was the only person they knew who got more energetic the more she drank. It must be where they got their stamina from.

Rachel shrugged and grabbed two cups for herself and Erica.

"Maggie's birthday is next week...I'm going to put together a little party for our last night. The Mackie's will come, and I'll see if some of the other neighbors around the lake can come. And," she paused to take a breath and gulp of her coffee.

"And?" Erica asked.

"Pierre. I managed to sneak his number off her phone earlier and I've contacted him to see if he'll come." Mom could read their faces and doubt crept in. "What? No good?"

Erica left to put some cream in her coffee, an excuse Rachel saw right through.

"Um, gee mom. I mean, do you think Maggie will want that?" Rachel asked.

"He's her husband! I know they're fighting right now, but I'm sure they just need the chance to reconnect a bit. He travels so much, and the girls were born so close together—they've probably just had a bit of a rough patch."

Erica remained silent.

"Well, who knows if he can even make it, right?" Rachel said. "You're right, he is so busy."

"He said he's coming already…" She sat back in her chair. "Girls, what are you not telling me? Is this a bad idea?"

"Look, I'm just a bit tired or hungover or something…whatever you want, mom," Erica said heading into her room. They heard the door latch and her radio switch on.

"Ray Ray, what's going on?" Mom asked.

"Look, I don't even know all the details, mom, but Maggie seems pretty pissed with him. I just worry forcing them into a reconciliation might blow up in our faces."

"Okay, well for now, let's keep it a secret. With so many other people here, I'm sure it'll be civil and at least he can see his kids. I mean, no matter what is going on between them, a father has to be involved in his kids' lives, right?"

"Sure Mom, that sounds like a plan." She didn't want to be the one to make ripples right now, she was enjoying being back together with everyone and wanted to draw it out.

"I might also have a little cat nap in the hammock, okay? Dad didn't forget about heading out on the skis later and I need to sleep off this champagne!" She laughed.

Mom nodded but was already deep back into party planner mode, emailing e-vites to their friends and looking up menu ideas.

If there was one thing Rachel knew, nobody threw a party like their mother, and this party would really be unlike any other.

36

"That was fun wasn't it, Joshy?" Margot asked as they pulled onto the dirt road and headed back to their cottage.

"You mean the drive home? We men weren't invited to the nail salon," he grinned.

"Yes, but I mean, just reconnecting with the Woodses. Your father and I have always stayed in touch with Judy and John but you kids have all moved around, created your own lives," she said looking out at the passing trees.

"True. Shame about Rachel's divorce," he said lifting an eyebrow over to see his mom's reaction.

She smiled and turned to him. "Yes hon, but you know what that's like. Hasn't been a piece of cake for you either," she said giving his arm a pat. "But she's always been such a sweet girl. Independent and fiercely driven. That's definitely a good thing." Margot had always worked as psychotherapist herself and loved seeing this next generation of women taking over the world.

"Yes, that's true. Did you know she has a gig at the New York Times? That sounds like the white whale for any journalist," Josh said feeling a small burst of pride in talking about her.

"I know! Something Diana seemed to be lacking," Margot said quietly. As a professional, she liked to push boundaries, but as a mom, she knew where to stop.

"Mm," Josh agreed, as a therapist himself, he knew he should talk about it more but he felt enough closure to leave it in the past.

"Well, Judy did mention she was planning some big surprise party for Maggie in a few days on their last night. Will be nice to go."

"Yeah sure," Josh replied. "So, they're leaving on Sunday I guess? Shame, I wonder when we'll see them again."

"Well, you know they haven't been in the best place these days."

"Oh?" Josh asked.

"Yes, I didn't realize that they had barely even heard from Rachel while she was in London. Seems that ex-husband did a real number on keeping her away from them. Something also happened between Erica and Maggie…Judy didn't go into details but they haven't spoken much since Rachel's wedding." Margot stopped to take a breath. Josh couldn't believe all this drama from the Woodses…they always seemed so overwhelmingly close!

"Maggie's marriage seems to be on the rocks and of course Max is raising adorable Chloe on his own after Kailey bailed on them to go to California. Now add to that poor John's health and it seems they've had a bit of a hard time lately."

Josh pulled into their driveway, waking a sleeping Woody up on the step. Within seconds his wagging tail was smacking his driver's side door.

"Thanks, hon," Margot said as she opened her car door and headed into the house.

Josh turned off the ignition and opened the door to Woody. As he was giving him a scratch, he was going over everything his mom just dumped on him in the car. He couldn't believe Rachel was dealing with all of that and yet still so…happy. So approachable, still so driven and forging ahead with her life. He was in awe of her.

After the way things ended with Diana, he became resigned to be a bachelor with Woody by his side. Maybe not the healthiest option but the months following his divorce weren't exactly the brightest times in his life. Maybe it was time he started taking his own relationship advice.

Josh was in the kitchen of his small townhouse in Brooklyn, staring around at the empty spaces left after Diana had moved out. His phone started to ring.

"Hey bro! Come on, we're going to the game. Tailgate first with the Johnson's and then hitting the pub after," Devon shouted down the line, trying to pump his brother up.

He was going to have to try harder than that, he thought.

"Uh, I'm not feeling so great, Dev, I might sit this one out," he said mustering up a cough and sniffle.

Pathetic, he thought.

"Nope, we are not taking no for an answer."

Before Josh could give another excuse he heard keys in his front door

Damn, why did I ever give him that spare key?

"See, cause I'm here and the cab is waiting outside for us so let's go!"

Begrudgingly, Josh put a clean shirt on, gave Woody a little scratch behind the ears and headed out the door with his little brother.

"This has been going on too long man, you gotta stop letting Diana live rent free up here," Devon said poking his brother on the forehead. "That chick was bad news bro."

Josh let out a groan. He was tired of everyone telling him that, as if he didn't know.

"I mean, it's not like she cheated on you but that chick was all about living a lifestyle funded by you and that's just not cool man," Devon must have had a few Red Bull's with his pre-drinks as he was talking a mile a minute.

"Hey, I know okay? The divorce was my idea remember? She just changed so much once we got married. Like, what if every girl does that once you get married? Maybe all those crazy clients of mine were normal once too and then some ex-wife screwed them up," Josh said waving at the bartender for a pint. They were at the pub down the road now and Josh was starting to feel a bit better. This was the most interaction he had in weeks.

"So what? You're suspicious of all women now?" Devon asked taking a sip of his own beer.

"No, not at all. There were so many warning signs. As a therapist, I should kind of be able to see those, no?"

"Love really is blind, dear brother."

"Okay so we get married and she tells me she wants to quit her safe, reliable nursing job to focus on being a good wife and just do this online thing on the side. At first I thought it was kind of sweet."

"Yeah, red flag one, nobody wants someone just bumming around all day. I mean, it's the dream, don't get me wrong, but I'd probably kill myself out of boredom eventually," Devon said flagging their waitress down. "I'm gonna get some hot wings, line the stomach, ya know."

"Okay, red flag two was what then?" Josh asked, enjoying not being the one to over analyze for once.

"She wanted kids, yet was constantly partying or planning weekends away with her girlfriends on your dime. Doesn't sound like something a mother would do," Devon explained.

Josh was nodding along, almost seeing it all in a new light.

"Then she threatened to leave a bunch of times unless you stopped working so much. God, she even stayed at her sister's up state for a month or something, didn't she?" Devon asked getting more animated.

"I almost forgot about that," Josh said sitting up. "How was I meant to support her lifestyle but work less?" he asked, getting angrier.

"Exactly! See, now you're seeing the light, bud," Devon said giving him a smack on the back.

It was only once she returned home from one of her girls weekends in Cabo that Josh knew they had to end it. He wanted to be a dad, he wanted to come home and talk about their respective jobs, he wanted a wife that was in tune with the world around her, not running away from it.

"Then the girl hires lawyers, with *your* money, to try and sue you for half of everything," Devon said waving to friends who had just walked into the bar.

"Thank god my lawyer was better," Josh said staring down at his beer. He didn't exactly make off like a bandit but sadly Diana's true colors had come out during the divorce. He was happy to see her go—what he was struggling with, was being divorced. He loved being married. He loved the idea of sharing his life with someone. And now, he was back to square one. Back to bar nights with the guys, blind dates—and god forbid, online dating.

He ordered another beer before the rest of the guys sat down. For now, he'd have another beer and enjoy being out with the guys.

37

Back at the lake, Max found Rachel and Erica chatting on the patio over a bottle of rosé. "Pop is a bit tired so he's going to just take the girls for a little cruise before dinner," he said. Noting his sister's wide eyes, he reassured them. "He's got some energy back, just not ready to slap on the skis. I'll probably head out with him. You wanna join?"

Erica pointed to their nearly full bottle. Looks like they'd be sitting this one out.

"Is Maggie going to join you guys?" Rachel asked. She had been keeping a low profile since they got back from the nail salon and she was worried about her.

"She said something about wanting to have a bit of a nap. I'll take the girls with us to give her a bit of a break."

"Aren't you just the best big brother?" Erica smiled up at him.

"Well, I'm definitely the best one you've got," he said leaving to round the girls up.

"Hey, save me a glass will you girls?" Dad asked on his way down to the dock.

"You got it, Pop!" Rachel said, happy to see him out and about.

"Might be from the next bottle." Erica laughed, topping up their glasses.

"Ever think we do this too much?" Rachel asked her little sister, eyeing the very large glasses she had just poured them. Erica shot her sister a look.

"Ok ok, do you think everything is alright with Mags then?" she asked staring down at her wine glass. She didn't want to dampen the mood but she was annoyed for abandoning her sisters. How could she be so self-centered and not know her sisters needed her?

"I'm sure she just needs some space," Erica said squinting into the sun. "And you pinky swore you wouldn't say anything."

"Pfft, when did I do that?" Rachel scoffed.

"Well, it was sort of unspoken, you should know that," she said matter-of-factly.

Dammit.

~

Maggie was lying in the dark on her bed staring at the ceiling. After hardly any contact in the past year, she now had seventeen missed calls from Pierre. Based on the texts she read before throwing her phone across the room, he was atoning for his sins. And sins a plenty there were.

Her head was pounding. She could not drink like she used to. How much champagne did they have at the salon? God, too much.

She didn't know what to believe. How many other women were there? I mean, if he slipped up before they were even married and again at her own sister's wedding, she shuddered to think how many others there were in the woodwork. She felt sick for even considering allowing him to come home.

But she had kids with the man, how could she just cut him out? They were happy at one point, right? She let her mind drift back to their courtship days. How they had bonded over their love of Paris and the French culture; their initial dates strung out between Pierre's visits to the city and hours spent texting and on video chat. It didn't hurt that Pierre was older and already very successful—the way he took care of and made her feel like the only woman in the world. And like a lamb for slaughter, she drank it all up.

She closed her eyes and rubbed her pounding eyes. She couldn't keep doing this. Going over every fucking detail.

The girls were with Max and Dad. She should be capitalizing on this free time. She remembered all the days she used to spend running and hitting the gym. The endorphin rush was so addictive to her once. Then she took on a new role and had to be the perfect mom who was always putting the kids first.

She jumped out of bed, popped a Tylenol and grabbed her running shoes.

It was time she remembered who she once was.

"Going for a run, see ya in a bit, mom," she said waving from the front door.

"Have fun, dear," Mom said, barely looking up from her computer. She was still deep in party planning mode.

"Did you hear the door?" Erica asked Rachel. "Mom! Who's here?"

"Maggie just went for a run," she hollered back.

Rachel and Erica looked at each other and raised their eyebrows. Maybe a change really was a coming.

"Well, do you think you'd say yes?" Erica was setting the table with Rachel and trying to get details on the Josh situation.

"What is everyone's obsession with setting me up with the boy next door? Nobody was very keen on the last guy so pardon my hesitation in bringing any poor new soul into the mix," she said grabbing the salad from the fridge.

It had been a long day with far too much booze. Thank god everyone had agreed on a teetotal dinner and to hit the hay early. Dad still appeared drained, and an hour on the water with three little girls seemed to send him over the edge.

"Sparkling waters all around?" Erica asked. "I whipped up these Bloody Mary's too." She smiled. Rachel gave her a look from across the island. "Don't worry, they're virgin," she said proudly. "So, you know…tomato juice and celery."

"Ugh, I don't know about you girls, but I'm looking forward to giving my liver a bit of a break," Max said getting the girls set up at the kids table with their chicken fingers.

Thankfully, Max had interrupted Erica's prying and Rachel could avoid the bigger questions for now. She needed a good night's sleep to get her head clear before she could attempt to discuss it with anyone else.

"Daddy, when can we have wine?" Chloe asked dipping her chicken into ketchup.

"Oh god, don't you girls start," Max moaned. "When you're much older, and your hair is grey."

"Oh, wow," she said wiping the ketchup off her face with her white shirt sleeve. Rachel beamed at the girls. She had missed so much with her nieces. It was so crazy to think that at one point, they wouldn't have really known who Aunt Rachel was. She hated that.

"Dinner's ready!" Erica shouted out back.

"Thanks, kiddo," Dad said coming in off the patio.

"Spaghetti and Caesar salad, a classic!" Mom said closing her laptop. Her afternoon had been very productive getting the party set. Maggie had been too busy to pay much attention and assumed mom was figuring out Facebook again.

"How was your run, Mags?" Rachel asked as she came in fresh from a shower.

"Oh my god, I feel old," she said and then gulped down some water.

"At least you attempted a workout. I need to get back into my routine," Rachel replied.

"Oh yes, what'll it be, cardio kickboxing? CrossFit? Jump rope to hip hop?" Erica asked.

"What are these things? Sports? Now I feel old," Mom said grabbing some garlic bread.

"Our little Ray Ray took up a number of new sports in foggy ol' London it seems," Erica said.

"Nothing so crazy—a gym membership would be a good start once I get back to the city."

Whoa, Rachel had kind of gotten used to the bubble of the cottage. She had totally forgotten about New York and having to start all over on her own next week. She shook the thought from her head. "Pass the salad please, old man," she said to her dad.

"So, Mags, someone's birthday is coming up," Mom started.

"Don't remind me, Mom. I am not looking forward to getting older," she said moving her food around on her plate. She was starving after her run but now had no appetite.

"Oh, come on, dear, it's exciting! You've got two beautiful girls, a successful husband and all your family around to celebrate!"

Maggie shot Rachel a look that said "save me".

"Sounds like me on my thirtieth!" Rachel tried changing the subject. "Ending my twenties as a divorcée wasn't exactly my life plan." She laughed, yet when she looked up, everyone looked sad. Shit, that didn't seem to help.

"Yeah, didn't you wake up hungover in Paris with your girlfriends or something?" Erica asked.

"Yup! I thought going to Disneyland Paris would be the perfect antidote to turning thirty, yet we got a little too tipsy on the Eurostar on the way over and kind of missed the whole theme park after that. Thank god no one threw up, well except Susie from my spin class, but she's a bit crazy anyway." Rachel inhaled. She hadn't realized she was talking so fast. But it seemed to work and switch the conversation for a seemingly drama-free dinner.

As soon as the kitchen was cleaned, Maggie headed to bed with all three girls. She claimed the champagne and run wore her out but Rachel was sure something else was going on. She excused herself and went outside to the bonfire pit where Max was starting a fire.

"Perfect night for a fire," she said spying the s'mores ingredients on the side. "Thought you'd leave them for us big kids then?"

"Chloe's gone through about four outfit changes today so we can save the gooey marshmallows for another night," he said spearing a marshmallow for her to roast.

"Thanks bro," she said grabbing the prong. "How's that all going anyway? Are you managing as a single dad?"

"I don't know if *managing* is the right word, but we don't have too many accidents or calls to the doctor so I must be doing something right!" He grabbed a graham cracker and started building his s'more.

"Oh man, I thought I smelled s'mores," Erica said, joining them out back.

"Mom and Dad in bed?" Max asked.

"Yeah, I kind of forget their age sometimes, shouldn't they be doing early bird dinners and wearing their pants up over their ribs? Not waterskiing and toasting champagne at midnight?" Erica laughed.

"I prefer the latter version, it reminds me of the mom and dad we grew up with. 'Hospital Visit' dad is not one I want to see again for a long time," Rachel said staring into the fire.

38

"John, John! Can you hear me?" the color had drained from Judy's face as she stood over John, collapsed on the Home Depot floor. It was summer and nearly a year after Rachel's wedding, with the stress taking its toll on everyone.

"Huh? Jude…why are you yelling?" he asked, coming to.

"Thanks so much, I think we're okay here," Judy told the poor seventeen-year-old part timer who was panicking beside them.

"Now why did you get that pimply faced kid all worried?" he asked, taking his time to get back up.

"Dear, you terrified us! Don't you remember? We were looking at paint samples and had just flagged him down for help. Then boom!" She snapped her fingers. "You were on the floor."

"Weird," he said trying to brush it off.

"No, John, I'm worried," she said, her eyes moistening.

In the months following Rachel's wedding, the stress of not hearing from her, and knowing their kids' lives were totally turned upside down, was starting to weigh on both Judy and John. The stress kept her up most nights and she had dropped down to a measly 99 pounds on her five foot five frame.

"Oh dear, come on, don't start with the tears here, Jude, come on," he said straightening out his jacket and grabbing her hand. "Let's go get a coffee, okay? This fluorescent lighting just got to me is all."

She wiped her eyes and squeezed his hand. In times like these, she just remembered the strong jock she fell in love with so long ago. Underneath all their wrinkles, he was still that same big burly man that cast a shadow anytime he stood over her.

"Are you taking the pills?" she said as they walked toward the car. The six month follow up with the doctor had resulted in a prescription for Beta-blockers to help control his blood pressure, but which John had proved unreliable in taking on schedule.

"Jude, don't start with that again."

"Well! John, look at me." She stopped to face him.

He wanted to keep walking but was forced to turn and look at her. He had to admit, she was looking like a shadow of her former self.

"Ok, to be honest, I forgot. I took them on the weekend and must have missed a few this week." He hated seeing more worry cross her face on his account.

"Where are they?"

"In the bathroom, top shelf. When we get home, I'll take them right away. Promise. You can even watch me," he said holding her shoulders.

Despite herself she couldn't stop a smile from creeping across her face. "Okay," she said standing on her tiptoes to kiss him, "but you're having decaf."

He smiled as he opened the door for her. "Yes, dear."

Rachel looked at her phone. Another missed call from her mom. She knew she had to answer one of these days but it was still just too painful. It had been about nine months since their wedding and she had hardly shared more than a few words with her family. It was only when she got hounded by the same person that she finally picked up with a quick excuse as to why she had to hang up. They weren't stupid and the message was being received loud and clear.

She may have felt utterly betrayed by them at her wedding, but she was also struggling to keep her own doubts at bay. Hearing the truth come out by the time vows had been said, dinner had been served and the deed was firmly done, what was she supposed to do with that information?

To know her family didn't approve, or welcome her new husband into their tight family circle, she started to feel like an outcast herself. Seeing her mom's number a second and third time started to pull at her heart strings.

"Hey mom, what's up? I'm about to go underground so can't talk long," she said, hating hearing her own shortness with her mother.

"Oh Rach! I'm so happy you picked up, dear, how are you? How's the new job? Oh my god, I just haven't heard your voice in so long." She spoke quickly.

Rachel could hear her mom's voice catch and knew she was probably on the verge of tears. She stopped in the middle of a busy London sidewalk and softened. "Hey Mom, yeah sorry, it's just been crazy. I've been meaning to call you guys."

"Oh dear, I know, I'm sure you are incredibly busy getting set up over there! We just miss you so much. And Ray, we feel just awful about how things ended at the wedding."

Rachel stared down at her shoes on the concrete. "Mom, let's not do this now, okay?"

She sensed she might be losing her daughter all over again so she changed the subject. "So tell me about the job, The Times right? Nice office and colleagues? I'd love some photos when you get a chance…"

Rachel spent another five minutes filling her mom in with the bare minimum details, making sure to leave Peter out of the conversation for now. "Mom, I really should go though, lunch is almost over and I don't want to be late. Say hi to everyone."

She hung up before Mom could say goodbye.

Judy had tears in her eyes as she put her cell phone back in her bag. John had gone in to get the coffee and Judy had wanted desperately to tell Rachel about John's episode yet she didn't want her to worry while so far away.

John came back to the car and could see Judy had been crying. "Oh Jude, what's up? It's not still about that little fainting spell, is it? Come on, I told you, it's nothing…and look," he said holding up his cup proudly, "decaf!"

She smiled. "No, I just spoke to Rachel…" she started and welled up again.

John leaned in and gave Judy a kiss on the forehead "I've told you, she'll come around dear, she just needs her space right now."

Judy nodded and took a sip of her coffee. She was sure he was right.

39

Rachel was the first one up the next morning. The damn jet lag was still playing with her sleep patterns and it was 5:07am when she finally decided to stop tossing and turning and just get up.

She wandered into the kitchen and started to put the coffee on. She absolutely loved this time of the day, before the world was awake and you felt like you were the only person in the world—the whole day lay ahead with such promise. She felt like she could accomplish anything. Even if today that meant just making coffee and enjoying the sunrise on the dock.

It had been so hectic since she arrived she hadn't actually had much time to herself to just take a breath and reflect on being home, surrounded by her family.

Divorced.

Starting a new job.

Getting a new place.

Alone.

All at once her day of promise transformed into stress—and worse, the caffeine hadn't even had a chance to work its magic! She poured a hot cup of coffee, quietly slid open the patio door, and headed down to the dock. The sun was just rising above the lake. It was such a spectacular view. She settled into one of the big Adirondack chairs, turned her head to the sky and closed her eyes, allowing the sun to warm her face. There was absolutely nowhere else in the world she would rather be than right here.

She took a sip of her coffee and watched a loon glide across the lake. The steam was rising off the calm water as the sun cast an orange glow as it crept across the skyline.

She thought back to the last time her family was all together. Her wedding was such a disaster. Rachel was never sure whether she really believed in destiny or signs, but if she did now, there were plenty of red flags and omens before the fiasco that was her wedding. It had been so difficult to get Peter to so much as meet her family for the first time, let alone get them to warm to him. They had such different familial backgrounds and he had always hated how close her family was, to such a point that she began to question it at times. Maybe it was weird or codependent the way they all leaned on each other?

And so she pulled away. He made it so easy for her by whisking her off to London and providing a bubble, away from the friends and family that knew her best. The longer she was away and drifting from her family, the easier it became. Before she knew it, Rachel didn't even recognize herself.

To think that just less than a week ago, she was dreading this trip. Dreading seeing her family and walking into a complete nightmare trapped in a remote cottage with no escape. And yet now that she was here, her life had begun to feel far more normal than it had in years. What's that saying, you can't go home again? Rachel was beginning to challenge that one and felt she just might win the battle.

"Hey little sis, thanks for the java!" Maggie said walking down the stone steps. "Mind if I join you?"

"Please, be my guest," Rachel said snapping out of her thoughts.

"Didn't think anyone was crazy enough to be up at this hour, let alone someone without kids!" she said settling into the chair beside Rachel.

"Jetlag, my own burden to bear."

"Ah yes, that's one thing I won't miss with all the back and forth with Pierre," Maggie said setting her cup on the armrest.

"You mean, you think it's over for good?" she tried.

"Who knows, but how long can I stand beside someone I know is blatantly cheating on me? I have to find my backbone again," Maggie said more to herself than Rachel.

"No one else can judge what you're going through. Trust me, it works both ways," she replied.

"True. Considering everyone else's drama, we have barely gotten the lowdown from you on your divorce," Maggie said, watching her sister to make sure she was okay.

"Ah yes, the long sordid details…boring, trust me," Rachel said, brushing it off.

"Well, I'm guessing he didn't cheat on you repeatedly."

"Oh really? You think there was more than one?" Rachel tried to pry.

"Trust me—there were others and I didn't need Erica drawing attention to things at your wedding. I still don't know what happened between them and I'm not sure I can handle it."

"I get that Mags, but you've got to hear her out at some point right? We may not know exactly what happened that night, but we know our little sister and I think you need to give her the benefit of the doubt." Rachel felt bold but knew she was starting to overstep.

"Look, I just want to enjoy my cup of coffee before I have to be mom all day again," she said curtly.

Rachel felt bad for fucking up such a nice moment with her older sister. "I can't believe how old the girls are looking," she said, knowing the kids would be a safe topic.

"Oh god, I know, right?" Maggie said snapping out of her bad mood. "I'm dreading the teen years." She giggled.

"Oh my god, we were the worst." Rachel laughed.

"Who was the worst?" Erica asked joining them on the dock.

"Wait what? It's before 11 a.m. What are *you* doing up?" Maggie laughed.

Rachel was relieved their earlier talk didn't cloud Maggie's interaction with Erica.

"I heard giggling and started to get FOMO." She smiled putting her coffee cup on the dock beside her. She dipped her feet into the lake and let the cool water rush around her toes. The little minnows sitting in the sun darted away at the intrusion.

"Remember when we stayed at that god-awful cottage down in South Carolina that one summer?" Erica said squinting up at the girls.

"Oh god, mom said she got an amazing deal on it but when we showed up…" Rachel burst out into a fit of giggles.

"There were dead rats everywhere!" Maggie finished with a shudder.

"Turned out it was so cheap since it was heading into foreclosure." Rachel was laughing hysterically now. "And mom tried to make the most of it, by sweeping up the vermin and making dad start a fire to distract us from the shutters falling off and the rusted pipes in the bathroom."

"That took foreeeeever to get hot!" Erica laughed.

"Ah sorry kiddo, that's because you were the youngest so by the time we all *showered*," Maggie said with air quotes as the shower was more akin to taking a sponge bath with its weak water pressure, "there was nothing left for the runt."

"Aha! Truth comes out now," Erica said giving Maggie a splash with her toe.

For a second the tension and drama faded away and the girls felt like themselves again. But Rachel was holding her breath, waiting to see Maggie's reaction.

"Okay-okay, truce," she said holding up her arms. Erica stopped laughing and really looked at her eldest sister.

"Truce?" she asked. Just that one word carried the weight of the hundred times she had wanted to pick up the phone and dial her sister, trying to say sorry and losing her nerve, wishing she could take everything over the last three years back.

Rachel thought she was going to burst but didn't dare make a move.

"What's all the giggling out here then?" Mom interrupted before Maggie could reply.

Rachel was sure she was about to soften and let Erica back in. Now when would that opportunity present itself?

"Oh, we were just talking about that cottage on the beach we stayed at the first year Max was off at university," Rachel said standing up to let her mom have a seat.

"You girls are never going to let me live that down, are you?" she said taking a seat.

"I still have an unnatural fear of opening cupboards after seeing a family of cockroaches dead under that kitchen sink." Erica stuck a finger down her throat. "Those things are supposed to outlive nuclear holocausts, and yet…no match for the house at 521 Cedar Lane!"

"I can't believe you remember the address," Mom smiled down at Erica. She took a long slow slip from her mug.

Rachel always loved watching her mom drink coffee. She could remember being a little girl at the breakfast table and wishing so badly she could have a mug of coffee like her mom and dad. Mom used all her senses to drink a cup. A big inhalation before that first gulp, a soft "mmm" as she let the black liquid slide down her throat. Rachel thought it was the most glamorous thing to do—wake up, put a fresh pot on, and read the paper with your husband.

"I've redeemed myself a little, no?" she said casting her hand around the view in front of them.

"I'd say so!" Erica said raising her mug. "Seriously mom, you've outdone yourself." She was happy their mom arrived when she did.

"I'm just so happy to have everyone under one roof again," she said, as she felt her eyes moisten. "These past years have been a lot for a mom, ya know? All we want is to see our kids get along and having everyone home for the holidays makes my heart so full…" She let the tears fall freely now.

The girls all looked at each other. Everyone guilty of their own role in their mom's broken heart. Rachel had abandoned her family for what turned out to be a possessive and terrible choice in a husband. Maggie cut Erica out of her life for forcing Maggie to acknowledge her husband's infidelity. And Erica, unable to make sense of how things unfolded, went on with her life unable to mend things with her older sisters.

They huddled around their mom and embraced her. Before they knew it, they were all crying.

Mom started laughing. "This is so silly! Look, we haven't even had our coffees yet!"

The girls laughed and wiped their eyes. As if in unison, they picked up their mugs for a sip.

Mom inhaled into her mug, "mmm" she said as she took a gulp.

Rachel grinned.

"Sorry to break up this big old hen fest," Max shouted down from the back door of the cottage. "But I've got three hungry little girls, and only two hands so why don't we move this party inside?"

Maggie smiled. "Guess that's my cue! I'll put a fresh pot on. Mom, where's Dad? Still sleeping?"

"Not after Max's outburst," Erica shouted back jokingly to the house.

"I heard that. And the old man is already in his seat, working on his crossword," he hollered back.

Rachel smiled. People from small families would just never understand the comfort that came from a million conversations being shouted over one another. It was soothing to Rachel.

As Mom and Maggie headed back up to the house, Erica shot a look at Rachel.

"Oh my god, I didn't breathe for like a full two minutes back there! What do you think Mags was going to say?" Rachel asked, reading Erica's mind.

"Fuck if I know, but I'm getting palpitations. Surely the only twenty-five-year-old to suffer a nervous breakdown by this stage in her life."

"I think she was going to let bygones be bygones," Rachel said, bending one leg in and dipping her own toes in the lake. "Ugh, I wish we could stay here forever."

"Whaaaaat?" Erica said surprised. "I thought you were 'Miss City Girl

This Small Town Ain't Got Nothing On Me?'"

"First of all, that name needs some work." She splashed Erica as she brought her foot back up on dry land.

"We can't all be writers."

"I don't know, maybe I'm searching for something in the city that was at home all along." She could hear the chatter and clang of dishes up at the house.

Erica looked at her sister, standing tall in the morning sun. She searched her face for meaning.

"Could what you've been searching for, come in the shape of a tall cute blonde boy next door by any chance?" Erica asked.

"Oh god, would you rather just be pushed into the lake?" Rachel teased.

"Well come on, you've moved home, taken your dream job in the city…I thought you wanted to live that hustle and bustle, girl," Erica said.

"Oh, don't get me wrong, I can't wait to start next week. Just being home around everyone after so long away, I feel so stupid for feeling like I was better than the life mom and dad worked so hard to give us, better than this town, or these people. Who the fuck am I?" Rachel said.

"I know what you mean. I'm realizing the reality isn't always as great as the dream either." Erica leaned back on the dock and propped herself up on her elbows. "I thought by now I'd be a Victoria's Secret Angel, or at the very least, a winner on America's Next Top Model."

"Is that show still on?" Rachel asked, totally oblivious to American reality shows these days.

"Pfft…there goes the air out of my last dream." Erica chuckled. "You're not second guessing your job though, right?"

"Not at all. I hate to admit it, but part of me is so excited just to prove Peter wrong. Do you know, I don't think he never really believed in me? I always thought he did since every move or opportunity he painted as being great for my career, when really it was just for him. So selfish," Rachel mumbled.

"What really happened there? Come on, it's me…the one you used to get into a ton of mischief with, who showed me how to sneak in after curfew or get drunk off Mom and Dad's peach schnapps," Erica said.

Rachel laughed. "Oh my god, you have the craziest memory. It was just one thing after the other and I was tired of convincing myself to choose him and us over…well, mostly over my family, but also my own dreams and my own goals. I totally forgot who I was somewhere along the way." Rachel watched as a dragonfly flew by and landed on the deck beside her foot.

"I can't even imagine what you went through, all alone over there?" Erica said, putting her hand on Rachel's.

"It sucked not being able to talk to any of you about it. He *hated* me sharing any personal details with you guys."

"Still, how did you finally, just get up, and move out?" Erica asked.

Rachel sighed. "Don't freak out and don't say anything to anyone…but he actually hit me. One night. We were having a massive fight. Just months and years of letting the unsaid boil up and it just started spilling over."

Erica's jaw dropped. "That little fucker! I never liked him, Rach. The way he treated you. I'm shaking. If I ever see him, I am giving him the hardest junk punch."

Rachel laughed. "Thanks sis, nice to know you have my back."

"So, he hits you and then what?"

"It was like one in the morning and he was late…yet again. Stood me up for dinner and came home smelling like whiskey. We got into it, he slapped me and got in the shower. He felt bad for like a second and while he was showering, I just packed my bags and walked out. I couldn't look back, couldn't talk to him, couldn't even collect my things. I knew if I saw him, he'd somehow convince me that I made a massive mistake, that I was nothing without him. And for the first time in a long time, it was like I saw life through a new lens. I knew I didn't need that toxic energy in my life and like that," she snapped her fingers, "it was like a switch."

Erica was staring at her sister. "Who the hell are you?" she smiled. "That is so badass, I really admire that."

"Hah, it's not that incredible, life's too short, ya know?"

A kayak emerged in Rachel's peripheral vision. She recognized the dog laying on the bow before the man paddling.

"Morning ladies!" Josh said with a wave.

Rachel straightened her shoulders and gave a subconscious brush over her hair. *Why did she have to wear her ratty old NYU sweater down to the dock?* she wondered.

"I'm gonna go check on that second pot of coffee," Erica said with a little twinkle in her eye.

"Aren't you guys the eager beavers?" Rachel asked as he got closer to the dock. As soon as Woody heard her voice, he jumped off the kayak and swam toward her. She laughed as he made his way from the beach to knock her down and smother her with kisses. By the time he laid beside her she was soaked.

"Doesn't exactly know how to play it cool, does he?" Rachel laughed.

"Never been his MO." Josh smiled.

Rachel smiled despite herself.

"So how is Ms. Woods today? Shit, is it Ms. Woods, or?" Josh said, worried he put his foot in his mouth.

"You are correct, Mr. Mackie, I am proudly a Woods once again," she said giving Woody a tummy rub.

"Good. It suits you."

She reached for her coffee cup to do something with her hands. Dammit, it was empty. Why was she so nervous?

"Oh dear, fresh out?" he asked.

"If you can believe it."

"You guys were always pretty obsessed with your coffee," he said. "I'm more of a tea drinker."

Rachel's jaw dropped. "Damn, you were almost cool there for a minute."

"Too early for jokes too then? My veins run black, don't worry." He smiled. "In fact, have some of mine," he said grabbing the travel mug on his lap.

As she reached for the mug their fingers touched. A shiver ran through her fingers all the way down her spine.

"You're sure you can spare a drop?" she asked.

"Oh don't worry, I know where you live if you take more than your fair share."

She took a long sip. He was smiling as she handed the mug back.

"You know you always make that 'mmm' sound right? I remember when we used to get the elusive invite for brunch at the Woodses back in the day," he said.

Rachel was shocked. Not only did she not realize she picked up this same trait as her mother, but here was a man who paid attention to such tiny details. This was new territory.

"I really am becoming my mother, aren't I?" She laughed.

"That's not such a bad thing, Mrs. W is hot." Josh joked.

Did he just call her hot? She blushed.

"Well either way, thanks for the extra hit. I may just be able to make it up to the house for another cup now." She smiled.

"Well I won't keep you from such pressing matters." He whistled and Woody jumped back on the kayak. "My mom said you guys are planning some big party here tomorrow night?" he asked before pushing off the dock.

"Yes, it seems that way. Although I have my reservations."

"What's this? Rachel turning down a party with the promise of champagne? Say it isn't so," he said raising his hand to his heart.

"I've splashed one person already this morning," she teased, "don't make me up that number. I'm just worried Mags won't be very keen on a big party." She sighed.

"Oh yeah, the possible divorce…we just may have enough people for a support group on this lake."

"Considering the drama everyone has been dealing with the past few years, a big party may not be the best place to work through all that," Rachel said running her fingernail through a groove on the dock.

"Hmm, if only you knew a good therapist nearby that was a pretty decent listener," he said scratching his head. "That's a toughie."

She looked up at him. "I'm not sure I need to burden you with this Woods drama on your vacation."

"Seriously, Rach, I'm always happy to listen to you," he said, staring up at her from the lake. "Or anyone in your family…just let them know I'm here if they need."

"Thanks Josh, I will."

There was a pause so Rachel decided to get up and make her way back to the cottage, slowly, hoping for a bit more conversation before he left.

"But um, you're doing alright otherwise?" he tried.

That would do, although even Woody looked disappointed in their poor ability to flirt.

"Yeah, I think so…" she started. "A bit weird being back, ya know? So much has happened these past few years. And yet, in some ways, nothing has changed. That sounds cliché, doesn't it?"

"Not at all. You're talking to a fellow divorcé, right? You almost go from a bubble back to the familiar—some people say you can never go home again but I'm not sure I believe that," he said.

Rachel's eyes softened as she beamed at him. "I literally just had that thought this morning."

He smiled, back to the good banter. "Well, I'll let you grab that extra shot," he said starting to paddle away.

Rachel didn't want him to leave. "Hey, what are you guys up to later?"

"No real plans, you?" He stopped paddling.

Fuck, now she had to make something up.

"I guess I'll figure it out with a little more caffeine…jet lag ya know?" She laughed trying to sound casual, though she feared she sounded anything but.

"Well, maybe see you guys on the water then?" he asked.

"Yeah for sure, I'm dying for a swim with all this heat."

"Cool, yeah, I'll probably go for a swim too…say around 11?"

"Weird I was also thinking around 11!" She smiled.

"So, maybe you see then." He waved. As he paddled away Rachel watched his wake spread over the calm water.

"Ooooooh maybe I'll see you then my looooooover! Parting is such sweet sorrow!" Erica was heading down the lawn with a fresh pot of coffee.

Rachel cocked her head to one side as she turned to face her sister. "Oh fuck, don't start. How much of my pathetic attempt at flirting did you hear?"

"Enough to know you're crushing hard on the boy next door." She filled Rachel's mug. "Come on, dad started the bacon and eggs, if you can call soy bacon, bacon? And you're gonna need your strength for that steamy sex sesh later."

"Ernie!" Rachel laughed giving her sister a shove.

As they walked up to the house, Rachel realized she was starving. Trying to sound aloof, casual and flirty was much harder work than she realized.

40

"Rachel pick up the goddamn phone. I've left you like million messages. Call me back."

It was Peter. Rachel was still at Ellie's flat and had no further clarity on what she was going to do about her marriage.

"Is it him again?" Ellie asked carrying a bottle of wine and two glasses in from the kitchen. Ellie had the cutest little flat above the market on Wimbledon High Street. It was a tiny studio where she barely had a wall separating the kitchen from her bedroom slash living room, but it was all hers and Rachel admired that.

"Ugh, yes…" Rachel said flipping her phone over. "So, they didn't miss me at work today?" After such a restless night, Rachel couldn't force herself to get up and face a busy office that morning.

"Nah, they bought my whole terrible case-of-diarrhea story." Ellie laughed. "I can't believe I still haven't even met the guy. Most of us think he doesn't even exist." Ellie smiled pouring two very large glasses of sauvignon blanc.

"Yeah well that's Peter…no time for anyone or anything but work," Rachel said with a shrug. She took a big gulp of her wine, "probably not good for my explosive diarrhea." She laughed.

"So what do you think you're gonna do? How was the call earlier?" Ellie asked tucking her feet up on her little blue sofa.

"Just more apologies. I barely spoke to him earlier, it just made me so angry listening to his excuses. I spent all day going over it all and I just don't think I can go back. It feels like I finally came out of a really toxic trance, or something." Rachel was staring into her wine glass as she spoke.

Ellie took a sip of her wine. "Dramatic much?" she joked.

"I suppose that did sound heavy. Maybe I spent too much time today over-thinking."

"No, that douche has hurt you enough times and the fact he hit you last night? You're lucky I managed to talk Will down—he was about to show up at the dude's office and kick the living shit out of him," Ellie said. Her boyfriend, Will was a semi-professional rugby player who doubled as a bouncer. Not the kind of guy you wanted to piss off.

"I know, please thank Will…I may need his services one day," she managed a small smile.

"How is your cheek by the way?" Ellie asked moving Rachel's hair aside. "I can definitely still see it. What a prick. No man hits a woman."

Her phone beeped again. Another text from Peter.

Rachel please please talk to me! I didn't mean to do that baby, you know I love you! I only work so late for you! For our dream life! Everything is for you Rach. Baby please come home to our place, it doesn't feel right without you xxx

Rachel held her phone up to Ellie who rolled her eyes. "Oh convenient, now it's your place too?" Ellie had gotten an earful when Rachel arrived in the middle of the night. She had constantly been showing the perfect exterior to friends and family. Knowing how much Peter hated airing his dirty laundry, she never let anyone in.

"Have you told anyone in your family yet?" Ellie had seen a plethora of Rachel's old family photos on her Facebook profile but recently, she had spoken very little of them.

"Things are still so weird there," Rachel said. "I wouldn't even know where to begin with them…" she trailed off, her voice shaky.

"Oh god, no, okay let's not talk about it! Trashy reality TV?" Ellie asked topping her glass.

Rachel smiled. "Yes please…people with lives more pathetic than mine."

41

"So, what's on everyone's agenda for today then?" Mom asked as they cleared away the breakfast dishes.

"Isn't that intricately laid out in the itinerary for today?" Maggie asked wiping Abby's face before she could run off after her sister.

"Well, the week has had a few surprises so far and so I just wanted to see if anyone had other plans?" Mom replied. "But, if we're so keen to stick to said itinerary, there's a beautiful little beach on the other side of the lake. Maybe we could cruise over with a picnic?" she suggested.

"What time, mom?" Rachel asked, not wanting it to conflict with her swimming date. Or was it even a date?

"Maybe around 11?"

"Yeah Ray Ray, you don't have plans, do you?" Erica said smiling down at the newspaper she was reading.

"Nope, just curious," she lied.

Rachel headed out to the patio and pulled out her phone. She scrolled and found Josh's contact.

Hey!

No, too excited. She deleted the exclamation mark.

Hey you!

Oh god, way worse.

Hello, I regret to inform you that I will be unable…

Way too formal. She put the phone down and laid back in her chair, welcoming the gentle breeze on her face.

"Rach, honey? You okay?" Mom poked her head out on the patio.

"What? Oh, yeah." Rachel let out a little sigh. "Sorry, just taking five in the sun."

"I think the beach is a good idea, don't you? I think it would be good for your father to relax a bit and the kids can make some sand castles," she said quietly. Rachel thought her mom sounded nervous.

"Mom, of course it's fine! Is everything okay with you?" Rachel was sitting straight up now, suddenly nervous for what her mom might say.

Her mom sat down and let out breath of air. "I know your dad is absolutely fine, I don't want you kids to worry, you get that, right?"

Rachel nodded.

"But these past few years…" She started to tear up but willed herself to go on. "They've just been so stressful and to have everyone here, under one roof now. It's just a mixed bag of emotions I guess!"

But Rachel knew it was more than that.

"I hate to think of the hell I put you guys through," Rachel said as she reached out to squeeze her mom's hand.

Her mother shook her head.

"But you're sure we don't have to worry about dad's health?"

"Dear, I just said," she pleaded.

"Don't give me that, Mom. Look, I know I haven't exactly been around and for that I'll never forgive myself, but what happened here the other day… that's not normal," she whispered.

Her mom's shoulders slumped down as she put her face in her hands. Her composed exterior starting to crack. "He's going to be just fine. You know how I know? Because he *has* to be just fine." She squeezed her daughter's hand, wiped her tears, and got up from the table. "So, you'll be dressed and ready to go in about thirty minutes? I could use some help with the picnic, if you don't mind?" She smiled quickly then returned to the kitchen to be the stoic matriarch she'd always been.

"Hey, mom?"

Mom stopped and turned.

"You know I love you guys, right? That didn't change while I was away…I just wish I could take it all back." Rachel felt on the verge of a breakdown.

She smiled again. "Rach, there's no need for any of that. You're home now and that's all that matters." She blew her daughter a kiss before sliding open the patio door and slipping back inside.

Rachel felt a bit of a weight fall off her shoulders. She had been dreading this holiday ever since her mom suggested it. She was worried she would be crucified for turning her back, cutting her family out—hell even for getting divorced. And yet, she was welcomed with open arms.

Her phone beeped, interrupting her thoughts.

Hey Rach, heading out on the boat toward MacDougall's point. Hope to see you there ;)

It was Josh! Thank god she didn't have to write first.

Hey there! Turns out Mama W had plans for a picnic today on White Sand Beach. I hate to cancel so last minute but think I really just need to stay with the family today...

She re-read it a million times. Finally, Maggie came out with the girls who wanted to play tag in the backyard. "You look like your head is about to explode."

Rachel handed Maggie her phone. "Please tell me what the hell to write."

"Aren't you the writer?" she asked taking the phone happily. Maggie read her text. She quickly tapped out a response and gave it back to Rachel for approval.

Hey! Turns out Mama W had plans for a picnic today on White Sand Beach. I hate to cancel so last minute but think I really just need to stay with the family today...rain check? :)

"Perfect, knew I could count on you." No sooner had she hit send when her phone beeped again.

No worries, family comes first :) am sure I will see you soon

anyway x

Rachel was beaming down at her phone.

"Guessing it was a good reply?" Maggie asked.

Rachel held up her phone and Maggie smiled. Abby was heading down toward the dock so Maggie had to return to being a mom. "Shit! Abby wait up!" She called as she chased after her girls. Rachel loved seeing her older sister shine as a mother. Even as kids, Maggie had only ever wanted to be a mom. They had spent countless hours playing house until Maggie hit the tween years and became too cool for her baby sisters.

"Funny seeing her be a real mom, isn't it?" Erica had come onto the deck and saw Rachel smiling at her nieces.

"I know, I just can't believe how big the girls are! I mean, I saw photos and had the odd Skype here and there but…" Dammit, Rachel was crying again!

"Whoa, what's going on, sis? That time of the month?" Erica said smiling.

Rachel laughed. "Probably due any day with all the emotions I've been having lately!"

"Yeah, it couldn't have anything to do with the big family reunion after years away with an elephant sized block of tension in the room between everyone? I mean it couldn't be all the family drama, surely not."

"Yeah, yeah, let's just go help mom with the picnic." Rachel shoved her baby sister on her way back inside. "And after a pretty dry day yesterday, you better be planning on making your famous Bloody Mary's on the beach."

"Need to drown those sorrows from your missed date, big sis?" Erica teased.

<h1 style="text-align:center">42</h1>

It was a lovely brisk autumn morning and Judy was on her way back from the hospital where she'd left John for another round of tests. He had insisted she leave him and take the afternoon off to get a manicure, grab a coffee, or do anything but sit in a sterile hospital. She fought him on it, but in the end, she knew he was right. He'd only had one other fainting spell since their afternoon in Home Depot, but that was two more than Judy could handle. They now had a referral to a heart specialist, who promised to get to the bottom of John's condition. The past two years had seen a constant stream of doctors and tests to get some answers. What started as a 'weak heart condition' they learned, was actually creating the perfect storm within John's heart for coronary artery disease and years of hypertension taking their toll.

As she sat in Starbucks scrolling through old photos on her phone, Rachel's wedding photo popped up and Judy smiled. If she just ignored what happened mere hours after this happy photo was taken, she would think she had everything she wanted. Lucky enough to marry her high school sweetheart, attend their second daughter's wedding, a grandchild in tow, and Maggie pregnant with number two. The love between those siblings knew no end.

Sure, they fought like crazy as kids but as adults her heart swelled to see them become best friends. John didn't speak to his two siblings and Judy was an only child who had desperately wanted a little brother or sister to play with. She vowed one day her house would be filled with laughter and chaos. And she smiled knowing they had that once.

Would they ever get that back, she wondered? When John's health first started acting up, Judy dreamt of their summers at the lake and how carefree everyone was back then. With Maggie not speaking to Erica and Rachel hardly speaking to anyone, Judy had her doubts she'd be able to pull it off. Maybe it was time to stop fretting and take action. It had been over two years already and still her family was struggling. Judy thought it was more important than ever for grand gestures to bring them back together.

"Ma'am? Your phone is ringing." It was the barista interrupting Judy's thoughts. She had been so lost in thought on planning a big reunion, she hadn't even heard her phone ringing in her hands!

"Oh my goodness! Thank you and sorry!" she said to those nearby, as she quickly grabbed her coffee and took a seat by the window.

She saw Rachel's name flash up on the caller ID. She hadn't heard from Rachel since a quick Skype for John's birthday at the end of September. Her excitement quickly faded to panic; she feared something might be wrong since things had been so strained.

"Rach, honey, hi! Is everything okay?" Judy was trying to sound upbeat and not too much like the panicked mother she was.

"Mom?" Rachel had been crying. She could tell right away.

"Honey, what is it? What's wrong? Are you hurt? Is Peter okay?"

"Mom, I'm okay," she started then took a deep breath. "But it is about Peter, we've…I mean I've…we're getting a divorce, mom." Rachel exhaled.

Judy's hand froze midair with her coffee steaming in front of her face, her mouth gaped open in shock.

"Mom? Are you there?" Rachel had managed to quell the tears now that the truth was out. She could already feel the load getting lighter and lighter.

"Oh honey, it's not about what we said, is it?" The years may have passed but Judy could recall every detail of their fight at the wedding. Every word spoken, every awkward pause and hurt expression.

"Mom, no. If anything, you were right. All along."

"Are you sure, dear? What happened? Please tell me," she urged.

"It was just a lot of things…his working all the time, very focused on himself, and well, if we're going to be honest about it—he hit me one night and I haven't seen him since. I filed the divorce papers here in London on Friday and it's done. The process has started and I *won't* go back."

Judy was stunned. "He did what?" She tried to remain calm as she gently placed her cup back down. She thought quickly of John's heart and whether he'd be able to handle this news.

"Look mom, I don't want to talk about it. I just wanted you guys to know. I'm staying with a friend right now, Ellie, remember me talking about her from work? But looking for my own place. Please can you let everyone know? Not about the slap, just the divorce for now, okay?"

"Of course, but Rach, honey, you're sure you don't want to chat about it a bit more?" Judy tried to cling tighter as she felt her daughter pull away.

"Maybe another time, okay mom? It's late, thanks for passing the message on."

Judy put the phone down and stared at the photo looking back up at her. It was the wedding photo she had open before her phone rang.

Now Judy only felt rage at the smiling Peter staring back at her. The anger soon turned to sadness as she thought of Rachel alone on the other side of the world trying to manage this on her own. She hated the way the call ended and sensed bitterness from Rachel. She wiped her eyes and wondered how to make things right once again.

Well, that settles it, she thought. I'm booking a cabin for the summer and I'm going to put this family back together again. She jumped up from her chair, tossed her cup in the trash, and headed back to get John. She'd tell him about her master plan. Of course, she knew he'd love it.

43

"Hey Ernie, where we at on those Bloody Mary's?" Maggie seemed to be feeling more like herself after a mid-morning nap on their way to the beach.

"I got you, girl! Here you go." Erica passed around her fresh batch of drinks.

Rachel smiled hearing the old banter come back between her sisters. The sun was high and beaming down on them. After years of British weather, Rachel forgot what it felt like to have a proper summer filled with endless sun, high humidity, and enough heat to make one forget about the east coast's brutal winters.

"You read my mind," Rachel said squinting up at Erica as she handed her an ice cold Bloody Mary.

"Grampie, build us a sand castle!" Abby called. Rachel had to admit, her father was looking much better than a few days ago. His color and energy had made a comeback, not to mention his social side.

"Coming granddaughter!" he said as he cha-cha'd over to the girls. "By the way, I passed Devon swimming in the lake when Max and I were testing out the motor earlier. Did you know that guy does two miles every morning? Insane!"

Erica waved away her dad's comment. "Oh ya, he's a regular Michael Phelps."

"Anyway, I told him to bring the famjam over for a barbecue later…they're bringing burgers to go with the million salads you girls made. You do know your old man can still process meat right?" he shouted back as he continued his dance down to the surf to help the girls.

Rachel immediately felt four sets of eyes on her. How was it that her dad seemed to be as clueless as ever teeing up all of these situations? Rachel took a long, slow sip of her drink trying to avoid eye contact.

"Well, at least we know how to light the beach barbecue—we'll just have Rachel stand near Josh and let the sparks fly," Max joked.

"Ha ha. Nice dad-joke, bro." Rachel squished her face up at him. But as she stood to take her drink into the water, she couldn't help but smile. She needed to cool down and not have everyone waiting for her reaction. How the hell was she supposed to play it cool with everyone expecting something? This was not what she signed up for this week!

She started to feel a little bit angry at Josh for imposing on her family time. He was a goddamn psychologist, didn't he understand the high stress she was under already being around her family after the past few years drama? Didn't he think it was a bad idea to pile on? Or assume she was ready to date so soon after her divorce? Wait, was she ready to date?

"Helloooo…earth to Rachel…" Erica said wading out to her.

"Oh! Hey Ernie, sorry didn't see you there," she said turning around.

"Nice try. I asked if you were okay with the Mackie's coming?" Erica asked sitting down in the shallow water. Rachel had no idea how she could drink the amount she did and still have a perfectly svelte figure. Her long legs seemed to stretch into her tight abs from weekly kickboxing, giving her young sister the perfect size 0 the modeling world demanded.

"Yeah, of course, why wouldn't I be?" Rachel lied.

"Yeah, yeah, no one can hear us over here. Dad stole my iPod and has his playlist blasting through the Bose."

"I think you creating that playlist with his favorite tunes has slightly gone to his head." Rachel laughed as "Don't Stop Believin'" started blaring over the beach.

"Meh. If the old man is happy, then we all are." She laughed.

Rachel looked at her sister sunning herself in the water like her favorite Disney Princess, Ariel.

"So, he's been pretty chilled these past few years?" Rachel asked. She hated to admit it but every once in a while on this trip, she felt like a reporter that was checking up on a story she covered years before.

"Oh yeah, I mean these past few years haven't exactly been a dream for anyone, have they?" she asked without needing a response.

Rachel nodded.

"Then there's the heart stuff. I had no idea they were dealing with that," Erica said pulling handfuls of sand up and letting it fall through her fingers into the water.

A pang of guilt rocked through Rachel. "I'm sure I didn't help matters. Why not tell people what's going on though?" Rachel said letting her guilt turn to anger.

"Come on Rach, we're rug sweepers! You know that."

Rachel frowned. "So, how's this beach party going to go then?"

"Just keep the sexual tension to a minimum and we'll be good," Erica said. "Don't do anything too sexy…no one needs to see little Joshy's boner poking through his shorts again."

"*Erica Mae*!" Rachel shrieked as she threw sand on her shoulder. "I can't believe you just said that. And what do you mean by *again*?"

"Oh, come on, you didn't notice it that day we were all on the dock?" Erica mimed her index finger going up and up as she burst out laughing.

"I knew you were full of shit." Rachel laughed.

"Well, what do you think? Is there potential there?" Erica asked taking a final sip of her cocktail.

Rachel took in a deep breath. "I mean, I'm obviously attracted to him. Which is odd since he's always just been this neighbor kid who used to throw worms at us as kids. Then as we got older, he had this psycho girlfriend-turned wife so it isn't like I ever looked at him that way. Plus, our families are so close, I don't need everyone in my business, even more than they already are. And then we're both divorced, which I suppose is a pro in some ways? But he's a therapist—could I stand being psychoanalyzed the rest of my life?"

She paused and took another breath to look at Erica who was staring at her with her mouth agape.

"A simple yes or no would do in future." She smiled.

"Clearly you can tell I have no idea what the fuck I think then?"

"Look, it's obvious you're attracted to him and I am sure going through a divorce can't be easy, but I think for now, just have fun and see where it goes. I mean you were so focused on school, then wrapped up in Peter, you haven't exactly had the opportunity to be single and ask yourself what you really want, have you?"

"When did you become the wise old owl?" Rachel asked.

"I've learnt a thing or two in my day. Come on, want another?" she asked standing up.

"Definitely, I might switch to some mimosas though. A good fizzy buzz will take the edge off."

As they walked back to their family under the shade, Max was already topping off glasses of prosecco with orange juice.

"Did you read my mind or something?" Rachel asked.

"I just thought it was time for something more suitable for toasting," he said as he nodded toward the water.

The Mackie's were dropping their anchor in the shallow water just off the shore. Josh jumped off the bow as Rachel looked over. She heard Erica's voice in her head, *Just have fun and see where it goes*—and goddamn if he didn't look good in his surfer shorts and unbuttoned linen top.

"Hey Rach, you happy to see me, or Woody?" Josh asked as he caught her staring. Erica snorted from behind. Thank god Woody wasn't far behind as Devon let him down the back of the boat and he started swimming to shore.

"Obviously, my main man Woody!" she yelled. Already Woody was making his way up the beach toward her and in a flurry of moments he toppled her over then covered her face with slobbery kisses.

"Come on bud, let the lovely lady up," Josh said shooing Woody away and grabbing Rachel's hand to help her up. "Sorry about that, he doesn't understand the concept of playing hard to get," he said as he pulled her up and they stood face to face.

"Ah, it's overrated anyway," she said with a cheeky grin.

"I couldn't agree more," he said, giving her hand a squeeze before letting it go.

She was definitely going to need that drink.

"Mimosa?" As if reading her mind, Erica was behind them passing out drinks. She gave Rachel a nudge before handing out the rest.

"Well look, I think it's time for a toast!" Frank said raising his glass. "To a totally kismet week at the lake!"

Rachel smiled and looked around at everyone standing on the beach. The girls were building sandcastles in the surf, Devon was helping Max get a bonfire built and their parents were laughing away on the lounge chairs. That left Erica and Maggie…shit, Rachel couldn't quite hear them but it looked like they were deep in conversation. Josh had started to head to the bonfire to chat with the guys so Rachel tip toed up to the girls.

"Has she said anything else to you about the divorce though?" Maggie was whispering to Erica.

"Just that he did actually hit her!" Erica confessed as Maggie's jaw dropped. "I always knew he was an abusive asshole."

"Yeah, I don't want to pry too much since mom made us promise we wouldn't say anything," Maggie said setting salads out on the table.

"Is that so?" Rachel asked from behind them, her face long and red with betrayal.

Erica's face dropped as she spun around. "Shit, Rach, I'm sorry, we just wanted to make sure you're okay and mom asked us to go easy on you. She was worried it might scare you away if we all came on too strong," Erica babbled.

"So, mom told you?" Rachel asked curtly.

"Just when it all happened. We couldn't believe you'd just walk out, you always seemed so happy…from a distance anyway," Maggie said.

"And when she asked us to just act as normal as possible, we didn't know what you expected or wanted us to do…" Erica shrugged. "And you only just told me about him hitting you yourself, shit! I don't know what I was thinking."

Rachel took a deep breath. "I expected my sisters to act normal. This is the exact kind of shit that pushed me away in the first place. Everyone tip toeing behind my back, acting normal to my face and then gossiping behind my back. I mean, what the fuck?" Her voice was rising.

The crackling wood in the fire drifted across the beach, disturbing the now silent beach. Rachel glanced from side to side—all eyes were on her.

"Rach, please, we didn't mean anything by it—this is all for you!" Maggie said taking a step toward her.

"Just save the perfect mom crap, okay? I don't need you guys lying to my face anymore." Rachel grabbed her flip flops and headed down the beach.

"What happened?" Mom asked leaving Margot and the men lounging in the sun.

"Sorry Mom, Rach overheard us asking whether either had gotten any more details about Peter. She heard me mention about the slap and I guess she feels betrayed we've been hiding things again," Erica said defeated.

Their mom's face fell. "Don't worry, it's my fault for asking you girls to act differently. Oh god, I hope we haven't ruined everything." She put her face in her hands.

Dad came over and put his arm around his wife. "Let's just give her some space," he whispered. "Come on, let's freshen everyone's drinks…who wants another?" He shouted back with a smile to the crowd. She obliged but handed him a Perrier before grabbing some snacks for the group.

Max gave a look to Maggie asking if everything was okay. She shrugged.

"I'm just gonna take Woody for a walk up the beach," Josh said to no one in particular. Yet on his way, he grabbed two beers from the cooler and whistled to Woody. He rounded the bend and approached Rachel who was sitting on a big piece of driftwood. She looked beautiful with the wind blowing her hair across her face, the sun beyond.

"Hey, want some company?" he asked as Woody ran over to her.

She broke into a smile as he slobbered all over her face. "Well, how can I say no to this face?" she said giving him a scratch behind the ears.

"I can just leave these beers for you two if you'd prefer," Josh chirped.

"Thanks, but I wouldn't mind a little human company too," she said taking the beer from his outstretched hand before twisting off the cap.

"To the inaugural meeting of the Divorce Club of White Sand Beach," Josh said before taking a swig.

Rachel burst out laughing.

"It's nice to hear you laugh again," Josh said taking a seat beside her.

Their bare thighs brushed together and Rachel's stomach did a tiny flip.

"That makes me sound like an old spinster who forgot how to have fun." She smiled.

He chuckled. "That's not what I meant at all. I just know how intense these family reunion things can be…not to mention after moving back home, getting a divorce, and starting life all over again. I may know how one or two things feel but it must be a lot all at once. It's just nice to see you having fun in between all of that."

Rachel sipped her beer and looked out at the lake. "Yeah, Mr. Therapist would know."

"Okay, if I take off my big therapist cap, can we just speak as, I don't know, friends?" Josh asked looking at her.

She turned so they were looking directly at each other. Her breath was shallow as his eyes bore into hers. He was so close to her. Was he going to lean in for a kiss? His eyelashes fluttered as he gently chewed the side of his lip. Time was standing still, she hadn't taken a full breath in what felt like ages.

She closed her eyes and felt a big wet kiss on her cheek.

"Woody, my man!" Josh laughed shoving him off Rachel. "Sorry about that," he said as Woody ran back into the water.

"You have to give the guy credit for jumping on an opportunity." She giggled as she wiped her face.

"Anyway, I just wanted you to know," he said leaning back comfortably again. "It's just been nice spending time with you guys again. And, if it all gets to be a bit much, you've got a friendly outsider you can unload, if you need or want," he said glimpsing up into the sun.

"Thanks Josh, that means a lot," she said, putting her hand on his. She immediately lost her nerve and pulled it away. "Overhearing the girls talk about the finer details of what happened between Peter and me. I mean, I told my mom to relay part of the message but had heard barely anything since… and then I hear them whispering about it. And that my mom asked them to not approach me. It just reminded me of the wedding all over again." She didn't realize it would all spill out of her but Josh made her feel so at ease.

"Okay, as President of the White Sand Beach Divorce Club, may I raise two questions please?" he said raising his hand.

Rachel laughed. "Yes, Mr. President, you may."

He smiled. "So, what exactly happened at the wedding?"

She gave him a quick rundown of the events that night—what she could remember anyway given the champagne she'd consumed.

"I imagine overhearing your family wasn't a fan of your new husband must have been a pretty big blow in the middle of your wedding." He said turning his beer bottle in the sand, watching the tiny grains stick to the sweat on the bottle.

Rachel was gently picking at the label on her beer bottle. She nodded. "I guess I felt a bit stupid for not picking up on it earlier. Not only was I now questioning my new marriage, but I was a bit sad we weren't actually as open and close with each other as I had always thought, you know?"

"I get that," he paused, "but, I'm not sure it should discredit your closeness as a family. I mean, put yourself in their shoes. I'm sure if they critiqued your relationship before that, it may have driven a bigger wedge, no? You are a strong and independent woman, Rach, I've always known that about you. If someone told you that you couldn't do something, you almost want to prove them wrong."

She pulled her eyes away from the sand and back to meet his.

"Shit, sorry, did I cross a line?" he asked. "That was supposed to be a compliment."

"No, not at all. It's nice to hear and to be honest, I never really thought of it that way. And you're right. However, so were they and it could have saved me a few years of grief and an expensive divorce." She laughed.

"Hey, now that, I know something about!" Josh grinned.

"Yes, your turn Mr. President. What happened to you and Diana?"

"Hey, I had one more question!" he pleaded, giving Woody a belly rub as he rolled in the sand beside them.

"Yes, but this is more fair—you ask one, I ask one and so on." She smiled, leaning over to pet Woody. Her arm grazed his. She was worried he could feel her goosebumps.

If he did, he didn't let on. "Diana just wasn't who I thought she was when we got married. And unlike you, my family did voice their opinions and I reacted in that defensive, overprotective way claiming they just didn't know her like I did." He took another sip of his beer. "Family knows you better than you want them to sometimes. We got together, she quit her job, just started bumming around, traveling with the girls a lot, acting more like a teenager than a wife. I think she just wanted to be a doctor's wife at the country club, not really part of a partnership." He said, letting little clumps of sand fall through his fingers.

"Yeah, but you're not a doctor," she said with a grin.

"Touché Ms. Woods!"

It felt good to laugh while telling their stories, it seemed lighter somehow.

"That must have been hard though, lack of ambition is really not attractive in my books," Rachel said.

"Yeah, I mean, look at you. Making such a big move to the city, landing a dream job, after spending a few years in one of the world's biggest cities, writing and living out your dream. That takes gumption."

She smiled up at Josh. "Gumption, huh? I'll take that one as a compliment too."

"Good. It was intended as one." He returned the smile. "So, I didn't forget my other question. What led to the divorce?"

"Well, like you, it was a few little things that built up. He was never home… always chasing a dream, a bigger deal, bigger house, bigger fish. Claiming it was all for me but I was just some pawn along the way. Good job, good wife, good house. And then I suppose it all came to a head when he hit me, and just after all the smaller mental abuse, I had finally had enough." She rushed out the last part, and downed the last sip of her beer.

Josh shook his head in disbelief. "I'm sorry, back up for a second—you're telling me he laid a hand on you?" His jaw clenched.

"Yeah, actually the last night I ever saw him. He left me alone, yet again, at a restaurant for a planned dinner but he had to work late. We started fighting when he got home after midnight. He claims he got 'caught up in the moment', kept apologizing, blah blah blah…I left."

He was still shaking his head when she turned to him. "There's just no way to sugar coat what happened." She shrugged.

"I want to—" he paused, throwing his hands in the air. "I don't know, spit in his food or something!"

She couldn't help but laugh. "That's sweet, but I'm okay," she reassured him.

"I know you are. Trust me, the way you explain that whole situation and how you handled it…gumption. Exactly that." He nodded.

"Well, thank you…" she said bumping shoulders with him.

Josh smiled at her. "I still wanna fucking hit that guy though."

"Get in line. If my dad or Max, hell, even if the girls see him, I'm sure there will be no shortage of hits coming his way."

"See? You know everything they do is coming from a place of love, right?" he asked.

"Wait! When did you put that therapist cap back on? Is this what a *breakthrough* feels like?" She threw her head back laughing.

As she leaned forward again, Josh was leaning in closer than before. She took in a small breath and closed her mouth. He leaned forward and brushed her lips softly. *Holy fuck, I'm kissing Josh,* she thought. She realized her eyes were open and closed them as she leaned in to kiss him back. Josh moved his hands up her face to cradle her cheeks in his hands. She was giving in completely to him and it felt so good—until Woody jumped on both of them.

They broke away laughing.

"Yeah, he gets a little FOMO," Josh said giving him a reassuring pet.

They could hear the sound of bottles clang together in the distance. "There you guys are!" Devon said walking around the corner of the beach.

Thank god, he didn't catch them! Rach didn't need a million more questions this trip.

"I'm on drink duty and thought you guys might want a refill?" he asked carrying a couple of beers.

"Thanks man!" Josh said jumping up and grabbing two for them. He handed one to Rachel.

"Thanks Dev, I'm actually going to go find the girls. Catch you guys later," she said giving Josh a lingering look as she walked away.

Devon caught the exchange and raised his eyebrows to Josh. In return Josh flashed his brother a knowing smile then sipped his beer.

Erica walked up to meet Rachel as she turned the corner. "Fuck, Rach, I'm so sorry, honestly, we weren't talking behind your back it's just all been so strained and Mom was desperate to make sure we didn't scare you off so soon after coming back," she said in one breath.

"Rachel held up her hands. "Stop, it's okay, honestly." She pulled her sister in for a hug. "Let's just be open about it all, okay? I have nothing to hide and I'd just like to keep everything out in the open from now on."

Maggie and Mom were running over to them in the sand. Pretty soon it was a big group hug of all the women in Rachel's life and she felt strong and fierce for the first time in a long time. She heard Josh's words echoing in her head and smiled even wider.

"Now come on, I'd die for some bubbles instead of this beer." She laughed.

"Got ya right here, sis!" Max said popping the cork on an ice cold bottle of prosecco. She leaned in as he put his arm around her and kissed the top of her head.

Rachel let out a long contented sigh. The rest could be left unsaid and in future, it wouldn't need to be.

"Thanks for such a great night!" Margot slurred as she made her way back onto their boat. Night had fallen, the black sky lit only by moonlight and the bonfire's remaining embers.

"What a hoot!" Mom laughed sloshing through the water, her hands full with leftovers.

"You help Mom onto the boat, son, and I'll throw water on the fire," Dad said running back up the beach.

The kids were fast asleep on the bow as Rachel carried the last of the bottles onto the boat.

"See you guys tomorrow…maybe," Josh said with a little wave to Rachel as he started up their engine.

"Looks like your party is all over, huh," Rachel joked pointing to Devon passed out on the bow, his parents slumped together behind him.

"Yeah, well at least we can sleep in." He stuck his tongue out at her as he backed their boat up. She smiled and waved.

As she turned back to their boat she could feel Maggie and Erica's eyes on her. "Ooooh what happened there?" Maggie teased.

"Huh? Oh nothing, just good to chat to Josh a bit earlier, ya know?"

"Yeah, that's not what Devon said," Erica raised an eyebrow.

"Shut up!" Rachel jokingly shoved her sister. "What did he say?"

"Oh, just when he found you two, you were scrambling to put your clothes back on."

"*Ohmigod* no!" Rachel was still laughing.

"So, that's not what happened?" Maggie gushed.

"There may have been a kiss…" Rachel's smile threatened to split her face in two.

"OMG!" the girls shrieked together.

"Yeah just tell me now if you hate the guy," Rachel joked. "It will save me a big legal bill."

The girls laughed. "He definitely gets our stamp of approval," Maggie said. "Good job, good family, good values." She was ticking off items on her fingers.

"And still a babe," Erica concurred. "And, most importantly," she said in all seriousness. "Good kisser?" she whispered conspiratorially.

"Oh, hell yes," Rachel said.

They were all giggling as Dad jumped on the back of the boat and gave Max the all clear to head back home.

"Music to this old man's ears," he said as they started the short cruise back to the cottage.

44

As they cruised home over the lake, Devon drifted in and out of sleep and reflected on the last time he had seen any of the Woodses. He was just back from another humanitarian trip in Africa and happened to bump into Erica at the airport—him landing, she off on a modeling gig. Devon laid on the boat, staring up at the bright stars remembering the conversation he had with his brother three years ago.

"So, D, now that you're back from Botswana, what's the big plan?" Josh was sitting at the diner catching up with his brother who had just returned from another humanitarian trip. It had been a year since Josh's wedding and he found himself alone yet again—Diana off on some girls weekend in the Hamptons.

"Finally time for my MBA I think, bro!" Devon said after devouring his milkshake. "It just feels good to have normal food again." Josh looked in awe at his younger brother, sporting a long scraggly beard in front of him.

"Well good for you, man, I would love to be able to do some of the trips you've done. You still thinking advertising after grad school?" Josh took a bite of his French fry. He suddenly felt undeserving of his food. He hadn't earned it like his baby brother.

"Yeah, I think so. It seems a safe career choice. Hopefully I can get a good gig with a non-profit and help them raise money and awareness on a bigger scale." He took a big bite of his burger. He felt like he hadn't eaten in months. This last trip had only been two months in Bostwana but after seeing how the less fortunate live, he had subsisted on bean stews and the occasional goat from one of the nearby villages. Was it wrong this burger felt like the best meal he'd ever eaten?

Devon looked at his brother who seemed happy enough to see him, yet a million miles away. "So how ya been, man?" he asked between mouthfuls.

"Good…married life is good." He shrugged. "Diana just took a step back from work to focus on the house a bit, and she's off with some friends this weekend at a spa to relax."

Devon stopped chewing. "Relax from what…the stresses of her soaps?"

"It's a lot of work maintaining the home I guess. She looks after Woody and helps when I've got a lot of research work to get done." Josh was struggling; even he wasn't sure what she did with her days since she quit selling her jewelry online. When they first met, she had been a driven nurse at the local hospital, so fulfilled working in the neonatal clinic. As soon as they got serious, she ditched that to get into some MLM thing Josh was still confused about.

"Just careful there, bud…" Devon said gently.

"Yes, I know you're all concerned, but it's under control," he said firmly, stopping any further conversation on the matter. "Now tell me, any girls on this trip? Or a bunch of old ladies and undergrads again?"

Devon laughed. "There really isn't much of an in between is there? Not this time, but you know who I ran into at the airport when I landed, of all places?" he asked. "Erica Woods!"

"Really? What a small world," he said, pouring some more cream into his coffee. "Was she alone?"

"Yeah, sorry bud, your first love wasn't around," he said joking about Rachel.

"Oh shit, come on, not that again, we're both married and we never even dated."

"Sure, but it was always the dream of the houses of Mackie and Woods." He laughed.

"Anyway, Erica doing good then? Where was she off to?" Josh asked, changing the subject.

"She looks awesome, she's been modeling in New York. Was on her way to a show in L.A. Might meet up for a beer when she's back. Or green juice—do models eat these days? I can't keep track," he said before shoveling six French fries in his mouth at once.

"Yeah, you should…it'd be good for you to make some friends in the city before you start school."

～

As they cut across the smooth lake, Devon wondered why he never did take Erica up on that drink. Whether he must have lost the nerve to get in touch with her, or they were just too consumed chasing their own dreams, he was glad this week had offered an opportunity to see her again.

Unlike his brother, he hadn't been harboring some crush on her since childhood. That wasn't to say it wasn't nice to reconnect with a friendly face and see where things might go. The dating game in the city was depressing at the best of times, and grim at the worst. Dating apps, people climbing the business ladder, and the excessive nightlife had started to wear on him. Or maybe he was just getting old. But tonight, they were able to really reconnect…

～

"So, I thought about what you said the other day," Erica said as they sat in the sand by the bonfire. Maggie and Max were busy sorting s'mores out for the girls and their parents were dancing seventies style in the sand to Dad's (now over played) playlist. Springsteen's "Born in the USA" was on full blast as they all sang off key.

"I say a lot of clever things." Devon laughed grabbing another beer and handing her one. She shook her head, opting for a sip of water instead.

"Maybe, but the only clever thing you said to me was about being a fashion designer. I might just look into that when I get back to the city."

"Oh really?" he asked taken aback. "That's awesome. I think you'd be a great designer," he said sincerely.

"Yeah, I'm not totally giving up on the modeling, but there's a course near me in Brooklyn that starts up in the fall so I'm going to look at a late application. At least a good fallback, ya know? I didn't do so great on my undergrad degree, so want a little refresher."

"It doesn't need to be a fallback, you know so much about fashion and you've got so many years in the business; if anything, it gives you a stronger outlook than most other people," he said encouragingly.

"Well, thank you for that, and for the vote of confidence." She gave him a little nudge with her shoulder. "And what do you think you'll do when you get back to the city?" She hated to think of the summer ending. She felt like a kid at summer camp with the cooler winds bringing thoughts of school and falling leaves.

"To be honest with you," he said. "I'm not sure on the whole advertising thing. I initially thought it would be a great way to help non-profits get more coverage and funding but turns out, not as many people feel the same way so jobs are incredibly limited." His regard remained fixed on the sand. He was bummed things weren't turning out as he planned.

"Hmm," Erica said thinking. "How many humanitarian trips would you say you've been on?"

"Maybe around ten? There were one or two in high school, a handful during university, and one every year or so since then…"

"That makes ten different companies you've worked with, know well, and whose goals and missions you understand, right?" she asked.

"Definitely, I've stayed in touch with just about everyone from each trip."

"Why not just create your own company? Be a consultant for all those companies and build awareness for them?"

Devon cocked his head up to the sky then turned to look at her. "Well damn, why have I never thought about that? I could become a consultant and work independently for each and every one. Pick and choose which companies I believe in and help them grow," he said thinking out loud.

"Exactly! You're already so well connected." She smiled.

"My, Miss Woods, you've really hit the nail on the head there!" He speared two marshmallows. "And for that, I'm going to treat us to some s'mores."

She chuckled. "Hey, happy to share my own wisdom back."

He smiled as the lights of their dock came into view. He'd look into incorporating himself tomorrow and hit the ground running when he got back to the city. He hadn't felt this fired up in a long time and it was all thanks to Erica.

45

Judy was up at 5:30 a.m., unable to sleep for all the last-minute planning she still needed to get underway for Maggie's party.

"Jude? What time is it sweetheart?" John asked groggily.

"Too early, I'm just going to send some emails for this party—remember… top secret! Maybe later you can get Maggie out of the house with the kids?" she asked throwing her robe around her. It may still be summer but the mornings were starting to feel more and more like fall. Judy looked over at John snoring peacefully again. Guess her marching orders would have to wait.

She tiptoed into the kitchen and switched the coffee pot on. It would be a day fueled by caffeine.

She booted up her laptop as she heard the coffee start to percolate. She scanned her emails with final RSVP's for the party. Confirmation from the caterer and florist. Everything was running on time! Even she was surprised at how well she had been able to pull this off in only a couple of days.

One email made her pause and hold her breath.

Pierre Beaufort - Today's party

Judy went to pour herself a cup of coffee. She would need it before reading his reply.

Bonjour Judy,

Thank you for the invitation to Maggie's birthday party tonight. As you know, things have been strained as of late, but I plan to be there for her and for our girls. My flight lands late afternoon but I will hire a car and be there as soon as I can.

Cordialement, Pierre

For someone who was so forward in person, his emails couldn't have been more formal. Judy leaned back in her chair and wondered if she was doing the right thing. She remembered Rachel's warning that things were a tad more strained than Maggie let on. But Maggie hadn't mentioned anything about divorce, or Pierre leaving. Weren't they just going through a rough patch? Over the years, Pierre tended to stay away from most family gatherings and Maggie seemed a little more on edge every time Judy brought it up—alas, eventually it was dropped.

"Mom? What are you doing up so early?"

Judy slammed her laptop shut hearing Maggie's voice from behind. "Just couldn't sleep so researching the new heart pills the doctor wants to put your dad on," she lied.

"Is that why you can't sleep?" she asked, pouring herself a cup of coffee and sitting on the couch across from her mother.

Phew, she clearly hadn't seen the email. "No no, just too much fun lately I think. Had to pee from all the wine last night and at my age, once you're up, you're up!"

"It isn't just your age, mom," Maggie said raising her coffee mug. "Abby woke up to pee too and with the three of us in that little bed last night, once one is up, I'm definitely up." She yawned. "Are you going to read the paper?" she asked, still in a fog.

"No, you go for it, dear. It's still on the step," Judy said relieved she'd be able to get back to her RSVP's.

"Thanks, I'll take it on the patio," she said shuffling to the door.

Judy opened her email again. She made a quick scan of the replies and updated the caterer with final numbers - 37 in total with the Mackie's, Pierre and a few friends and relatives that could make the trip to the cottage. It wasn't going to be a huge affair but she wanted to make sure there was enough food and booze for everyone and that John wouldn't have to be strapped to the barbecue all night.

Speaking of John, she wanted to make sure he was aware of what she had planned to avoid causing any undue stress. He may like to think he was strong as an ox but the man had been hospitalized only a few nights ago. Judy could feel the pull to go down the rabbit hole by Googling the on call ER doctor's suspected diagnosis—Stage D heart failure—meaning they were running out of options. She shook her head softly at the screen, willing herself not to search the internet yet again for answers. There had been enough times that John caught her and made it known there was nothing to worry about—he wouldn't have her creating mountains out of molehills.

It was just all the horror stories she had heard of what could happen to people (especially older men) with hypertension and years of high cholesterol. When did they stop becoming molehills and become actual mountains to move? She took a sip of her now cold coffee and went to get a refill.

She saw the clock on the stove: 6:12 a.m. At least it was a more godly hour to be up. She could hear rustling from…was it Rachel's room? She peeked around the corner to see her third born walking out of her room, throwing her hair up into a messy bun. No matter what age her kids were, every time she looked at them, she swore they were frozen in time at a particular age. For Rachel, it was the rambunctious seven-year-old who rode her bike everywhere, flying down the block laughing her head off trying to keep up with her older siblings, or was it to shake off her baby sister, who followed her everywhere?

"Hey Mama," Rachel said as she leaned in to give her mom a peck on the cheek. Mom handed her a mug and Rachel smiled. "The service here is really top notch."

"Just be sure to leave a good review, will ya?" She laughed. "What are you doing up so early, my daughter?" She filled up her coffee mug and started to put a second pot on. Mom had decades of experience fueling her family and knew this would be the second of many pots today.

Rachel let out a big yawn as she sat down at the breakfast bar. "I'd like to blame it on the jet lag but I think I'm running out of steam on that excuse."

"It does take our bodies awhile sometimes," Mom said. Never being much of a traveler, Rachel wasn't sure what experience she was basing this on, but she still liked to believe her mom knew best about everything.

"I think I'm a bit worried about the party tonight…just don't want any big drama, you know?" Rachel tried to lightly let her mom in on the fact that not everyone may be thrilled with the guest list tonight.

"I'm sure that's just because you'll be seeing a lot of people for the first time in a few years. And don't worry, I'm sure people won't be asking a million questions about Peter. Most of them know you divorced and to leave it at that." Mom said now putting out some fresh fruit, a new batch of scones (when did she ever find the time to make those?) and fresh orange juice.

"I hadn't actually thought about those questions…" Rachel had been so concerned for her sister's welfare at the party, she hadn't stopped to think she might be subject to questioning as well. "And I'm feeling sad about having to leave here tomorrow. It's been so nice just escaping for a bit." She grabbed a raspberry off the top of her mom's fruit salad.

"I hear ya! I wish we bought land on a lake years ago. We could have camped there every summer, then built a little cottage when we had the money. That way we'd be thinking about retiring out here instead of downsizing to a condo."

Rachel nodded, "Condo? Wait, what?" She snapped up. How could they be selling her childhood home? No matter what happened, she knew she could always find her parents at 2561 Apple Orchard Lane. Where would she visit them now? Some vapid retirement community with a bland events room and regular shuffleboard tournaments?

"Rach?" she heard her mom question. "Did you hear me? We haven't decided on anything, we've just discussed it. It's such a big house with all of you gone. Might be time we thought about getting some place a little more suitable." She shrugged and grabbed a stray blueberry on her way back to the fridge.

As though she was mentioning how nice of a day it was meant to be today or that she was thinking about switching toothpaste brands. Not that the only constant thing in her whole life was about to become obsolete.

Rachel took a sip of her coffee. Still the best part of any day.

She decided the day was going to be filled with enough drama as it was so she made a mental note to continue this discussion another time with her parents—what a beautiful thought. How things can change in such a short period of time—not long ago, her parents were totally removed from her life and decision making process. And not long before that, they had been her rock, her trusted therapist, mechanic, chef, student advisor, doctor, etc., all rolled into one. Now once again, she'd be only a quick train or car ride away. Never again would she lose that time.

"So, any last minute help with the party?" she asked.

"You know it!" Mom said, bringing her laptop over to the bar. She peeked outside. Maggie was leaning over the newspaper, enthralled with the latest Arts news, nursing a coffee.

"I was going to get your father to sneak Maggie out of the house later when we have guests arriving, but maybe I could keep Erica here to greet and entertain. That way you and Dad can go get ice cream with her and the girls or something?"

Rachel was nodding along until she realized that was a terrible idea.

"Why don't Erica and I both take Maggie out? She was just raving about how nice it was to go to the salon. We can either go for a boat ride to relax on one of the islands or head back into town?" Rachel suggested hoping her mother took the bait.

"Yes, that just might work actually!" she agreed. "We'll offer to watch the kids so she can enjoy her last day of holiday, a little pre-birthday gift. Now, what to do though? We just did the spa so she won't be up for that again," Mom drummed her fingers on the island.

Rachel had a crazy thought. "Leave it to me mom, I know the perfect thing and that will just have to be another surprise for the day. Might just throw her off your scent." She smiled smugly.

"Okay, I'll leave it in your capable hands then. Tick!" she said, making a mental note to her checklist.

Rachel whipped out her phone to Google: *Zip lining Stowe*. She was sure she had seen a sign earlier. And didn't they always joke about doing something crazy like that before they were all old and grey? Rachel turned her eyes upward, knowing that wasn't true as there were a few white, scraggly hairs popping up more and more lately.

She refilled her mug and grabbed an extra cup before running off to fill Erica in on the plans.

46

"So, wait, I'm going bungee jumping today?" Erica said, wiping the sleep out of her eyes and stifling a big yawn. She greedily grabbed the mug from Rachel and downed the delicious black elixir.

"No, not bungee jumping—I want to do something crazy, not die." She laughed. "Zip lining up at Stowe, remember how they always offered that in the summer? I just Googled it and we can just show up!" Rachel was grinning from ear to ear. Erica knew that look and knew she better jump onboard.

"Okay, I'm in. Can I finish my coffee first, please?" she asked, leaning back onto her pillow.

Rachel sat quietly and waited for Erica to finish a few more sips before starting the next topic she knew had to be addressed. "And what about you? With the party today?" she asked from the side of her bed.

"It's okay, sis, there's no need for a mega dose of valium…although we still have some of those handy, right?"

"Yes, don't worry." Rachel raised her mug. "I got you girl."

"And anyway, we don't even know if *he'll* show up," Erica said referring to Pierre.

Rachel's face sank. Erica could read it right away. "Just tell me," she said.

"Mom just told me he confirmed…" she tried to hide behind another sip of her coffee but she could feel Erica's eyes on her begging her to change her response.

"Well fuck."

"That's why I thought it would be an excellent idea to get us girls out of the house; we can avoid any one person at any time and with a big party, you might not even cross paths." Rachel shrugged, knowing that was a weak rebuttal.

"Two things," they heard Max comment from the doorway. "Where are the girls going?" he asked running his hands through his thick hair, wild with bed head. "And two, I assume I am part of the girls in this scenario?" He said throwing his hands under his chin and batting his eyelashes.

"Absolutely if you want!" Rachel jumped up. "Zip lining—two o'clock, be there or be square."

"Yeah, you don't want to be an L-7 weenie," Erica said making the symbol for square in front of her face.

"Oh my god, did you ever leave the nineties?" he asked her. "It's too early and I haven't had enough coffee for that." He turned to wander into the kitchen.

"Now we just have to convince the Birthday Girl," Rachel said following Max into the kitchen. She poured another mug for Maggie and headed into the basement where she could hear her getting the girls dressed.

"Hey big sis, coffee?" she asked holding out the mug.

"As if you need to ask," she said trying to get a wiggling Abby into her bathing suit.

"There. Go find Grampie and ask him to take you girls swimming!" she shouted as they ran up the stairs to find Chloe and their grandfather.

"What's that look for?" Maggie asked suspiciously.

"What? A look? From me? No…" Rachel tried.

"Sure, sure…couldn't have anything to do with a pending birthday of mine could it?" She asked taking a big gulp of coffee from her steaming mug.

"Oh, is that coming up? Gee, I had no idea…" Rachel smiled.

"You know I hate surprises. Tell me there's no big party planned or some god awful theme event." She rested her head in her hand as she looked at Rachel.

Rachel would side step the surprise party comment for now. "We might have a little surprise for you, just the siblings though!" A white lie would be okay as it was for the greater good.

"Hmm, okay." Maggie still seemed skeptical.

"Just chill this morning, we won't be heading out until after lunch. Unless you wanna grab lunch in town?"

"Yes, that would be ideal! Would kill for a drink away from it all," she said, throwing her long blonde hair into a bun. Rachel was always slightly envious of how her older sister could look stunning any time of day at any age. She couldn't even spot a wrinkle on her porcelain skin.

"Totally get that, let me talk to my co-conspirators." She smiled and bounced up the stairs.

"Okay, I've had another thought," she said to Max and Erica when she found them eating breakfast in the kitchen. "The Birthday Girl would like to grab lunch with us so let's head to zip lining this morning then find somewhere to eat. I'm thinking booze beforehand may not be wise…"

"Very good plan—good for the nerves but I don't feel like puking hundreds of feet in the air onto poor unsuspecting hikers," Erica said spreading a big dollop of butter onto her warm blueberry scone.

"Okay that settles it then. Check!" Rachel said ticking off her own mental list and throwing some bread into the toaster.

"Okay, Mom," Erica joked.

Rachel smiled, she really enjoyed that comparison.

"So, where should we go for lunch?" Max asked looking up from the paper.

"What's that little one with the patio on the sidewalk in town?" Erica asked. "They always seemed to have a good menu."

"Was that McLean's? The little pub that has karaoke on the weekends?" Max asked.

"No, that's a dive." Erica scoffed as she pulled out her phone. "Ah, Nina's! That's it," she said finding it on the map.

"Yes, let's book a table for four at noon please," Rachel stated. "I simply must dine there today." She laughed.

Erica threw a carrot muffin at her head which Rachel luckily caught before it could hit her square in the eye. She took a big bite out of it and smiled triumphantly at her sister.

"I'm gonna go shower—assume I'll be designed driver?" Max said.

"Is that even a question? We girls are gonna be on the rosé all day!" Erica said busting a move in her PJ shorts and thick socks across the kitchen floor.

255

47

"Thanks for watching the kids, Pop!" Maggie said as she ran out to hop into the passenger side of Max's car.

"No worries, kiddo, I've got the matches and scissors at the ready so plenty for them to play with." He smiled.

Maggie tilted her head at their dad and let out an exasperated breath.

"Kidding, they're gonna help me drive the boat—donuts and waterskiing, right?" He gave a thumbs up.

"Nice to know he hasn't lost his sense of humor," Max said as he started the car.

"So, do I get to know what this big birthday surprise is?" Maggie said pulling out her phone. No missed calls and no texts from Pierre. After a near relentless onslaught from him lately it seemed strange for him to finally have gotten the message. But did she want him to finally back off?

"You'll just have to wait and see, Mags," Rachel said giving her shoulder a squeeze from the backseat.

"Well, as much as I love all you guys, I'm looking forward to a drink in town away from the kids, and Mom and Dad," she said looking out the window at the passing trees. If she hadn't felt so drained from having to function as a single parent lately, or from overthinking her marriage, she would have found the surrounding forest incredibly peaceful.

"It's definitely on the list, don't worry Birthday Girl," Max said as he rolled to a stop.

Left would take them into town where Nina's was. To the right led to nothing but farm fields en route to the mountains. Max flipped his turn signal and headed right.

"I thought we were getting lunch. What the hell is this way?" Maggie asked, looking back in the direction of town.

Nobody said anything.

She looked back to Rachel. "Cricket, give it up, what's the big deal?"

"Can't you wait another ten minutes? You never did learn patience, dear sister, did you?"

Maggie crossed her arms. Frustrated, she then flipped on the radio for a distraction.

"I love this one! Crank it," Max said turning the dial way up. "Take Me Home Country Roads" blared through the stereo as they all sang along.

"Remember when dad would play this on the way home from every road trip growing up? You'd think he wrote the song just for us or something," Erica said nostalgically.

"Oh god, yeah. I couldn't listen to it for the longest time since it was so overplayed." Rachel laughed. "Now it's on dad's playlist, I'm sure it will get burnt out yet again."

"Ahh let the old boy enjoy his tunes," Max smiled in the rearview.

Erica fidgeted with her hands in the back seat. Rachel looked longingly at the passing cars out the window, contemplating the future of their patriarch.

"Boy, this bunch is a real riot today," Maggie said sarcastically. "Look, guys…if Mom says he's fine, then I'm sure he's fine. Lord knows she cannot keep a secret."

"True, remember when we got Champ? Thought she could surprise us with a puppy and then on the way to get him, she blabbed and we all started making up names." Erica laughed.

"He was the fluffiest little golden retriever ever!" Rachel said. "Man, I loved that dog. Was so heartbroken when he had to be put down."

"Let's make a deal, it's my birthday—technically speaking anyway," Maggie said matter-of-factly. "So, can we just have some fun today? No talk of ex-husbands, or kids, or health issues, or dead dogs for that matter….just the four of us, having a laugh and cutting loose a bit? Life has gotten too fucking hard as we've gotten older and I just need to remember how to have fun." Maggie looked around the car at everyone.

Max nodded and put his hand over hers as he drove onward to Stowe.

"Of course sis…it's your day." Rachel smiled.

Erica nodded, happy to have a clean slate ahead.

"Good." She smiled and turned back toward the front of the car just in time to catch the sign: *Zip lining next exit.*

"Holy shit, no. You guys…you're kidding me, right?" Maggie shrieked. "I'm too fucking old to go zip lining!"

"Rubbish!" Rachel said. "If you're too old, we're all too old and that's even more reason to grab life by the horns and go for it!"

"Carpe diem, Mags!" Erica said punching the air.

"Exactly! You're bogged down with marriage issues and busting your ass to raise your beautiful girls, time to say yes to you, too!" Rachel said.

Maggie took a deep breath. "Well when you put it all that way…okay. Let's do it!"

Aaah!" the girls shrieked.

"OMG!" Max said with a girly shriek. "I am like soooo excited!" They all laughed as he took the off ramp.

After Maggie had asked for thorough reviews, stats on injuries and faulty equipment replacements, they were finally on their way.

"Who's up first?" asked their guide, Jake, a twenty-year-old college student home for summer vacation.

Everyone looked at each other. Erica stared at Jake's golden amber eyes and perfectly tousled hair.

"No takers?"

"Fuck it. I'll go first," Max said. "In order of birth!" he shouted.

Always the tried and true way to decide the order of things growing up.

"Someone will look after Chloe, right?" Max joked before shoving off.

"Wahoo! This is so awesome!" His voice drifted farther and farther away.

The girls felt better about their own turn after seeing Max's pure joy.

"So, are you just home for the summer? Where do you go to college?" Erica asked, thrilled there was life outside of the cabin: hot, young life.

Rachel smirked at Maggie and they burst out laughing.

"Weird to think we'll all be single together for the first time as adults," Maggie said looking off into the distance at the tiny dot Max had become as he landed safely on the other side.

Rachel was nodding. "Wait, what? So, you're for sure going through with the divorce?" Rachel was shocked to hear this but even more so knowing Pierre was on his way to the cabin to surprise her.

"Yep. I just can't do it anymore, Rach. I mean, I'm sure we'll make plans to get together for the kids once we're all back home but I don't think I can respect myself if I do, you know? The only thing is, he can be very persuasive."

"Sorry to interrupt, but looks like you're up, Birthday Girl," Jake interrupted them before Rachel could get more details. She stared after her sister getting harnessed up. Her questions would have to wait.

"See you bitches on the other side!" Maggie said suddenly exuding total confidence.

Erica looked at Rachel. "I thought she was petrified? Did you give her some kick ass pep talk or something? If so, give it to me…I'm starting to chicken out."

"Big strong Jake didn't make you feel better?" Rachel said pouting her lips.

"Oh god, you know, being the baby sucks, you can't even talk to someone without your family marrying you off."

"I'm kidding! Trust me, it's good to be out and see other people. I know I've only been home a short while and don't get me wrong, it is going way better than I ever thought it would, but there's gotta be a limit to family time sometimes," Rachel said.

"So, not looking forward to the party tonight?" Erica asked as she put her hands up to shield the sun. Maggie was nearly to the other side and after her initial "Fuck!" on the way down, she seemed to enjoy herself! So much for that confidence.

"I kind of forgot people may ask a million questions about the divorce, plus feeling like a failure—and then there's Maggie who just said she'll likely file for divorce when she's home, then of course knowing her husband is showing up later…" Rachel kicked a pebble and watched it cascade down the cliffside.

"It's going to be a shitshow," Erica said matter-of-factly. "Did you expect anything less at a Woods family gathering, dear sister?"

Rachel smiled. "Touché," she said climbing up to the platform.

"Carpe diem, right?" she looked back at Erica for reassurance.

"Fuck yeah!" Erica said as she threw up the rock and roll symbol with her hands.

Rachel took a step off and her other foot followed behind as she sat back in the harness. Her stomach nearly jumped out of her throat after the first leap but once she finally exhaled she was able to look around. She was on top of the world. The tallest trees she had ever seen felt like they were miles below her dangling feet. The sun was beaming onto her cheeks, and she could see the mountains peeking through the horizon. She was flying, totally free and alive. For the first time in a long time, Rachel felt like she was relearning how to breathe. With a final whooooooooosh! She was safe and sound on the other side. It was all over so quickly. She wanted more!

"What did you think, sis?!" Max asked as they unbuckled her harness.

"I wanna go again!"

"Right!" Maggie agreed from behind Max. "But let's save it for another day. This mama only gets so much free childcare and she wants to have a big glass of wine now."

With one final flirtatious wave to Jake, Erica was sailing over to her siblings.

"Considering the massive grin on your face I'm assuming you enjoyed yourself?" Max asked Erica when she landed safely on the other side.

"Or did Jake ask for your number?" Maggie said with a nudge.

"K, dude is basically still in diapers—college boys are so immature," Erica said with a flick of her hair.

"To Nina's!" Rachel said as they were ushered toward the exit. "But first… we'll be taking copies of these, please," Rachel said to the cashier who had their photos on display. Max was mid-scream, Maggie had her eyes squished shut, Rachel was smiling up at the sky, and Erica was screaming with her hands in the air.

"Really captures our essences, no?" Erica laughed as they headed back to the car.

48

"Definitely the large glass, actually you know what? The bottle and likely we'll need a refill," Maggie said as the waiter asked for their wine selection.

"Guess we're getting right to the point, then?" Rachel teased.

"Yeah, it might not be a milestone birthday but it's nice to be out with all my siblings, kids are looked after, no marital drama…for anyone right now!" Maggie laughed.

Rachel looked at Max and Erica pleading for someone to ask for more details. But it was too late, the waiter was pouring their glasses and Maggie had already taken a big swig.

"So, is this how you thought you'd be spending your birthday, Mags?" Max asked tearing into the bread and butter.

"Pfft, Pierre wanted us to be in the south of France celebrating," she said tracing the rim of her wine glass with her red manicured nails.

"*Excusez-moi*, but France has got nada on this group, or this second-cheapest bottle of wine!" Rachel laughed.

"Don't I know it!" Maggie chuckled.

"So, um what is going on with you two?" Max asked. Rachel was thrilled he picked up the gauntlet finally.

"With Pierre? What's there to tell?" Maggie said, reaching for a piece of bread. "Turns out he's been a serial cheater. If it wasn't his secretary, it was some skank from another office, or god knows who else. I mean who does that?"

Erica's foot was tapping nervously on the pavement. Rachel did some calculations. Maggie was about a glass and a half deep into her wine, as was she. And she was going to need a big dose of courage now.

"About that Mags…" Rachel started and Erica put her hand on hers.

"Rach, no. Don't."

"Don't what? Stick up for you?" Maggie asked. "Look, I'm trying to move on, okay Ernie? I really hate all this garbage between us but I look at you and sometimes I just can't get over it. The unanswered questions, I mean, why were you with my husband that night? Are you really capable of something so low? Not only that, but I felt completely abandoned by my sisters when I needed them most." Maggie's voice was rising with each sip of her wine.

Rachel shook her head at Erica. "No. It's time you knew the truth…"

"Why am I always the last to know everything?" Max asked with a mouthful of bread.

"Mags, you know Erica was just looking out for you and would never even think of laying a finger on Pierre. And what's worse? She found him with Leslie! At my wedding! And when she confronted him, he threatened her. Said if he ever tried to get between you two again, he'd make sure her modeling career was over for good; or worse…move you and the girls to France making it harder for any of us to see you and the girls again."

The bread fell out of Max's mouth. Maggie nearly spit out her wine but managed to keep it down. Rachel was worried her eyes were going to pop out of her head.

"Oh my god," Maggie whispered.

"Look, I knew it would come to this. It's stupid, Rach. I know you want to help but no one believes me and I'd just rather it all went away." She made to leave the table but someone caught her arm. It was Maggie—she wrapped her up in a huge hug and they cried together, quietly at table twelve, on a patio filled with people.

Rachel had to admit, even she had tears in her eyes as she felt the tension lift.

"Excuse me, but what the actual fuck?" Max was using his big brother voice.

The girls stopped saying sorry to each other and pulled apart.

"No, I'm serious. This guy…he threatened you? And you've been letting him parade around for years dragging your reputation through the mud with Maggie, destroying relationships with your family, and making you feel like actual garbage? I swear to god, I will kill him if we ever cross paths again," Max stated.

Rachel shifted nervously in her seat. The impending reunion with Pierre was no longer a 'what if' but a firm date they'd all have to see through. Thank god Max was driving and wouldn't be totally hammered by the time they got home.

"Let's allow everyone to digest this new information, okay?" Rachel tried. "Plus, it's Maggie's birthday and I'm not about to let that prick take any more time from us than he already has."

Maggie wiped her eyes. "Hell yes! Cheers!" Maggie said raising her glass for another toast. Maggie on the other hand, was well on her way to being absolutely shit-faced before her surprise party.

49

After a surprisingly uneventful lunch, where Rachel ordered pizzas for everyone to soak up as much booze as possible, they were on their way back to the cottage. Maggie and Erica were blasting Spice Girls on the radio and singing horribly off tune but surprisingly, Max was smiling and even signing along.

"Scary was always my fave!" He shouted, cutting shapes with his free hand.

Rachel pulled out her phone. A text from her mom.

Guests have started to arrive. Pierre running late but still coming. What a surprise for our birthday girl!

Rachel was worried her wine was going to come back up at the thought of Pierre in their presence. Her worry wasn't only about what Maggie or even Max would do once they saw him, but how big the line would be before she got her own chance to give him a piece of her mind.

About five minutes away, so make sure everyone is nice and hidden :)

Rachel replied to her mother. Their mom had assured her everyone parked down the road to not raise suspicion. She was hoping Maggie was in a nice sweet spot of *just drunk enough* to be flattered and feel the love, without being too far gone to breakdown and never speak to anyone ever again. That wasn't too much pressure on the powers of wine, was it?

"I can't wait to get into my bathing suit and have a nap on the dock!" Maggie said swinging her legs out of the car. "Reckon mom and dad will babysit all afternoon or have I pushed my luck already?" She laughed as her bare feet crunched on the rocks.

"Just had to take the shoes off, huh sis? Not even wearing heels." Erica laughed as she grabbed Maggie's arm in hers. Rachel smiled, then realized it may be more for Maggie's own stability than anything else.

"Think we'll pull this off?" Max asked as he raised his eyebrows at Rachel. They were pulling up the rear with the camera ready for Maggie's reaction.

"Worst case, it only hurts for a minute, right?" Rachel shrugged. "Plus, if we can get through everything else, what's another couple hours? It'll all come out in the wash." Max cracked a smile as he followed his sister inside.

"SURPRISE!!!!!!"

The sound of about thirty-five people met them as soon as Maggie opened the door.

Geez, mom, if thirty is a "few" guests, I dread to think how many more may be coming by later, Rachel thought.

"*Ohmigodohmigod!*" Maggie squealed as she dropped her purse on the floor. She looked back at her siblings. "You little shits! You knew all along!" But she was smiling so Rachel knew they were in the clear.

"Don't look at us—it was all mom's idea," Erica said trying to extricate herself of any blame.

Mom and Dad ran up to give their daughter a kiss.

"Mom! This is epic even for someone with your hostess powers!" Maggie gushed as Dad put a glass of champagne in her hand. The entire living room and kitchen were adorned with silver and teal balloons, while little strands of tulle had been carefully taped to the ceiling, creating a little bubble for celebrations.

"Sprung for the good stuff, kiddo," he said with a wink.

"Happy birthday, mommy!" Abby and Anna cried in unison running over in their matching pink floral party dresses.

"Oh my girls!" Maggie wiped her eyes.

"Auntie Maggie!" Chloe was running behind her cousins in another matching dress.

"Mom, no one can say you don't enjoy having granddaughters." Max laughed leaning down to scoop up Chloe.

"Guilty!" Mom said raising her hand. "Now come on in, the bar is fully stocked!" She gestured to the bar on the patio.

"Erica, we need your help, kiddo, how do I get my playlist on this thing?" Dad asked shaking the iPod in front of him.

"Sure you're not sick of it yet, Pop?" Erica laughed.

"No way, I got a real hankering to blast some Queen. Ray over there doesn't believe you can fit a thousand songs on this little thing so I'm about to prove him wrong," he said with a smile as he made his way through the crowd.

Soon Queen's "I Want to Break Free" was booming through the speakers and Erica was silently wishing the same thing, dreading Pierre's impending arrival.

"You look like you could use a drink," Devon said coming up behind her and handing her a glass of champagne.

"You're the perfect kind of mind reader," she said raising her glass to meet his.

"So…looks like a blast from our childhood," Devon said glancing around the room at all of their parent's friends. "I guess most other kids tend to move on from their families—all but us, that is." He laughed.

"We must have missed the memo." She smiled looking around for people she might recognize. Her eyes stopped on Rachel's pleading eyes.

"Oh crap, looks like Rach has been cornered by old man Reggie. Probably grilling her on her divorce and wondering if a thirty year age gap is really such a big deal." Erica took a quick swig of her champagne then put her glass down to go rescue her, when she saw that had already been taken care of as Josh gently took Rachel's elbow and excused them.

Rachel and Josh practically ran across the room to meet Erica and Devon. "Thank god for you," Rachel gushed. "Reg was just asking how old was too old of an age gap for a second marriage."

"What did I tell ya?" Erica smiled smugly at Devon.

"Good thing we didn't put money on it."

"So where's everyone's kids?" Josh asked.

"That's what I just said," Devon laughed. "Looks like we're the only ones who are still codependent."

"I'll take it. I can't face anyone else asking me about the divorce. Even though it was only old man Reg over there. How did you deal with it?" Rachel asked looking over at Josh.

Josh smiled down at her. "Well, as a therapist I should tell you to confront the feelings head on. Address the underlying reasons you don't want to discuss the divorce openly." He was using his hands animatedly, as if delivering a presentation at a conference.

"Before I smack you, what would you tell her, as a friend?" Erica asked.

"Deflect, deflect, deflect." He laughed with a raise of his glass. "I find humor works well for me, but you may want to try a few different techniques."

Rachel giggled. She felt better having someone in her corner that knew what she was going through. Erica grabbed her arm mid-laugh. "Ouch! Ernie, a little lighter on the grip," she said. But when she looked up, she saw the color had drained from Erica's face and followed her eyes to the door.

Pierre.

Rachel's breath caught in her throat.

Fuck.

"Whoa, did someone see a ghost?" Devon joked looking toward the front door.

"That's Maggie's husband, right? Is it not a good thing he came to his wife's birthday party?" Devon asked confused.

"Long story…" Rachel started but Erica was already dragging her out of the living room, her champagne sloshing over the hardwood floor on their way to the patio.

"Shit, shit, shit…shitshitshit," Erica was chanting as she nearly ran into Max.

He saw the look on her face and knew right away. "Where is he?" he asked in a face Rachel had never seen before. Overprotective big brother, with a dash of father of a daughter, and sprinkle of very active imagination, he clenched his jaw as he scanned the room.

"Max…wait!" Rachel jumped in front of him.

"Ray Ray, that is a very bad idea," Max said through gritted teeth.

"Just let Mags at least see him first, okay? She deserves to address him first and foremost, no?" Rachel said trying to diffuse the situation.

"What the hell is he doing here?" Rachel could hear Maggie screech over "Summer of 69".

Even Bryan Adams couldn't save them now.

"Maggie….*s'il te plaît*…" Pierre was putting on his best doting husband act.

"Oh, there he is! Pierre, we're so glad you could make it!" Mom said trying to usher them into the hallway and away from the guests.

"No! I want this selfish prick out of here," Maggie said, her hands balled into fists by her side.

"Hey Sugar Bug, why don't we just have a drink and chat in the other room?" Dad whispered, stepping in and putting his arm on Maggie's shoulder.

"I don't think a drink will fix this one, Pop," Maggie said still staring straight ahead at Pierre.

"Oh come on now, babe, we've all been there. Right Jude?" he asked looking at his wife. "Marriages are tough. But let's just take our drinks into the other room, where you can talk privately." He was desperate now.

"Okay, dad. You're right." Maggie said.

Dad relaxed.

"Let's ask the crowd how they would deal with this in their marriage. Say you find out that your husband has been sleeping with other women before you even agreed to the second date. Oh, but infidelity isn't the main thing here folks…no," Maggie was shouting now.

Thank god all the kids were downstairs watching a movie. Rachel hoped against hope the volume was too loud and making their eardrums bleed *just* enough to block this out.

"No, I'd like to know how the guests would have dealt with the fact that their husband, father of their two beautiful girls, decided on yet another affair at his sister-in-law's wedding? Or how, when confronted by her protective sister, Erica, he threatened to destroy her life and move his family across the world to be away from them?" Maggie's face was bright red but her voice was steadier than ever.

Mom dropped her glass, sending champagne sprinkling through the air, a quizzical look on her face as the past three years suddenly made sense. Why Pierre was absent from so many events, why Erica seemed adamant to just leave her sister alone.

Dad's jaw locked. Max was standing behind him with the same *don't you fuck with either one of us right now, or we will dump your body in the lake and never look back* face.

"*Margaret, non*! Pleeeez, you must listen to me," Pierre pleaded, ignoring the dozens and dozens of eyes on him.

"You don't want to finish that sentence," Dad said calmly. "You need to go. And if I ever, *ever* find out you've tried to contact anyone in my family, it will be the last thing you do."

Pierre looked to Maggie. Erica had moved inside and was standing with Rachel who had formed a group behind Maggie with her brother and dad. Rachel put her arm around her shoulder and gave her a squeeze.

In a room filled with nearly forty people, the only sound was Aladdin's voice, echoing up from the basement.

"Oh Pierre," Mom said, finally finding her voice. Pierre looked up hopefully. Everyone held their breath. "Don't forget your party gift," she said making her way to the door. Rachel couldn't believe it. If ever there was time to forget your manners, this was it mom! She walked up to Pierre, grabbed the wedding band off his finger, and punched him square in the nose. His head flew back from the shock, finally wiping the smarmy look off his face.

Nobody moved.

"You don't deserve to wear this. You'll be hearing from our lawyers." She said before he turned and ran through the door. He held his bloody nose in his hands, nearly tripping on the welcome mat with his expensive Italian loafers.

There was a quiet cough from the back of the kitchen as the Woodses turned around, remembering they had a house full of guests. Their old camping friends, the Jensen's shifted uncomfortably from foot to foot, not sure how to react. Guests quietly pretended to be in deep conversation, waiting for queues on how to react.

"To the Birthday Girl!" Mom exclaimed, putting her best hostess face forward.

"Woohoo!" the cheers rang from the crowd. Josh ran over and turned the music back on. Somehow in all the commotion, it had been turned off.

Mom ran over and scooped her family in one giant group hug. They all had tears in their eyes as the crowd faded away and it was just them once again. The original six, who would always have each other's backs. No matter the distance, the dirt or the drama, this was one piece of wood that wouldn't break.

Tom Petty's "Won't Back Down" started blasting through the speakers. The party resumed its normal noise level with the past ten minutes feeling more like an apparition than reality.

Rachel started to laugh and looked over at Josh with the iPod in his hand.

He shrugged. "Seemed pretty fitting no?" He smiled.

She walked over to him with a sudden burst of confidence. If this week taught her anything, it was to not waste any time. To not play games. To be open. And to live with your feet firmly planted on the ground, your eyes and heart wide open.

"Very fitting. And I hope you won't back down either." She smiled looking up into his hazel eyes.

"I won't fight you on that one, Ms. Woods," he whispered before placing her head in his hands and leaning down to kiss her deeply.

Rachel was a million miles away. Floating above the crowd. A crowd that included people that were at her wedding only a few short years ago. And her family, who not too long ago, knew nothing about her life. Rachel loved being able to let the world in. Let her family back in.

"Alright alright, get a room you two. I don't want to have to kick another sister's boyfriend's ass," Max joked as he walked by them to the bar.

Rachel broke away laughing. "I figure, if you guys didn't approve of Josh, he wouldn't have been invited to all those family events over the years."

"I suppose we're stuck with him whether we like it or not," Dad said coming over and shaking Josh's hand.

"But that's my Cricket over there, son," he said pointing to Rachel. "And you do not want to see me angry if you screw this one up," he said with a straight face. "Or Judy for that matter." He motioned to his wife, with a bag of frozen peas on her hand.

Josh felt sixteen again, as if he was meeting his girlfriend's parents for the first time. "Yes sir."

He burst into a smile. "Oh, that was fun! I never got to do that with the last one. Too precious," he sighed, throwing his arm around Josh. "You know I'm kidding…plus I know your dad so you guys can't get away with nothing," he yelled over his shoulder then walked back toward the party.

"I'm so, *so* sorry…you girls have no idea. Why didn't anyone tell me?" Mom was pleading between Erica and Maggie.

"Mom, you've got quite the right hook!" Erica cheered.

"It only just came out mom, don't worry, okay? It was the final push I needed to have that man out of our lives," Maggie said dabbing her mom's eyes with a tissue. "And to get my family back." She smiled over at Erica. She nodded and grabbed another hug with her girls before gliding through the room, topping up drinks, and apologizing for the interruption.

Rachel leaned up against the island. She cast her eyes over the party. Max and Devon had Erica and Maggie in hysterics over some story. Her mom, the life of the party, and their dad, despite his health scare and all the unknowns, was cracking jokes on the patio. Josh was making his way back from the bar with fresh glasses of champagne.

"What are we toasting?" Rachel asked with a smile.

He smiled and thought for a moment. "To a week at the woods," he said before giving her glass a tap.

"You know I'm a sucker for wordplay." She smiled and let the cold sip of bubbles snake down her throat. She couldn't believe that only six days ago she was popping valium to get through the front door.

50

"So, everyone's all packed up?" John asked as he did a final check of the dock.

"Looks like it, Pop," Max said tossing him the boat keys. "Don't forget to put these in the mailbox with the other sets."

"Girls are all locked and loaded!" Judy said rushing back into the kitchen to grab the last of the groceries.

"I can't believe it's all over," Erica said sadly, nursing her cup of coffee so they didn't have to leave.

"I know, Ernie, but we're grabbing a coffee next week in the city right?" Maggie said rushing by with her bags.

"Definitely," she said beaming.

"Hey, don't leave me out!" Rachel said as she shoved the last of her clothes into her bag.

"As if we could ever do that." Erica tittered.

"Can you believe we're all going to be in New York City at the same time?" Rachel shrieked excitedly.

"Well…I have to see about schools for the girls but I'm excited to get back to reality." Maggie laughed.

"Come on girls, let's wrap it up. Kids are getting impatient," Max teased from the door.

"Aww is someone else feeling left out?" Rachel jeered.

"Well, it would be nice to be asked to coffee." He looked sadly at his running shoes.

John and Judy were standing at the front door looking at the scene unfold. John put his arm around Judy and she laid her head on his chest.

"How did we get so lucky, Jude?" he said as he kissed her on top of the head.

"I was just thinking that." She smiled.

"They must take after their father," he said.

Judy gave him a playful shove.

"Who knew a week in the woods could get us back here?" he said.

But Judy just smiled. She knew what would happen getting her family back under one roof. They might be loud, they might be crazy, but she also knew there was a whole lot of love here.

Once everyone was loaded into their cars, Judy did a final check over the house. She saw where her granddaughters had giggled and played in the backyard. Where her four grown children had laughed and fallen asleep together in Rachel's room. Where John had collapsed and she thought her world was ending. But then she heard the laughter and excited chatter shared over copious bottles of wine, and she smiled at the memories they created. She'd take the good with the bad, as long as she knew it was with this incredible family she had created.

Epilogue

"I can't believe we managed to get the same cottage for the same week this year!" Maggie squealed bursting through the door with Anna and Abby close behind.

"I know, right?" Max said from the kitchen. "Hey girls!" he said giving his nieces a big hug. "Chloe is downstairs unpacking if you want to join her!" But the girls were already flying down to the basement to join their cousin.

"Any news from the girls?" Maggie asked, unloading her groceries on Max.

"They left the city around the same time as you so I reckon they should be here any minute," he said popping open a beer. He handed one to Maggie.

"Cheers Maxy," she said. Before she could get her first sip down, the door burst open again.

"Gang's all here!" Rachel shouted from the door, running up and giving Max and Maggie a big hug.

"Relax sis, we just saw you last week for dinner." Max laughed.

"I know but it's just good to be back." She smiled.

"Hey no fair! You guys started the party already." Erica stated gesturing toward the beer in Maggie's hand.

"Catch," Max said throwing her a bottle.

"Thank god for my years of softball!" She shrieked catching the bottle with ease.

"So Michelle didn't want to tag along?" Rachel asked Max.

"Nah, I thought I'd leave her out of the full-on family festivities so soon out the gate! It's only been a few months but she did meet Chloe last week and it couldn't have gone better."

"You've worked together for years though, right?" Maggie asked.

"Yeah, but last time I rushed something, we all know what happened," he said gesturing toward Chloe who had wandered upstairs for a yogurt.

"Fair enough!" Erica said.

"How are the single ladies of New York making out?" Max asked, diverting the attention.

"I'm not sure it's all cosmos and one night stands," Maggie sighed. "I'm so busy at the bank and daycare is not cheap in Manhattan…let me tell you!"

"I barely even survived this year at school," Erica said after a taking a sip of her light beer.

"Liar, she is absolutely thriving. Who's the top of their class right now?" Rachel said popping open a beer and flopping down on the couch.

"The results are in?" Max asked giving her a clap on the back. "Well done, Ernie! Knew you had it in you," he said proudly.

"It's only a college course, plus between that and my modeling contract, I barely have time to eat, let alone date."

"Isn't that what everyone in the fashion world wants? To not eat?" Max teased. Erica threw a pillow at him and laughed.

"I thought I heard some commotion up here!" Mom said as she came into the kitchen from the backdoor. "Everything looks good out back. Just like last year!" She beamed.

Rachel gave her mom a big hug. "Oh, hi my girl. How are you? Busy before leaving the paper for the week?" she asked.

"Yes, they can spare me for the week don't worry. Not like I'm Deputy Editor or anything," she said confidently.

"What? You got the promotion? OMG!" Erica jumped up and gave her sister a big hug.

"To Cricket!" Max said raising his beer.

"Hear, Hear!" Josh cheered from the patio door.

"I didn't think you guys were coming up until tomorrow!" Rachel said running to him. She kissed him but was quickly interrupted by Woody.

"Now there's my real love!" She laughed bending down to give Woody a belly rub.

"He gets withdrawals if you're away too long," Josh said lovingly. "I'll leave you guys to it. We're just getting unpacked but call me if you need me, okay?" He asked softly, holding her hand in his.

Rachel nodded as he kissed her on the cheek.

"Did he say Devon asked about me?" Erica said as Josh made his way back down the dock and into his boat.

"I thought you weren't interested?" Rachel smiled.

"I said I'm too busy! That was a legit answer," Erica said. "I wouldn't even be in this school right now if it wasn't for his push." She smiled, twisting the cold beer bottle in her hands.

"Yeah, they're pretty good guys, aren't they?" Rachel said smiling as she waved to Josh.

"What do you think you'll say about his offer?" Erica asked.

"I think I'll say yes…" she smiled. "We've been dating for a year now and I think I'm ready to live together. What do you think?" Rachel asked.

"Well, I mean if not for him, at least for Woody, right?" Erica laughed.

"My thoughts exactly." Rachel smiled then sipped her beer.

"So, are we ready for this?" Max asked quietly.

Rachel took a deep breath. She was trying her best to forget the other reason they had come back to the cottage this year.

"How is she holding up?" Erica asked Maggie who had just come back to the living room.

"You know mom. She's a force to be reckoned with," Maggie said dabbing her eyes.

Mom came into the kitchen to find her kids all looking sadly at each other.

"Hey, guys come on, you promised. This is a celebration, right?" She smiled, trying her best to hide her tears.

"Absolutely mom, I'll go get the girls." Maggie kissed Mom on the cheek before heading down to the basement to bring the girls down to the dock.

Erica slipped her hand in her mom's as they headed out the patio door and Max went down to start the boat.

Rachel picked up the urn on their way out the door. "How about one last boat ride, Pop?" she whispered.

"Oh, I almost forgot!" Erica said at the dock, running back up to the house.

Everyone was on the boat as Erica came running back down.

She turned to hook something up to the stereo.

John Denver's "Take Me Home Country Roads" started to play through the speaker.

Mom laughed. "One of his favorites." She smiled grabbing Erica's hand.

As Max put the boat in drive, he turned the volume as high as it could go.

Erica passed around the drinks. "I still can't believe how much he loved to drink this stuff," she said choking back a sip of the whiskey.

Rachel raised her glass high. "To Pop, this one's for you," she said looking up. Everyone raised their glasses and took a sip.

As the sun sank into the lake, John Denver's voice was carrying them home to exactly where they needed to be.

Acknowledgements

If you have found your way to the acknowledgements page, I trust that you made it through to the end of my novel and for that, I thank you! I've long felt the call to write a novel and while it's been a passion project and something I've worked on during a very heavy workload, I've enjoyed it immensely. I see so much of my own upbringing in the Woods family and found myself just as excited to see where their story would end up. I hope you enjoyed reading it as much as I enjoyed writing it!

I would never have gotten to this day without the love and support of my own very large and loveable family! To my fiancé Rich, for not only tolerating my long hours holed up in my office writing and editing, but encouraging me and supporting me in this journey. I'm so lucky to be on this adventure with you. To my parents, Mike and MaryEllen for being crazy enough to have four kids and for moving us around so much. We may have moaned about it at the time but it fostered an incredible bond between us all and I am sure is the reason we love to make fast friends out of everyone we meet! My siblings, Scot, Amber and Sarah for always being there throughout the years - no matter the distance, ours is a bond that won't break. And my extended family of siblings, in-laws, nieces, nephews, and the countless dogs and cats, for always making family gatherings the loveable mayhem they are.

To my editor, Courtney Lochner for her tireless edits and being a source of amazing knowledge to me! Thank you as well to Ashley Santoro for my beautiful cover and the interior formatting. To all my friends and family who immediately wanted to read the first draft, my heart swells with the support and love that surrounds me.

And to you dear reader, for taking a chance on this novel and spending A Week at the Woods with me. Thank you, thank you, thank you.

About the Author

Rebecca Taylor has worked as a writer, journalist and marketing consultant in London and Canada for over a decade. After finishing her post-grad degree in English Literature at the University of London, she entered the world of luxury travel and yachting and continues to work as a freelancer in this industry among others. While not writing her debut novel, Rebecca can be found hiking, doing yoga, nursing a coffee in a local cafe or sipping a nice glass of red wine. She now resides in Ottawa, Canada with her fiancé, Rich and their beloved Rhodesian Ridgeback, Kingsley. Please check out her other works on her website rebeccataylorwrites.com and on Instagram @bectaylorwrites.

9 781777 307028